THE BIRDS

FRANK BAKER was born in London in 1908. From a young age, he had a deep interest in church music, serving as a chorister at Winchester Cathedral as a boy from 1919 to 1924. From 1924 to 1929, Baker worked as a marine insurance clerk in the City of London, an experience that he later fictionalized in *The Birds* (1936). He resigned in 1929 to take on secretarial work at an ecclesiastical music school where he hoped to make a career of music; during this time he also worked as a church organist.

He soon abandoned his musical studies and went to St. Just, on the west coast of Cornwall, where he became organist of the village church and lived alone in a stone cottage. It was during this time that he began writing; his first novel, *The Twisted Tree*, was published in 1935 by Peter Davies after nine other publishers rejected it. It was well received by critics, and its modest success prompted Baker to continue writing. In 1936, he published *The Birds*, which sold only about 300 copies and which its author described as "a failure." Nonetheless, after the release of Alfred Hitchcock's popular film of the same name in 1963, *The Birds* was reissued in paperback by Panther and received new attention. Baker's most successful and enduring work was *Miss Hargreaves* (1940), a comic fantasy in which two young people invent a story about an elderly woman, only to find that their imagination has in fact brought her to life.

During the Second World War, Baker became an actor and toured Britain before getting married in 1943 to Kathleen Lloyd, with whom he had three children. Baker continued to write, publishing more than a dozen more books, including *Mr. Allenby Loses the Way* (1945), *Embers* (1946), *My Friend the Enemy* (1948) and *Talk of the Devil* (1956). Baker died in Cornwall of cancer in 1983.

KEN MOGG lives in Melbourne, Australia. He writes on film and other topics. His recent publications include a chapter on "Hitchcock's Literary Sources" in *A Companion to Alfred Hitchcock* (Wiley-Blackwell, 2011) and a piece on "The Cutting Room" in *39 Steps to the Genius of Hitchcock* (British Film Institute, 2012). An earlier discussion by him of Frank Baker and Alfred Hitchcock appeared in the online journal *Senses of Cinema* (#51).

By Frank Baker

FICTION

The Twisted Tree (1935)*
The Birds (1936)*
Miss Hargreaves (1940)
Allanayr (1941)
Sweet Chariot (1942)
Mr. Allenby Loses the Way (1945)
Before I Go Hence (1946)
Embers (1946)*
The Downs So Free (1948)
My Friend the Enemy (1948)
Lease of Life (1954)
Talk of the Devil (1956)
Teresa: A Journey Out of Time (1960)
Stories of the Strange and Sinister (1983)*

NONFICTION/AUTOBIOGRAPHICAL

The Road Was Free (1948)
I Follow But Myself (1968)
The Call of Cornwall (1976)

* Available from Valancourt Books

FRANK BAKER

THE BIRDS

With an introduction by
KEN MOGG

VALANCOURT BOOKS

The Birds by Frank Baker
First published London: Peter Davies, 1936
Reprinted as a Panther paperback 1964
Valancourt Books edition first published 2013, reprinted 2021

Published by Valancourt Books, Richmond, Virginia
http://www.valancourtbooks.com

ISBN 978-1-939140-49-4 (*trade paperback*)
ISBN 978-1-948405-45-4 (*trade hardcover*)
Also available as an electronic book and an audiobook.

Set in Dante MT

INTRODUCTION

FOR ME, Frank Baker's *The Birds* (1936) is both a finely crafted suspense thriller that could show even Alfred Hitchcock a few things, and an authentic account of pre-War London. As London was where Hitchcock lived and worked, before going to Hollywood at the end of the decade, the Cockney director's many admirers have a double reason to read this book. Of course, they also have a more specific reason. Baker's "apocalyptic" novel anticipates Hitchcock's 1963 film of the same title. Both in particular details—like a woman attacked by birds in a telephone booth—and in broad situation—involving a male character and his widowed mother, and a smart foreign girl whose arrival in the family circle sparks the mother's jealousy—you could be forgiven for thinking that the novel inspired Hitchcock's film. Certainly it resembles the film more nearly than the latter resembles its official source, Daphne du Maurier's "The Birds," a short story first published in 1952. Indeed, Hitchcock instructed screenwriter Evan Hunter to forget the short story, to keep only "the title and the notion of birds attacking human beings." Yet there is no evidence that the director knew of Baker's novel until, in 1962, with the film already in production, the author wrote to him, seeking compensation (which came to nothing). The resemblances of novel and film can be attributed to several factors. Among these are a preference by both men to make exciting "soul-drama"— superior melodrama—that grips a general audience; and a mutual concern with visual storytelling.

Yet the novel *The Birds* also has its unique voice. Throughout his life, Baker (1908-1983) was aware of "two actors" contending within him, two halves of the one soul. Accordingly, although his novel was conceived, late one wintry afternoon, as a means of settling past scores—its author had just watched with a gleam in his eye a gigantic flock of starlings blanket a field in Cornwall—

the vengeful side of him was soon being admonished by its opposite number. You can see this happening in the scene where the
narrator apologises if he has given the impression that the world
was once "so miserably governed, humanity so dense and apathetic, that I never spent a happy moment in their midst." Several
charming passages follow. A typical one expresses longing "for
the roar of an underground train; the babble of humanity crowding in the refreshment-room of some theatre. . . ." Another must
have been added at the last minute, for it describes the funeral of
King George V, in January 1936, and begins: "Our people were
discovered at their best and simplest, whenever any special occasion called them to unanimity." However, in Baker's interior life,
unanimity was always elusive; the division there ran deep. You
could call it *eros* versus *thanatos*—the life instincts battling the
death instincts—yet Baker was scarcely alone in housing such a
civil war. It comes of being civilised! What was special in his case
was how keenly he felt it and the literary uses he put it to, including in a doppelgänger motif that surfaces in *The Birds* and whose
apotheosis would fuel another fine thriller, *My Friend the Enemy*
(1948).

    His ability, then, to construct drama out of his grievances and
intimate convictions distinguishes Baker's work. And although
his biographer Paul Newman sounds an admirable caution—
"Biographical details should never be turned against a writer
or masquerade as literary criticism"—even Newman concedes
that such matters in Baker's case "booby-trap his writings" and
were "burned into his memory." A reader of *The Birds* needs
to know some background, starting with the five tedious years
young Frank spent commuting between his parents' house in
north London and his first job, as a clerk in the marine department of an insurance firm in the City. The novel's hated Underwriter is based on a real person. So, too, clearly, is the novel's
narrator, referred to as the Elder because he is recalling events
many years later for his daughter Anna, but who features in those
events as a young insurance clerk with literary aspirations. One
fateful evening, the clerk is sitting alone with his notebook in a
busy London café when a "tall, thin man" enters and, seeing the
youth, comes straight to his table where he tries to show him

dirty pictures. The youth flees. When they meet again, in the novel's magisterial climax in St. Paul's Cathedral, it becomes evident that the man is the very Devil. In real life, though, he was one Alfred Rose, and in Baker's memoirs he apologises for the depiction. Then adds: "Yet in a way it was the highest compliment I could pay him; I think he would have appreciated it."

Rose was a middle-aged, lapsed Anglo-Catholic monk, apparently gay—but with two schoolgirl daughters—who effectively picked up young Baker on Ascension Day 1925 during the teenager's lunch break, when both parties found themselves attending a High Mass in St. Paul's Cathedral. That just about says it all! At least, it would, but for some further facts about Baker. First, he was a moral lad. Although he and Rose maintained a friendship, on and off, for about five years, and he often visited Rose's first-floor flat in Chancery Lane, almost certainly they never slept together. Baker was precocious in some ways—he was musically gifted and played a church organ on Sundays—but he was not ready for unorthodox sexual adventures. Not ready in one sense, at least. In his superbly humane memoirs, *I Follow But Myself* (1968), he explains: "I was dismally unaware of the nature of the [sexual] forces that bewildered me—infinitely less approaching maturity than my own sons at the same age ... I had come almost to despise my unfortunate parents." Nor, one gathers, had those benighted parents stocked their house with fine literature, something else which Frank keenly felt. (He had, though, discovered Dickens.) Accordingly, the urbane, well-read Rose now became like a surrogate parent and confidant to the youth, and the topics they conversed about ranged from the shortcomings of the Anglican Church to masturbation. (When Frank's sense of humour prompted him to pen a short ditty about onanism, beginning, "Now Onan was a naughty man and Onan he was wise," his mentor was delighted.) Nonetheless, about one sexual topic Frank seems to have remained uninformed—until painful new events exposed his ignorance and gave him further cause for grievance.

In 1929, when Baker turned 21, he felt emboldened to quit his job with the London Assurance. He had found two new positions: the main one as an assistant secretary at the School of English Church Music, Chislehurst, the other, another organist's job, in Holborn. Yet, within months, both positions were abruptly terminated. As Baker tells it, an innocent friendship with a 14-year-old choirboy was misinterpreted, so that one day he was informed by the Warden of the School that his intentions were suspect and that he must stop seeing the boy. When Baker and the boy secretly rebelled against this, they were reported. And Baker was summarily dismissed. "In less than a year," he writes in his memoirs, "I [thus] found myself sacked for a crime I had not only never committed but of whose nature I was totally ignorant." It was presumably Alfred Rose who duly informed him of its nature; certainly Rose was the only person to whom Frank could turn, for his parents, he says, "looked at me as though I stood in the dock at the Old Bailey." Whether directly or indirectly is not clear, but they pressured him to leave home. For a while he languished in a nearby flat in Stroud Green, north London, but eventually he turned his eyes to Cornwall and the real possibility of a writer's life.

Thus his path was set. Baker's first published novel, *The Twisted Tree* (1935), a melodrama about a girl, Tansy, half attracted and half repelled by a wandering artist, Chailey (who resembles Alfred Rose!), was written while Baker supported himself by playing the organ at the church of St. Just, near Land's End. The book's modest sale of a few hundred copies encouraged him, and he began *The Birds*. Something remarkable about the latter is how prescient it is. Like the 1936 film of H.G. Wells's *The Shape of Things to Come*, it foresees the approaching war. The climactic service in St. Paul's Cathedral not only invokes God's intercession against the increasingly pesky avians, but specifically requests that He "dispel the savage cloud that brewed a thunderstorm over Europe." Equally, the novel lays down a template for Baker's future life. Early chapters are candid about the narrator's sexual confusion. But then (1) he glimpses for the first time the Russian girl Olga, and (2) soon afterwards he makes a trip to Cader Idris in Wales—his and Olga's future home, as it turns out—where he receives a virtual "oceanic" experience. This impassioned chapter feels almost Biblical, both when the narrator goes up into the mountain and again immediately afterwards, when he has successive moments of temptation. There is a clear message:

> I came away then … With all my being I longed to press
> against me the form of another human person, young, beauti-
> ful, and desirable … that we could derive from each other the
> twofold act of creation, taking and giving …
>
> I remember how quickly I walked, almost ran past the
> lake and then homewards, for fear that if I lingered my desire
> would drive me to turn in upon myself; to take from myself
> and give nothing …

Did Baker first encounter such wisdom in Alfred Rose's apart-
ment, perhaps in some Catholic pamphlet he found (or was
handed) there? Well, then, God moves in mysterious ways!

About Olga now. She enters the narrator's life all at once and
by stages, so to speak. There is a passage in the memoirs, marvel-
ling how a period existed "when the partner who was to share
some of the most beautiful and some of the most stormy passages in the long voyage, was not even within knowledge." Olga
empowers the narrator (as, from 1942, actress Kathleen Lloyd,
Baker's future wife, would empower him). But she is adamant
that he must do certain things himself. Her previous boyfriend, a
bohemian poet (based on the composer "Peter Warlock"/Philip
Heseltine), had committed suicide, "because he could not face
himself as he really was." For a time, she mourned. Then one
evening in a café she had seen the narrator and detected something in his eyes which she knew was true. "Only—only it isn't
true until you see yourself." With those words, we reach the crux
of the novel, including what most provokes its avenging avians. It
is marred humanity.

* * *

I want to return to Alfred Hitchcock. Exegesis of his films,
including *The Birds*, seldom acknowledges that issues from ordinary life enter into them. (A notable exception is a recent article
by Mervyn Nicholson, "Alfred Hitchcock Presents Class Struggle.")[1] It sounds counter-intuitive that an "escapist" filmmaker

---

[1] *Monthly Review*, December 2011, pp. 33-50.

would concern himself that way. Yet in 1936 he was already declaring, "we grow sluggish and jellified . . . our civilisation has so screened and sheltered us that it isn't practicable to experience sufficient thrills at first hand." Frank Baker's novel not only illuminates that statement with much topical detail but can throw into relief life issues—as distinct from the structural and / or psychoanalytic ones favoured by Hitchcock scholars—informing the Hitchcock film. Furthermore, Baker grew up, like Hitchcock, in the era of silent cinema, and had enjoyed some of the early serials. For these and other reasons, his novel and Hitchcock's film overlap and can throw light on each other.

Their essential *modernism* has already been touched on. I have called them "soul-dramas." Recently John Gray[1] distilled what he sees as the lesson of Sigmund Freud. It is less psycho-analytic than existential. According to Freud, people harbour impulses that sabotage their self-fulfilment: compare the refrain in Baker's *The Birds* about "a man made to mar himself" (a phrase taught him by Alfred Rose). Freud's classic description, reflected in both Baker and Hitchcock, is of the war between eros and thanatos. But Freud did not see his job as being to intervene in that war. Rather, he sought "to effect a change in the mind through which both [elements] could be accepted." According to Gray, Freud echoed Nietzsche in envisioning a form of life "beyond good and evil." He once wrote a reproving letter to a colleague, telling him he was too virtuous. "One has to be a bad fellow, transcend the rules . . . and behave like the artist who buys paints with his wife's household money, or burns the furniture to warm the room for his model. Without such criminality there is no real achievement." Both Baker and Hitchcock would explore that idea— although in Baker's early novel his clerk is still very uptight, very "moral," as Olga laughs one day. Nor could Freud accept a self-transformation based on an "oceanic feeling of oneness." In Gray's words: "The oceanic feeling was real enough, but it could not be the basis for a way of living. Whatever moments of release they might experience, humans were fated to a life of struggle." After Baker's narrator has literally out-faced his Demon bird, by

[1] *The Silence of Animals: On Progress and Other Modern Myths* (London, 2013), pp. 83-90.

seeing *himself* as he really is ("I saw and I lived"), he understands the corollary:

> I stood up. My ankles ached, my limbs were bruised, blood was dripping from my chin. But ... I saw [now] that I had not to go to a mountain to fill my lungs with life. I saw that I made my world what it was; that all died around me if I died in my Soul; that all lived if my Soul lived.

There is a similar incident in Hitchcock's film, and it occurs at the end when Melanie Daniels (Tippi Hedren) goes alone to the attic and is attacked by birds. Crucially, they fly straight at the camera lens. Whatever else Melanie may be—for example, complacent at first but a quick learner, according to Hitchcock in interviews—she is a stand-in for the individual viewer. This was always Hitchcock's way. Instead of spelling out the existential meaning of a film's drama, his "subjective" camera would transfer that drama inside the viewer's head. Invariably his films (like *Rear Window*, about a bored photographer spying on his neighbours) posit some such existential dilemma. Then, as the comedy and suspense take hold, the viewer is drawn in. And because each film is a soul-drama, and Hitchcock is making what he called "pure cinema," the camera may emphasise eyes and the act of seeing. In other words, the film "targets" those eyes, *our* eyes, as at the end of *The Birds*. We sense that the existential dilemma applies to us, and we (rightly) feel ourselves complicit; thus the question arises, how might we, as individuals, deal with it? Not that the canny Hitchcock ever sought to pose such a question directly—with the possible exception of two wartime propaganda dramas, *Foreign Correspondent* and *Lifeboat*, which both called for more than usual direct action. Nicholson puts the matter well: Hitchcock will "show us what we need to know—but not *force* us to see it. We have to see it for ourselves."

With Frank Baker, his knowledge of cinema accounts for several of his novel's best stratagems. The employment of a well-known landmark for his climax emulates the silent serials and early feature films like Hitchcock's *Blackmail* (1929), whose climax occurs in, and on, the British Museum. Still, I find almost

eerie that both men chose to give their respective heroines identical shadings of foreignness, of wronged virtue, of superior
but wasted ability. You sense some archetype working. In Olga's
case, we learn that her parents died in the Revolution. After arriv-
ing in England, she found a job as a cinema attendant but was
soon being taken advantage of by the local lads; on hearing herself called "the Russian whore," she knew that she must move
on. In this context, Baker's narrator becomes her saviour, and
she (with her experience) his. Melanie, too, is a complementary
"other." Played by Ms Hedren, who was born of Scandinavian
parents ("Tippi" derives from "Tupsa," meaning "little girl" or
"sweetheart"), she is a sophisticated playgirl who nonetheless
has been mixing in dubious company, having just returned from
Rome where, reportedly, she would jump into fountains naked.
Her father owns a San Francisco newspaper but her mother long
ago abandoned them for another man. Melanie's accidental
meeting with lawyer Mitch Brenner (Rod Taylor) in a bird shop is
a "meet cute" situation that you just know will deepen into love
once the wild birds start attacking. Both heroines, then—vulnerable, defamed, but looking to improve themselves—invite our
interest and sympathy. Similarly, both heroes are given "prob-
lem" widowed mothers, no doubt to account for those heroes'
own peculiarities (and allow the pop psychologist in us to spec-
ulate) but also to raise further poignant issues of family and the
future. Marred humanity is the "given" here; eros and thanatos
underlie each story's existential situation. As for the respective
avians (whatever satisfaction Baker and Hitchcock derived from
inflicting them on us), they are ultimately mysterious. Simply
another given. Hitchcockians may think of them as the "reality"
that Norman Bates in *Psycho* (1960) could not face.

Finally, what we have here are two remarkable tales of suspense. In 1934, England had experienced a year of record heat;
inspired, Baker sets his novel during a long hot summer, and
the trying conditions collude with the gathering birds to drive
both the authorities and the populace to, first, distraction,
then to something like apathy and a nameless fear. But there
are moments of relief. For now, life goes on. A lovely passage
describes the young clerk's early-morning visits to an outdoor

public baths near the Alexandra Palace (where Baker's grandfather had played the organ). "At that early hour men were different . . . Here . . . with the fresh sun over them, they were alive, naked, and free . . ." As in Hitchcock's best films, the ebb and flow of suspense in Baker's *The Birds* suggests life in its full intensity that humans have lost touch with, and which both artists would restore to us, or at least remind us of. We are at one with the birds if only we could see it; they are not as "other" as our closed minds tell us. With delicious irony, both works delight in drawing bird/human parallels. Baker describes how one busy day in London a flock of birds kills a man; afterwards, "the birds rose into the air. The flapping of their wings; their harsh squeaking and gibbering—so curiously similar to the excited cries of the people—drowned the noise of the traffic . . ." Which invites a closing comment on the sheer technical skill both works show. The film's Tides Restaurant sequence, whose Bible-quoting drunkard is based on playwright Sean O'Casey, is an extended tour de force. But it is matched by the novel's two main café scenes, especially the second, which literally covers much ground with its equivalent of a "tracking crane-shot" and shows a musical influence when it implies the clerk's tipsy condition by means of a refrain about "peas in a drum." Splendidly accomplished stuff!

* * *

Baker wrote many more novels, including both the whimsical *Miss Hargreaves* (1940), whose success probably owed something to a wartime need for escapist fantasy and would later be adapted as a stage-vehicle for actress Margaret Rutherford; and the gently wise *Lease of Life* (1954), about a clergyman who learns he has only a year to live, which was filmed by Ealing Studios with Robert Donat. But a case can be made that the author was at his best when the "criminality" in his nature directly engaged him, and that "thrillers" were his true forte. Sadly, he wrote only two or three of those, with *The Birds* outstanding.

KEN MOGG

PUBLISHER'S NOTE

The Birds was first published by Peter Davies of London in June 1936. The print run was small: the book sold only about 300 copies and is all but unobtainable today. In 1964, in the wake of the popularity of Alfred Hitchcock's film *The Birds* (1963), Panther reissued Baker's novel as a paperback, which was labeled a "revised edition." For the revised edition, Baker marked up his own copy of the 1936 edition in pencil, making hundreds of deletions, alterations, and corrections; he also made several long additions, which were typewritten on separate sheets and inserted in appropriate places in the text. However, when the Panther edition was finally published, almost none of Baker's revisions were incorporated; only a small percentage of them, mostly very minor changes, were actually made, and these were not done consistently. For the present edition, the text has been prepared from Baker's own copy of the 1936 edition, incorporating his holograph alterations from that copy and the typewritten insertions. The Publisher is grateful to Mr. Gabriel Hughes, Baker's grandson, for providing digital reproductions of these materials, from which this edition has been typeset.

Though Baker's changes are many and result in a measurably shorter book, the alterations are almost without exception stylistic rather than substantive in nature, improving grammar, removing repetitive matter, and shortening some of the longer didactic passages, resulting in a much more readable text. A detailed comparison of the 1936 and 1964 editions with this one is beyond the scope of the present edition, but publication of this unique version of the book will allow future readers and scholars the chance to make those comparisons.

THE BIRDS

"O all ye fowls of the air, bless ye the Lord."
> (*From an ancient Hebrew hymn.*)

"Birds, birds, we gotta get rid of the birds . . ."
> (*Adaptation from an old American song.*)

AUTHOR'S INTRODUCTION

to the 1964 Panther edition

IT is the London of 1935 which is observed in these pages—the
world before the birds came; a world which had no television, jet-
planes or H-bombs. Yet it was a world which differs little from
ours of today, except that now there are many more people and
the rat-race is swifter. But the birds too are swift. If they came
today they would, I hope, be even more alert to the horrors
which devil our present society.

Let it be remembered, though, that the birds are our friends—
if we can learn to live up to them. To the reader today I say—
take them, if you please, as entertainment (of a kind). I would
not, perhaps, so readily destroy civilization as I did in 1935 when,
young and ruthless, I wrote this book. For there is much about
even today's world which I love; and if the birds do have to come
(who knows?) I hope their scourge will leave a cleaner land
behind them.

Read on. And be careful if you hear the tapping at the window.

FRANK BAKER

PREFACE

"Before the birds came" was a phrase commonly used by my father. As a child I paid little attention to the words; they were but a sentence in an adult language for which I cared nothing. But once, when I had done some childish act which was forbidden—I cannot remember what—he said to me with the humour with which he always modified his rebukes, "Anna, if you had been living before the birds came, you would have had to go to a place called a school where you would sit at a desk all day learning a number of dull things which were no use to you. So be thankful for what you have." And my mother added, "Yes, Anna. And instead of running about in the garden without any clothes as you often do, you would have had to wear ugly garments, however hot it was."

From that time my curiosity was awakened, and I began to wonder many things. Where had we all come from? Was all the world the same as I saw here—trees, fields, mountains, and cold rivers? What had my father and mother been like when they were young? Above all, what birds were those which had apparently changed life so considerably?

I asked my father these questions and many others. But he always turned away with a sigh and said, "It was too long a story. Was not the present enough without thinking of the past?"

I talked to my brothers about it, but they—being men and full of activity—did not care so much where they came from as where they were going. Their concern was with the future.

I married and left my father's home. I came back later with my three sons. My mother died. My brothers were away, married and busy with their own affairs. I found myself in daily contact with my father, more than ever I had been before.

Again I asked him, "Tell me about the birds?" And he said,

"Perhaps the story should be told. But it will take a long time, Anna, and you had better write it all down as I tell it."

Between us we devised a system of what he called shorthand, so that I could write quickly while he dictated. In the month of August, while the boys were gathering in the corn harvest, my father commenced his story, and I sat at a table by his side recording every word that he spoke.

I

THE BACKGROUND

PERHAPS I am the only man living in this island who remembers the birds. So many perished at the time; most of the few who remained must since have died. For some reason Providence has given me a long life. I do not complain of that—why should I? I am very happy with my children and grandchildren, like one of those old patriarchs of whom we used to read in a book of poetic folk-tales from which we extracted a great deal of false moralizing in the old days before the birds came. How long ago that is! Do you realize, Anna, that in October I shall be eighty-five? Yes, I always kept a record of the number of my years, even though the children laugh at me and pester me with questions about these birthdays—mysteries to them, of course, who never know nor care how old they are. I think there could be no happier people than those who forget their age—none so happy in the days of my youth as these children. Berin, Roger, Allan——

But if I waste time in vain comments upon my age I shall never find the courage to start at all. Let us get to work, then. And first let me tell you of that foolhardy journey I made some twenty years ago. I remember that Olga, your mother, had no sympathy for such a venture. "You are too old," she said. "It will disturb you too greatly." And she was right. For it awoke too many memories and started so deep a train of thought that, when I came back, I found it hard to talk of what I had seen.

I set off, you remember, with Fallow. She carried me well. I am not going to describe the journey in any detail. You know, from what I have told you, something of the road that I took—along the centre of this island, through what were known as the midlands, and towards the east coast. Little happened on the way.

The journey was a long one and wearisome, and the sun very hot that year. Often, passing settlements, communities such as ours, I claimed hospitality as is our custom, and was always courteously received.

Sometimes I slept in woods by the banks of streams, sometimes in the shells of houses where our forefathers had lived. I fell in with no companion on the way, and for that I was not sorry. Fallow was a better companion than any man. I remember one sad evening, when I kindled sticks in the ruin of a great building that had once been a temple of religious worship. Such places were called cathedrals; centuries ago, men had laboured for generations to establish in brick and stone some memorial of the goodness of their God. Many of these buildings were very lovely. This perhaps, had been one of the loveliest. I remembered it as I had last seen it, when its delicate silver spire had sundered winter clouds or carved an angle in a blue summer sky. Now it was nothing but a wall of splintered stone, like the spine of some fabulous beast, over which lichen, moss, and bramble trailed profusely. I brooded over it with many long thoughts and left it early in the morning, reminding myself that for a grain of beauty in the old world there had been a rock of ugliness. If the grain had to go with the rock, then it had to be.

I drew eastward to the outskirts of the old City. It was a wasted land that met me, desolate with the scattered ruin of house, church, factory, and shop. There were few settlements now. I followed the course of the river called Thames; that at least had not changed—though who from the old time would recognize now its banks?

So I came into the dead City. Immense and silent it is, with not a soul to tell why it is desolate. Not a soul. . . . Many buildings were still standing; they were hollow with fallen floors and broken windows, no more than traps for the wind that whistled through them. I found myself eventually in a great open square, across which sprawled the massive column of an old memorial to a sea-lord, an illustrious hero of this island. Often at sunset, when the lights of the City began to prick the darkness and the faint stars rose, he had been beautiful, poised like some remote God in the misty orange sky—a signal of this island's temporal power. Now he had fallen from the clouds and nothing remained of him except broken bits, shameful and small. My heart was like stone; I was cold. I wanted to weep, but I could not. To whisper my name was to summon ghosts around me. I could fancy that they reproached me for coming. Fallow was restive; it was hard to induce her any longer to pick her way over the scarred streets. Often we had to mount over piles of masonry clutched by thick masses of rank weeds. The air was very close; the wind that came from the river sighed without movement. To me, the wind was a lamentation, crying, *"Babylon, thy Babylon is wasted."*

I urged Fallow on quickly now, for I was afraid of the silence, so heavy with implied sound. I wanted to be back in this peaceful country, where silence is full of music. I had to cross the wreckage of a railway bridge that had snapped across my path. There was a little hill before me. I could not lift my head for fear of what I should see at the top. And when I did, it was only another ruin that I saw—but to me, so dreadful a record of the dissolution of the old society, that I did not like to look at it. What had once been the pride of our people—a temple capped by a magnificent domed tower—stood emptily before me now like a jagged eggshell biting into the sky. The columns at its main entrance were crumbled down the stone steps where pigeons had once flocked to receive food from men. Nothing was left of its grandeur.

I stopped by the steps, climbed to the top, sat on a scrolled lump of mossy stone and laid my face in my hands. And with my eyes closed, with my fingers pressed into my ears to keep out the thin sound of the wind through the temple, it seemed to my imagination that a youth stood at my side. "Why do you come, old man," he asked, "to torment yourself?" "Because," I said, with my eyes still closed, "before I die I had to see the ghosts that linger around the old places of men."

Then I opened my eyes, and in one brief flashing vision, I saw, as I had seen years before, the confusion and horror that had brought about the decay of my civilization. Like a shadow at my side, stood the youth. Through his eyes I saw people running wildly down the hill, falling over and tearing at each other in their senseless flight. Mingling in this crowd, drifted the black wings of a million birds, like no birds we have ever seen here. In the midst of this confusion was a grinding file of wheeled vehicles of all descriptions, tall, cumbersome scarlet cars, thick with people, and draped with the black shapes of birds who writhed in and out of smashed windows with a harsh beating of skinny wings; smaller cars, all colours and shapes. One man, regardless of the people he cut down on his way, drove his machine at great speed. I saw him crash into a building down the hill; I heard screams as his car overturned with a hissing of sharp flame. There were men on horseback in a blue uniform, and others in dirty yellow uniforms with hideous masks on their faces. Roaring low in the black sky were flying machines; there seemed to be some plan between these machines and the mounted men to restore order amongst the people. But no order could be established. The demented people, furious for their own safety, flocked densely into the crammed doorways of shops and offices. I backed aside as a thundering mass surged up the steps of the temple and broke through the doors, trampling on one another in their panic. There was a roar of engines and bewildered shouts, a rushing of wings, a wailing of those who could find no door to shelter them. Then a dying silence, a fading away of these hideous figures, a clearing of the black sky.

I was alone again, alone with the shadow of the youth in the desolate City. The shadow stirred, I thought. "Go home," it said, "go home, and tell them not what you have seen here."

So silently, quickly, without turning my head, I mounted Fallow and rode away.

For many seasons I could speak only to your mother of what I had seen and remembered in that place. Now you know. But the story I have to tell you is the story of that shadow who stood by me on the temple steps; the story of that youth who, sixty years ago, lived and worked in the great City.

*

In that old life before the birds came, I was a marine insurance clerk. You must try to picture me travelling morning and night to and from the City, descending to dark underground passages, penned in a chain of moving boxes together with thousands of my kind, male and female. We all sat and allowed ourselves to be shot from place to place under the streets of the City without a murmur of complaint. Were you enabled to study us from some timeless altitude, you would remark the pathetic inertia of our faces, so heavy with grief, unrest, ill-health, and pride, that if a natural smile broke upon the mouth of any one of us, we were in danger of being labelled eccentric. Yet you must not imagine that the people of this island were possessed of serious minds. If you examined their attitude to their work you would find that it rarely interested them. They blundered into it: often executing it with complete lack of skill; they discussed it flippantly and treated the gravest issues with a non-committal gesture, known as a "shrug of the shoulders." Any man finding himself in an awkward or dangerous situation, responded to the emotional pressure put upon him by a "shrug of the shoulders." I cannot imitate the action; I have almost forgotten how to shrug.

In those days very few people were immune from a spirit of aggressive nationalism. It did not only affect countries, it affected individuals, so that even a man's family was "better" than the family who lived in the house adjoining his. There was a complete absence of trust between individuals. There also existed a singular craving for inanimate possessions of all types. This fever, described by a poet as the *"mania for owning things,"* gave birth to a rivalry between those who possessed much and those who possessed little; and it entirely obscured the elementary principles of the brotherhood and equality of man with man.

At that time every nation, heavy with suspicion, feared oppression by another nation. For this reason, great armies of fighting men were reared at the expense of poor and ill-nourished people who, in taxes, were forced to support these entirely unnecessary bodies of soldiers. Factories all over the world employed thousands of people in the making of intricate machines capable of destroying large sections of mankind. The ingenuity of practical scientists was more expended upon this type of labour than upon anything else. Yet here is something more difficult to understand. The factories that made such engines of destruction were in the hands of a few rich men who, in order to sell their products, did their utmost to encourage the intense spirit of jealous rivalry between nations. The law—which could imprison a man were he to appear in public unclothed, or take a twopenny loaf from a baker's shop—had no power over such curious freaks of nature as these factory managers. Outwardly humane men, they had even been known to sell guns to the country engaged in warfare with their own country, at the same time simulating possession of the automatic national spirit. When I tell you, Anna, that this state of affairs existed only a few years following upon a great slaughter of youth in a war such as had never before been known, you will begin to perceive something of the singular stupidity of man. It cannot be understood, it can only be marvelled at.

This, then, was the temper of my world, and to the great seething centre of it I was delivered every day in a growing spirit of discontent. A certain day comes back to me very clearly; that fateful summer day when I sat on the roof of our office, eating my bread-and-cheese lunch, looking over the City and wondering how, from so calm a prospect, so much unrest could arise. For weeks we had suffered a drought not comparable in living memory; rain had not fallen since early in the spring. Now it was August. I was oppressed by my heavy clothes and tired of labour which seemed, like so many professions in those days, to be established upon the misfortunes of others. I had spent a busy morning copying at great speed numbers of risks of insurance served upon me by an endless flow of brokers, those who made it their business to go between the insured—that is the merchant—and the insurer, an important being known as underwriter.

Yes, I was weary—impatient for some green river-bank where a man could again relate himself to the natural rhythm of life. I could not be content with the company of my colleagues at the long desk in the underwriting room. I liked these people, but I resented having to be with them. So, instead of going to one of the many city eating-houses for my midday meal, I had brought bread, cheese, and fruit and climbed to the roof of the building where I worked. Here, all my thoughts were gathered up in contemplation of that beautiful city—its chimneys, domes, spires, roofs, and monuments softened in the trembling waves of a hot summer day.

My eyes were on the river, that fair Thames which at the port of the City widens out to the sea. I saw, trailing in the air above a small barge, a dense moving cloud as small as a man's hand. Travelling towards the bridge it grew larger as I watched it. An intense lassitude overcame me. The air was very still, smoke hung like cloth in the sky. I was aware that a group of people had gathered on the roof of a building opposite, and were pointing to the growing cloud that sailed along above the river.

I heard steps on the iron ladder behind me. Two or three youths came up and began to talk excitedly. Below in the street, a string of vehicles had stopped, waiting at a cross road; people on top of omnibuses were craning their heads out of windows and staring into the sky. The policeman who controlled the movement of the traffic had forgotten his duty, and stood with arms outstretched, his mouth agape, his face turned upward. Now the cloud had grown large above the City; the sun was partially obscured, it was as though there was an eclipse. I heard shouts and a quick spasmodic fluttering. It was no cloud that hovered above the streets and obscured the sun. It was a great company of small twittering birds of bright plumage. They circled round and round like creatures looking for a landing-place. Mingled with their piping voices and the fluttering of their little wings, were the cries of amused people and the strident signals of motor-cars. The traffic stream thickened. One man in a powerful car impatiently sounded his alarm several times; he did not seem interested in the birds. All down the street I saw people, running in and out of offices, and crowding on to roofs in order to obtain a better view of the birds.

Suddenly, with a swoop as though one of their number had given them a command, they descended. Regardless of the people they brushed in passing, they settled some few hundred yards away from me, in the great open square in the heart of the City, called Royal Exchange.

*

The sky was clear again now, and the sun intensely hot. For a few moments I stayed, trying to read a purpose into what I had seen. My companions had left me and joined the crowd. I saw

them pushing their way in and out of the mass of people below.
There were policemen attempting to coerce the crowd in other
directions and clear a path for the traffic. But they could do very
little. At last, I too went down and pushed my way through. The
Royal Exchange was a large building in the ancient Greek style—
of more antiquarian than practical value, for little business was
transacted within its walls in those days, though carols were sung
in it at Christmas-time. At the main entrance was a colonnade of
smoke-blackened pillars raised upon a lofty tier of stone steps.
Two streets branched away on either side: one, Cornhill—the
other, Threadneedle. Because of this singularly domestic title,
the large and important building, not unlike a prison, which ran
parallel to the street, was popularly known as "the old lady of
Threadneedle Street." It was an apt title. For this edifice was the
restraining influence over our national extravagance—a fortress
of formidable power. Its actual name was the Bank of England.

Bank? No, nothing to do with green fields or riversides. We
could spend a long time discussing it, but I must content myself
with no more than a passing reference.

It was a vast building with vaults in which were locked gold
bars. Upon these the country established its trade with other
countries. We actually no longer dealt in gold; we transacted
business with slim pieces of paper which were based upon the
value of the gold in the Bank.

It was thus a most important place, and although the control
of the country's affairs was supposed to emanate from some his-
toric houses in another part of London, called Westminster, few
governmental policies could be evolved without the assistance of
the Bank of England. It might be said that the actual seat of government was in the City of London, not in Westminster.

One other building, with the Royal Exchange and the Bank of
England, completed that trinity of temples to commerce which
were at the centre of the dying heart of the City of London. This
was the Mansion House. I do not know why it was ever given
that redundant and comic title, unless to lend more importance
to its annual tenant, a person known as Lord Mayor, the master
of London's merchants, who was elected every year by other
merchants who formed what was known as the Corporation

of London. He was always a popular dignitary, having usually mounted his way from shop or humble store to the Italianate corridors of his vast home. The original Lord Mayor had been one, Dick Whittington, an enterprising boy with a cat. Now he had become a legend, always remembered in the great sooty Mansion House which, like the Exchange, had a classical colonnade before it.

Here, then, were Royal Exchange, Bank, and Mansion House, and converging into the centre of these three main buildings, a bewildering number of streets, all thick with slow-moving traffic and slower-moving people. There were steps leading underground to the various subterranean railways which delivered people to their houses in the outer suburbs. Shops of all descriptions lined a street called Cheapside, which led westwards and ran parallel with another street of like nature, named after a recently reigning queen. Hemmed in by jostling shops, many old churches strove to raise their grey heads to the sky. They were refreshing haunts of solitude and peace in busy midday hours, many of them in those days, when orthodox religion was suffering a steady decline, offering entertainments of music as a bait to people who might otherwise have forgotten their existence.

This, then, is a vague picture of the whirlpool of activity into which I plunged that still summer afternoon. With urchins shouting in my ears news of the entire breakdown of all peace negotiations in Europe; with hot, bewildered people hurrying along Cornhill; with the engines of innumerable vehicles grumbling angrily, like beasts in cages unable to move more than a yard or so; with the unremitting fire of the afternoon sun, merciless as it can only be in a great city; with all this bubble of humanity fermenting around me; with no tree or flower in sight, to cool the passage of the sun's rays, I came to the Bank, there to witness the extraordinary spectacle of thousands of small birds, thick as a mighty swarm of clustered bees, twittering and ruffling their shining feathers, spread like an autumn fall of forest leaves over the steps and in the square before the Exchange. And all round, on every side, were people, pressed thick against each other, talking in quick, half-amused, half-timid whispers, full of wonder and amazement.

It was a strange scene.

*

I was hemmed in at the back of the crowd and could only catch an occasional glimpse of the birds. A messenger in a tall shining hat and a green uniform with brass buttons, stood beside me.

"Can you see them?" I asked. "What are they like?"

"Some say they're pink, some say they're purple, but I haven't been able to get near enough myself to see. Never mind, they'll tell us all about them in the papers to-morrow."

He referred to the daily printed accounts of current events which were published throughout the country. These journals were permitted a remarkable licence in their commentaries, all giving different accounts of the same event as it best suited their purpose—that is to say, the tastes of their particular section of the public. They told not only stories of the past, but prophesied concerning the future. And since any prophet, however false, has a magnetic power over people's activities, many of the events forecast in the Press actually came to pass. People, in fact, did what the Press told them to do.

I grew impatient, and began to push my way nearer to the front. Eventually I reached a line of policemen who struggled with outstretched arms to prevent the people from swaying into the midst of the birds. The policemen did not look happy; sweat trickled from their helmets down the sides of their faces. Nobody seemed to know what to do. There was no known law or remedy which could effectively cope with a sudden invasion of many thousand strange birds.

I was able to study them closely now. About as large as starlings, they were neither pink nor purple as the messenger had surmised, but an ambiguous shade of dark jade green. This colour, catching the bright sunlight, sometimes shone blue, sometimes purple. Each one had a little ruff of feathers round his neck which stuck out like a hat above his head. The brightest part of their colouring was in the breast, from the throat downwards, where the feathers were smooth and of a glossy sheen which seemed to reflect all colours. Their little beaks were curved, not unlike a parrot; they had sharp, very lively eyes which gave them an inquisitive, impertinent expression. Their tail feathers were rather bedraggled, so that from behind they appeared to be dull, squalid creatures. Whereas from the front they were alive and full of colour. Their behaviour was interesting. Lined in thick ranks up the steps, they did nothing but sit there, looking at the people who studied them, with almost critical intensity, as though they themselves were studying us. Indeed, the longer I watched them, the more I felt that it was ourselves, rather than the birds, who had no place in this City. They showed no sign either of aggression or timidity. They twittered occasionally and sometimes ruffled their feathers; otherwise they were silent. The noise they made was not very pleasant; much of it would have been intensely irritating. And the longer I looked at them, the more irritated I began to feel. That flamboyant colouring, that impudent little ruff which had first charmed me, began now to annoy me as would a person of great wealth who dressed in opulent bad taste. Yet I was too fascinated to try to break away from the crowd.

I heard a disturbance not far from me. An old woman was trying to push her way towards the police.

"I do wish you'd let me through," she kept snapping in a thin wavering voice. "I do wish you'd make way. All frightened of a few birds. They're hungry, that's what it is. They want a peck of seed, poor things."

She had a large paper bag in her hand.

"Now then, ma'am," said a policeman, "you leave those birds alone."

"Not me," she replied. Suddenly she plunged her hand into the bag, and threw a handful of seed into the midst of the flock.

They paid not the slightest attention.

Everybody laughed and people began to talk more easily. The old woman stood, perplexed, not knowing what to do.

"Try again, mother," urged a small boy near her.

"No," she whimpered, "no, I don't think so."

She clutched her bag and attempted to break farther back into the crowd, away from the birds.

I remember two things happening at once, which quickened

this inert mass of people to incipient movement. The Exchange clock struck the half after two; and one bird suddenly rose from the centre of the flock, impelled as it seemed by some individual urge, and flew straight towards that section of the crowd where the old woman was standing.

This had an extraordinary effect upon her. She screamed, darted her head down, and began to butt her way through the crowd. The bird flew above, low over our heads. Some tried to coax it towards them; some backed away as it seemed to approach them. The old woman's hat fell off her head; she paid no attention to it but pursued her difficult path.

"Let me out," I heard her scream. "I've never done no harm to anyone. Let me out."

This declaration seemed irrelevant. But her alarm was contagious. Two or three girls began to laugh hysterically; there was danger of some being suffocated in the seething mob. I myself, weary and sick with heat, made efforts to get away. But I could do no more than go where I was pushed. I saw the solitary bird, hanging above the people like a child's bright toy swaying from a cord. Somebody struck at it with a stick, missed, and struck again.

"Leave it alone," screamed the old woman. "Else it'll get me and pay me out. Leave it alone."

One of the policemen pushed savagely past me and forced his way to a telephone box.

Then suddenly, the entire flock of birds rose into the air, higher and higher, darkening, as they had before, the sun's light.

The crowd broke rapidly then over the courtyard and steps of the Exchange, where a moment before the birds had been assembled. Everybody looked up to the sky. From the jutting triangle of a jeweller's shop some hundred yards away, to the portico of the Exchange, the dense cloud of birds hung and diminished like a thick pall over the City. They seemed bound together by an invisible thread; not one straggler hung on the edge of their great company.

As we watched, they rose higher, smaller still, till there was no more that the eye could follow. They did not just fly away; they seemed slowly to dissolve like smoke till the sky was blue again.

I found myself talking excitedly to two or three people near me.

"There'll have to be a new clause in insurance policies," chuckled a shabby-looking old gentleman who held a long black wallet under his arm.

The crowd had quickly broken up, people were already hurrying back to their offices and shops, the released traffic sped along Cornhill as though to make up for lost time. Everybody seemed to have forgotten the old woman with the seed.

"What happened to her?" I asked somebody.

I was told that she had last been seen running down the steps of the underground railway. Curious about her, I ran quickly down to the cool labyrinth of passages that twined in and out of the Bank station.

That was a bewildering world. There were long passages, artificially lit and decorated by advertisements, (we will talk of advertisements later.) There were wash-houses and lavatories where the student of human abnormalities could observe the strayed twistings of the sexually-possessed mind, scrawled furtively on the marble walls of each little private stool. There were mechanically controlled stairs which conveyed the passenger to his train without his having to exert the muscles of his legs; and rows of telephone boxes where a man could talk with his friend miles away. I remember those small, close boxes with peculiar detestation. Many a time I had been penned inside them, sick with heat and the rancid fumes of sweat and tobacco smoke left by the previous occupant of the box. Yes, they are very vivid in my mind, those little boxes with their black breath-spangled speaking-tubes. Perhaps because of what I saw that afternoon. For when I drew near them, I saw a small group of people clustered outside one of the doors. A policeman dominated the scene.

The object of the crowd's attention was our old woman. I asked somebody what had happened. He was a small ragged boy who told me that the old woman, running in terror from the bird, had shut herself into one of the boxes.

But not before the bird had flown in too.

There followed, apparently, a furious conflict. The old woman had slashed right and left with her umbrella. I saw evidence of that in the broken glass; the gashed umbrella with its spokes caught in the wire of the telephone; the mouthpiece hanging and swaying from the coin-box; the torn and trampled directory.

"They got her out then," I said to the boy.

Yes, he said, they got her out. But she was in a faint now.

"What happened to the bird?" I asked.

He disregarded my question. There was a sudden hush over the people. Two men pushed their way through with a stretcher. Presently they emerged again, carrying her, with a cloth over her body.

Somebody whispered, "Poor old thing. . . ."

Again I asked, almost impatiently, for nobody seemed to realize the importance of my question, "What happened to the bird?"

Nobody knew anything about the bird. In the general disturbance it had been forgotten. Not a feather was left as evidence of its presence.

The old woman died that night in a hospital where they took her. There followed the customary inquiry into the cause of her death, and it was given that she had died of heart failure, following upon intense shock and alarm. It was also disclosed that she had been a procuress—that is, one who traded in the bodies of young girls for the sexual gratification of others.

*

I must interrupt this account of the birds over our City, in order to set before you, with more clearness, the scene in which I moved. Chiefly, I would like to tell you something about my mother— to re-create for you a character so full of whimsical charm, of erratic judgment, of instinctive wisdom, of great sweetness and bitterness combined—that no record of myself could ever be complete without reference to her from whom I inherited so much. She was a small frail woman at that time, with long, slender hands, graceful and expressive. I remember her long, pointed forefinger, with the rounded curve of a well-arched nail, always most beautifully manicured, the nail never protruding beyond the tip of the finger. I remember that finger, the shape of it laid over a keyboard as she played and sung, or bent round a needle as she sewed. Most do I remember it, forked inside the pages of a book she was reading; it recalls to my mind most vividly the characteristic habit she had of reading books backwards and forwards, from here to there, as her spirit dictated.

Although she was small, her head, with its greying mass of often unruly hair, made her appear larger than she really was. It was a massive face, stronger than the body which supported it. Her hair seemed to fly about her like some downy substance having a purely adventitious relation to her head and transforming the harshness of her features into a radiance—indefinably soft, warm, and shadowy. Her nose tyrannized over this tropical scene like a palm tree reared above soft ferns. My dear mother—how she would laugh could she hear me say that! Many were the jokes we had about her nose. It was large, crooked in the middle with a bridge—what was termed a Roman nose. In truth it was Jewish. There was something far away and vagabond in her appearance which suggested Hebraic ancestry. Her eyes were grey, with that quickening spirit of sensitivity which often distinguishes grey eyes. Her mouth was rather tight. She had, I remember, a determined jaw; one that could snap if necessary—and indeed, often when not necessary. She had high cheek-bones and, at times, a florid complexion which could agitate the tranquillity of that far away expression. It was not always a serene face. Sometimes it was quick with potential movement; alive with an odd, secretive humour, purely her own. It was strong; it was weak. It was generous; it was self-centred. It was soft; it was hard.

Sometimes, when she was reading, I studied her face and saw in it the power of an empress—cold, impersonal, aloof. Then it was a grand face. But best I like to remember it when she was listening to some trouble that oppressed me. Then it was so warm, so quick to grasp my meaning, so intuitive in understanding—I felt my trouble was dispelled without her saying a word.

We were much alike, in ill-humour and good. We used to quarrel at least once a week. She loved, as did I, the tense atmosphere that springs up around two people at odds with each other. It is significant that such explosions of temperament were termed "scenes." Our scenes were always a great stimulus to the love we bore each other; they always concerned themselves with trivial differences. In effect, they were only the clash of wills so alike as often to resent that similarity.

As a young woman my mother had been very beautiful, with a power to command which was never allowed to develop. Her mother had rigorously curbed in her every natural bud that should have flowered. Her education had been that of a young gentlewoman of those days. That is to say, she was taught to believe that she was incapable of any individual activity; that simple domestic tasks were not only beyond her, but beneath her dignity; and that her duty was to sit still in a chair, watching from behind the traditional aspidistra—always known as the Plant—with which such families would darken their windows, the passing to and fro of men and women in the workaday world. Had she been of a high intellectual capacity such a static pose might have been turned to good account. There had been other women before her, who from silent contemplation of a teacup were able to endow the world with incisive commentaries upon human behaviour. But my mother's whole impetus to life lay in her body, her face, her hands. She was intended for movement and adventure. She could, I believe, have ridden the fastest horse, swum the heaviest sea, or braved the fiercest gale. But she could not stand aside from life and make a record of what she saw. Her whole nature wished to expand, to give—not to imbibe and digest. And this repression of her natural qualities resulted later in the strange quixotic medley which composed the unresolved drama of her life. It was the reason why she was indiscriminately generous and at the same time, self-centred; why she loved youth and yet criticized it resentfully; why she read book after book in a sad attempt to recover that Odyssey she had barely glimpsed as a young girl.

My dear mother. . . .

She had lost her husband many years previously. I remembered him with affection as a man who rarely punished or rebuked me, but gave me rides on his shoulders, taught me how to swim, and led me for long walks in the country when I had been a little boy. No whim of his wife had been too much for him to indulge.

I was their only child, and she loved me as a mother does the one seed who has sprung from her. Loved me perhaps too much, yet who will dare question the extravagance of love in a world that saw so little of it? She gave her life over to me and lived in my development. She could not detach herself from me. I do not believe there was a single thing I did, a single emotion I felt, which she did not feel as acutely. And in return I gave, often, such casual treatment as sons are apt to give their mothers, accepting her as part of my life, but too seldom declaring my indebtedness to her with my lips.

We lived, my mother and I, in a long, long street in a northern suburb of the City, called Stroud Green. I do not know what Stroud meant and there was little enough green about it. On either side of that depressing street were houses—so many of them you would have said, had they been trees, this is a forest. They all looked exactly the same. The street rose up a high hill to a ridge from where on clear days you could see the distant spires and roofs of London. If you turned the other way you would see a colossal edifice composed of stunted towers, glass domes, and pinnacles, which was known as Alexandra Palace. This was, I believe, intended as a house of entertainment, though whom it entertained I could never discover. In my childhood I remember a menagerie of monkeys there; statues of slyly draped men and women with chipped breasts and noses; slot machines which never worked; painted effigies of the kings of England; and palm trees rearing out of shallow tubs to press themselves like stiff hands against the glass roof. In one great hall was a mighty instrument for making music, a machine called organ which my grandfather had often played many years ago. Now it was never used, and the whole place was like a gigantic mortuary.

The house in which we lived had a number like all the others, but not a name as many had. Our number was Three-hundred-and-ninety-six. This number; the name of the road—which I cannot remember—and the name of the district—Stroud Green, constituted what was known as our address. Inside it was very much the same as any of the other houses, although we boasted one or two pieces of inherited furniture of good craftsmanship. But it was crowded, airless, and unhealthy, receiving little sunlight.

One of our rooms was centred by a massive table with a red baize cloth on it. There were romantic pictures on the walls; one of Jesus, that good prophet you have heard me speak of, who constituted the foundation of our religion. Here he was shown praying in a garden at night, the supernatural light of God shining on his face. There were pictures of relatives who had died long ago—one of my mother's mother in a heavy silver frame, wearing a spangled poke bonnet.

There was another room, called drawing-room. It was used on Sunday afternoons, and occasionally when we had guests, rarely otherwise. The old walnut piano my mother loved to play to herself was in the warmer room. It is that room I remember. With all its lack of design and freedom, with all its close sealed-up atmosphere, its loud and ugly decorations, its entire inability to calm a mind as a room should, it is yet the one room I remember which changed Three-hundred-and-ninety-six from a house to a home.

And that is only because here my mother sat, day in, day out, working her needles, reading her books, eating her frugal meals, playing her old songs, and for ever thinking, dreaming, and praying for that one child with whom she had laboured twenty years earlier.

I must cease for to-day. The sun has tired me; my mind cannot unwind the threads of this tale until I have dropped from me the burden of an old lullaby my mother, Lillian, used to sing.

*

The evening of the day the birds had come, I stood in a long carriage, travelling underground towards my home. There were seats, two long lines of them facing each other, but they were already full of people when I boarded the train. Those of us who could, held on to straps that depended from the roof, in order to keep our balance in the jolting, swaying car.

At every station on the way, more and more people crammed

their way in. They had literally to use force to get into the car at all. Thus, on the hottest summer evening, one stood, attired in dark tight clothes, sweating all over one's body and breathing upon the neck or nose of a man or woman pressed tight against one. It is strange that this close proximity never caused people the smallest embarrassment, though had you taken two of them, male and female, and placed them in a large double bed, they would probably have been overwhelmed with shame.

Let us not stay long in this car. It is too hot to try to remember something a thousand times hotter and more airless. But before I leave it I should like to describe to you the advertisements which were framed above the seats of the carriage.

An advertisement was a fanciful and often highly artistic laudation—whether in words or pictures—of various commodities which manufacturers wished to sell to the public. Every possible article was advertised so cunningly, that very often people were induced to buy things which they did not really require. Nothing escaped advertisement—no, I am wrong. Two articles of universal interest, armaments and contraceptives, were, so far as I remember, never given the publicity of the advertisement.

That evening there was, naturally, a great deal of lively conversation about the birds. Speculation as to the origin of the birds ran wildly in various quarters. Some had it that they were emigrants from North Africa, where at that time a war was supposed to be in progress. Some affirmed that they had escaped from a private aviary. My paper announced that an eminent ornithologist would give his views on the subject the following day. As I came out of the train, gasping with relief to feel the evening air, I remember how the coming of the birds seemed to have cast an unreal shade over every familiar thing that I saw. I had to wait in a long train of people in order to mount an omnibus at a place called Finsbury Park. As always, there was a beggar-man. He was playing very sweetly on a violin, long drawn-out tunes of other years. I fumbled in my pocket for a coin, could not find one, and blushed because he had looked at me searchingly as my hand went to my pocket. I gave him nothing. The bus moved away.

As we passed away from the man, I identified his starved music with a message, a prophecy, a warning, though I knew not of what. For the rest of the journey home I could feel nothing but heaviness upon my spirit, even though the prospect of bearing to my mother the tale of the birds filled me with excitement.

I was oppressed, oppressed by something nameless. Even the deep-sinking blue of the evening sky where a half-moon lay like a trimmed cloud, seemed to me lifeless with a passive apprehension of change.

*

My mother was sitting beneath a sunshade in an easy-chair in the small strip of garden at the back of the house. Annie, the little creature known as the "maid," who waited upon us and did most of the housework, greeted me with her customary grin. Though this expression of hers generally warmed me, it irritated me that evening. I took little notice of her, but went out through the kitchen door and into the garden.

"What would you do, Mother," I asked, "if the sky was suddenly darkened by a great mass of strange birds like you had never seen before?"

I lay down on the grass beside her chair. Scrumpled up near her feet was her daily paper, and next to it the book she had been reading, its place marked by her spectacle case.

She threw down the other book she was reading—she often read from two at the same time—and smiling a little irritably, said she would love to see the sky full of birds.

"There are never enough in this place for my liking," she said.

A flying machine rumbled high up in the soft sky as she spoke, and I seized upon it as a continuation of my theme.

"Suppose the sky was thick with those things?" I suggested.

She shook her head.

"No," she said. "I can't bear them. They always remind me of the war."

My mother then asked me what made me talk of birds and aeroplanes, why I looked so worried, and why I had not kissed her as was my habit? I kissed her then, and showed her the evening paper. Presently I was deep in a description of the event of the day, telling her everything, from my first view of the birds over the Thames, to the carrying-away of the old woman from the telephone box.

"I was thinking," I added at the end, "what will happen to London when all these birds start casting their loads over us."

My mother asserted that it was a good thing they weren't cows, at which there was a raucous laugh from Annie, who had been standing in the doorway listening to us all the while.

"Go away, Annie," said my mother, with a slight frown. And as the girl went inside she turned to me and told me what she told me every evening: that she was sick of the habit the girl had, of hanging on the edge of our conversations.

"Of course she's in love with you," grumbled my mother. "They all are, silly things."

I assured her she was mistaken, though secretly I hoped they were.

Lillian complained of the heat, said we were going to have a thunderstorm, and that her stomach was all wrong again. Something she had eaten at lunch had disagreed with her.

"Like varnish it tasted," she murmured petulantly. "I don't know what's the matter with food. Like varnish."

"Aren't you interested in the birds?" I asked. With remarkable contempt she declared that no doubt they had all "escaped" from somewhere and would soon be caught.

I was irritated by her lack of interest and went into the kitchen to eat my supper of cold meat, salad, and tea. There, Annie encouraged me to give another and fuller account of the birds. This conversation between Annie and myself so enraged my mother that she stumbled impatiently into the kitchen, fussed incoherently with one of her most histrionic gestures over a minute tea-stain I had made on the tablecloth, and declared passionately that nobody cared for her, I least of all; her money was all I wanted; and she might as well never have been born for all the use she was in life. She shouted, she clutched things, she paced up and down. I sat and glowered and snapped dark cynicisms at her. And the strange thing is that all the time we were on the point of laughter. At any moment her mouth, twisting with abuse, could have broken into wild and lovely laughter.

I went out towards sunset and walked to the top of the ridge called Mountview, where there were seats overlooking brittle, sun-scorched lawns. Here a number of people, dressed in white clothes and holding instruments composed of networked catgut, were patting grey balls over sagging string nets. This was a diversion called tennis, very much favoured by City people as a relaxation from the labour of the day.

Gloomily I watched them playing. It was growing dark, and they could not see the ball very clearly. Laughter came from a group of youths and girls in the clubhouse.

I sat up there, thinking and wondering about the birds. The scent of lime trees hung in the air and small white stars began to pierce the deep veil of the sky. Spread out in the hollow beyond the tennis courts were all those haphazard pieces of roof, chimney, spire, and dome, which fell miraculously into the one great mosaic of London. Set in the middle, poised like a pensive judge over a babbling court, was the dome of the Cathedral. It seemed to be composed of some flexible substance, like a bladder of smoke, pausing for a while before it should disperse into the luminous green sky around it. Viewed from the ridge it became the heart from which all activity seemed to emanate. I could see the sumptuous and strangely Oriental tower of Westminster from which the immense clock struck its bells—those friendly quarterings of music which Englishmen all over the world remembered with the affection a son feels towards his parents. I could see steeples and bridges, towers and factory chimneys, and in the foreground the gloomy drum of a gas-container. Yet always my eyes remained focused on the Cathedral; almost unwillingly, because it made such a claim upon vision, my eye returned to that dome.

Whether it was a trick of evening mist I did not know, but as the sky darkened and the red glow of the sunset began to hold the City in an embrous flare, I thought I saw a thin, spreading shadow of fast-moving cloud. It was unlike any cloud I had ever seen. As it moved it seemed to prolong itself until it was nothing but a thin whip of blackness.

I turned to go. The people were leaving the tennis courts for the night. I heard their voices crying "Good-night" and "See you to-morrow." Some couples lingered arm in arm under the plane trees.

I came to our road. Before I descended the hill I stayed a moment looking at the sprawling shape of the Alexandra Palace, all its windows lurid with the last rays of the sun.

I felt in everything a dreadful sense of the instability of the mock-world we had set up in place of the real world which was our heritage.

A woman was walking slowly up the hill, without hat or coat. I saw it was Lillian, and ran to greet her. We were immediately in sympathy with each other's mood. She reproached me gently for leaving her alone so long, and said she could not rest, it was so hot. I told her I was sorry, and desiring to show her the City as I had seen it, took her arm and led her up the hill to the ridge.

"You're like your mother, son," she kept saying. "Like your mother."

But at the top there was no dying twilight City to show her. The sky was dark, the stars blotted out above the City. Only a pale yellow ribbon of light lay on the horizon. There was no breath of wind. The pavements seemed to thrust a sticky warmth up into our faces.

"Come, son," said Lillian, "we shall be caught in the rain and catch our deaths."

So we hurried down the hill, went into our house, and opened a bottle of red wine to quench our thirsts. We sat in the room till late, the windows wide open, the air so still that the curtains never stirred, and the voices of people talking in a little group at the corner of the road were easy to hear.

Lillian did not retire to her room till long after midnight. Although I went to bed before her I could not sleep. I lay naked, with one sheet half covering me, listening to the clock striking the hours and trying to assemble into some shape a hundred confused images that raced and twisted in my bewildered mind.

*

In the night while we all slept, the birds had come again. I had known it, of course, from the moment I had seen that long black line over the City, and tried to assure myself that it was a cloud. Lying in my bed sleepless for many hours, I had known the birds would come. Yet even to myself I would not admit this fact.

The next day was the last in the week, a half-holiday for the City workers. There were fewer people in the train at Stroud Green, because many were allowed the whole day in which to rest. Some carried tennis rackets or cricket bats. They would spend their afternoon on one of the many sports grounds around London.

This predilection for athletics possessed the English temperament to a remarkable degree and was probably the only part of their lives which many people considered with any real seriousness. Their national game, cricket, was so respected as to be discussed in the newspapers in a leading position together with international politics and celebrated crimes.

(Were crimes respected? Well, yes. In a sense they were. They gave employment, do you see, to a vast number of people— policemen, judges, lawyers, and such like, who would otherwise have had no place in society.)

I am afraid I rarely spent those precious Saturday afternoons on any playing-field, though once or twice I had played cricket in local games. But my team-spirit hardly existed. I could not bear standing in a field all the afternoon waiting to receive the ball. It seemed always so much more comfortable to lie down. Yes, they were tedious, those games, though I made many simple friends amongst the cricketers.

Most Saturdays in the summer I went into the country north of London where I could find a field in which to lie and compose those callow observations upon Nature which I called poems.

In the train, that Saturday morning, I drifted into conversation with some people from whom I learnt that the birds had gathered at an early hour, before dawn, in a place called Trafalgar Square and were, for all they knew, still there. Everybody was talking about them, although this new activity had not yet been reported in the papers, which were full of yesterday's invasion of the City.

As soon as the train reached the station I jumped from the carriage before it had stopped, and ran quickly to the office in Leadenhall. I expected to come across a scene of confusion similar to yesterday, and was almost disappointed when I found that everything was the same as usual.

The office was half empty. I had little work to do, and was in a perpetual fever to leave the place, take an omnibus to Trafalgar Square, and see if the birds were still there. None of us did much work. Every broker who came into the room delivered fresh and diverging accounts of the scene in the West End, as that part of London was termed. Apparently the birds were still there and could not be moved.

Eventually one o'clock came, the time when the office would close down for that day and the following day. I and a colleague, a youth slightly older than myself, ran out, scrambled on to a bus, and began to move slowly westward. As we drove along, it was soon apparent that some considerable disturbance held up the traffic at the other end. We left the bus near a station and walked, or rather pushed, towards Trafalgar Square.

I have already told you how I went there twenty years ago and saw the column of the sea-lord strewn along the ground like the splintered backbone of some great beast. To-day he was in his proper place, secure in the sky on his lofty pedestal, with four guardian lions below him to keep his enemies at bay.

But they had not been able to keep the birds at bay.

Covering the graven figure and clustered along his column, bound over the entire monument like a soft carpet of moss or lichen, the birds clung with a still tenacity that made one doubt whether they were not some furry growth that had sprouted from the stone overnight.

That was not all. As at the Bank, only over a far wider expanse, the birds had assembled. The crowd was thick, immense, and traffic was in complete chaos.

On the balustrade of the National Gallery I saw a party of schoolgirls. There appeared to be some excitement amongst them, though I could not see very clearly. I saw the girls running about, a small fluttering shape amongst them, and I heard distressed little cries.

My friend and I pushed here and there, trying to get closer to the birds. We found that the best thing to do was to climb to the top of a bus which stood stationary at the bottom of the Strand.

It was already crowded with people, and we mounted it with difficulty. Only by prying between the heads of people clustered around the open windows of the vehicle could we obtain any sort of view.

There were many more birds than the day before. They sat very still, though in several places I could detect a curious heaving of their ranks as though something below were trying to force a way out.

Suddenly we heard shouting. The crowd swayed aside to make a path for mounted police who had been summoned to deal with the chaos.

We watched, excited. Somebody shrieked in a thin, muffled voice. I saw something that looked like an arm, tattered with loose flesh and torn clothing, rise feebly from the mass of birds.

Then, with one precise movement the birds rose into the air. The flapping of their wings; their harsh squeaking and gibbering—so curiously similar to the excited cries of the people—drowned the noise of the traffic and the screams of those who were near them as they ascended.

From the National Gallery, from the monument, in one dense rank they took flight, straight as an arrow along the Strand. They were not more than a few yards above our heads. It seemed that all the Strand, as far as the eye could see, was overshadowed by this moving canopy of winged shapes. As they slowly diminished into the sky, a heavy silence fell over us all. Only when the birds had vanished out of sight did the crowd break up with excited chattering.

I turned and looked again at the empty square. The police were attempting to restrain the people from swarming towards objects that looked like mounds of dung-bespattered rags. The schoolgirls were running wildly down the steps.

I was faint with the heat and an offensive smell that had begun to pollute the air.

"Come on," said my friend, "let's get away from this. It's making me sick."

In Trafalgar Square they were reassembling on to stretchers the rags and broken bones, the crumpled flesh and blood that hours before had been the somnolent forms of destitute men and women who had been passing the night there. I do not know how many were killed. We did not stay to watch, as many did, the clearing away of their crushed, clawed bodies. We went quickly to a small sandwich-bar and sat, I remember, speechless for several minutes, drinking beer and attempting to think calmly.

★

The next day was a Sunday, often called "the day of rest," the day when the few practising Christians left in our island went to their churches to worship their God. I am not going to attempt to explain the religion of those times here; it is too complicated and would only become tedious. Yet I like to remember some of those Sundays, when I travelled up to the strange empty City and attended the evening service at one or other of the cathedrals. How well I remember walking over London Bridge on dark afternoons, with the glow of lamps bright in the quiet City, and the bells ringing noisily from every tower and steeple.

There was something staunch and defiant about those old bells of the City, like a dog who will bark by his master's corpse. I used to pause sometimes on the bridge and watch the dim lights of barges passing along the river. I could hear the swish of water inaudible in weekdays because of the traffic. Wrapt in gloom behind me was the immense pillar of the black monument which commemorated a fire that had destroyed the City centuries before. There was always a faint smell of fish and rotten fruit. I could see right along the river to the chain of yellow lights by the embankment near Trafalgar Square. How quiet, how retrospective it was—the tall offices locked till to-morrow, the few omnibuses half empty, the streets forlornly peopled by the dark shapes of strange, poor creatures whom one never saw at any other time. Where they came from, where they went to, nobody ever knew.

I would go to an old cathedral on the other side of the bridge, buried away under a railway arch, its beautiful compact tower scarcely visible because of the warehouses and railway lines that closed it in. It was pleasant to sit in the half-dark nave, my eyes held by the brass candelabrum that swayed slightly as though the breath of its candles had given it life. The singing was good here;

the music, I remember, better than in any other London church; the people who came were more devout, less flamboyant. The building was ancient and full of sombre beauty in dim roof and candle-gloomy chapel. Sometimes a train would roar over the bridge above. Then the quiet psalms and songs from the sanctuary were lost; I felt I was the adherent of some dying religion secreted in a catacomb under the earth.

Afterwards, with a warm glow of emotion spreading over me, I would sometimes go to the station tavern with a friend who came up from another part of London and with whom I had been at school as a boy. Here we would sit over the Sunday newspapers, discussing new books, plays, music, and political developments. They were pleasant evenings, good to recall. When I think of those Sundays I am reminded of one in particular which stands out vividly in my memory.

It was a Sunday when the birds assembled in enormous numbers in a large park in the west of London. Huddled thickly together amongst the trees and shrubs, they showed no inclination to move and were not particularly offensive. This more natural behaviour did not at first alarm people greatly. It was fitting, we felt, that birds should make for trees and grassy spaces.

After some time, however, the melancholy presence of these curiously inactive creatures, forever clustered in the branches of the trees and rarely flying or making any sound, began to be, to say the least, embarrassing. Fewer people visited the park. The eccentricity of the birds was admitted and became the source of much humorous commentary. But the humour was shadowed by a dubious edge of apprehension. What were the birds going to *do*? What were *we* going to do?

Here is the story of what we did, or rather failed to do.

I have often told you of the cruelties of that time and how it was termed "sporting" for a man to spend five or six months feeding young birds so as to make them tame, then, on a given day, ask his friends to come and shoot them. Every year in August there was a great exodus from London to the north where rich stockbrokers and others used to rent moors and with the aid of an army of men called beaters, murder a vast number of entirely harmless and attractive birds, called grouse.

On this Sunday in that fatal summer, twelve of the best shots in the country arranged a magnificent shoot. Having obtained permission from the authorities these twelve sportsmen concocted the following elaborate plan. At five in the morning, just as dawn was breaking, each of them armed with a gun, accompanied by a loader with a spare gun and a huge array of cartridges, would take up his position at an allotted place in the adjacent park called Kensington Gardens. They were to be dotted about the gardens at intervals of three to four hundred yards, and each, as was the usual practice, was to secrete himself as much as possible. One, I remember, hid himself behind the statue of a very popular little boy who never grew up; another behind a huge statue of a man on a horse; another in a garden belonging to a park-keeper, and so on. Each man stood with his gun loaded, his loader behind him with the spare gun, and one or two dogs lying at his feet ready to pick up all the creatures his master destroyed.

At 5.15 a huge army of men armed with sticks and flags were to enter Hyde Park from the opposite side. In one long line they were to cover the whole of the far side of the Park and advance in strict order and line towards Kensington Gardens and the waiting guns, meanwhile waving their flags and making any kind of sound designed to lure the birds forward. It was hoped that by these means the birds would be encouraged to fly towards the guns and that even if very few were actually killed, those who remained unhurt would be too terrified ever to return and plague us again.

This was the plan, and up to a certain moment, all went well. With the greatest courage—at least, so I thought—the army of beaters advanced. Yes, there were the birds, thousands of them clustered together in the middle of Hyde Park. A friend of mine who was one of the beaters, told me that at this point of the sport, he began to feel extremely uneasy. What would happen if the birds refused to move?

However, they seemed to know what was required of them. When the line of beaters came to within fifty or sixty yards of the birds, they rose with one accord, uttering coarse, derisive little cries and dropping a great amount of ordure. Then they turned and headed straight for Kensington Gardens. My friend swore that they formed into twelve sections. Any jubilation or excitement he might once have possessed sunk to a heavy apprehension of danger. A yell rang out from the line of beaters, and whistles were frantically blown as signals to the waiting guns that the birds were coming.

What went through the minds of the sportsmen and their loaders, I wonder? The usual excitement of the "kill"? The needle-thrill of zero hour? Perhaps a faint apprehension? One can picture the scene, the "gun" standing at the ready, eagerly scanning the horizon, the loader waiting behind to pass the second gun, the dogs lying still but for the faint movement of an excited tail. Suddenly the birds appear. Up goes the gun to his shoulder; finger to trigger. "Bang, bang," change guns, "bang, bang."

But nothing has fallen. And what is it swooping down upon his upturned face, making blood-curdling noises such as he has never heard before and will certainly never hear again?

Perfectly organized, the line of beaters advanced steadily. They heard the first and second volleys break the stillness of the early morning. Now, if ever, they would see the end of these birds. But why was there no third volley? Their hearts sank, a sickening dread overcame them, and they began to run fearfully towards the twelve sportsmen. My friend headed for the statue of the boy, since he knew the man whose stand that was. Sick with fear, he saw no birds, not even a feather; nothing but the figure of his friend lying at the foot of the statue, his clothes torn and spattered with blood, his face hideously unrecognizable, his eyes torn from his head. A few yards away lay his loader in the same horrible condition. His two retrievers, pitiful to see, sat on either side of his mutilated body, howling inconsolably. A miserable church bell suddenly cracked on the air; the little figure of the statue played unconcernedly on his pipe as though nothing had happened. My friend ran from the place and said he would never want to go near it again.

The news of this attack soon reached north London. I remember I did not go to the cathedral by the river that evening. I was afraid. Of what? Birds? No. Of something far deeper which I could not attempt to define nor dared to try.

*

The twelve sportsmen were not the only ones who made any organized attempt to rout the birds. At least two other attempts come to my mind.

There was the tragic and futile case of the gallant and ambitious colonel who took his courage in both hands, without waiting for authority, and launched a hurriedly organized attack with his battalion, armed with rifles, hand-grenades, machine-guns, and all the ludicrous paraphernalia of war. This attack took place on a bleak stretch of country which was reserved for teaching the pride of our forces how best to hate and kill all foreigners. All that resulted was a ghastly confusion. Many of the soldiers were badly hurt, some killed. No birds appeared to be damaged. The wretched colonel, realizing the extent of his folly, committed suicide.

In all parts of the world, as we heard later, similar things were happening. In a place called Japan, where suicide was considered a most honourable death, a hundred young airmen dived simultaneously in a furious headlong smash to a ground infested with birds. Their machines were soaked in some highly inflammable substance. According to plan, the airplanes burst at once into blinding flames; the men, however, had sacrificed themselves in vain. For the birds rose through the flames unscathed and apparently much amused.

But I am pushing events too far forward. All these stories belong to the later days of September and we are still in August.

Day followed day, wearisome and fierce with heat. London, shocked and disturbed by the sinister incident in Trafalgar Square, seemed to be waiting—waiting in unspoken fear for the birds to come again. But the days passed and they did not come.

They were tense, heavy days; days in which I found it harder than usual to concentrate on my work in the City. It occurs to me that you know little of that work, and since it is important for you to understand the nature of my existence in those days, I should tell you something about the business of Insurance in which I was employed.

Very well then.

The office, Leadenhall Street.

Leadenhall. Does it convey a picture of imprisonment masquerading under hospitality? The word seems to me appropriate. For we were chained and we had somehow to maintain a pretence of satisfaction, since we all possessed what was known in those days as a "good safe job with a pension at the end." Our work was known as marine insurance, and it dealt entirely with the insuring of voyaging ships and their cargoes. It was not uninteresting provided imagination could carry one's pencil beyond the boundaries of a registered voyage to the actual places—so far away, so magical in sound—that one had written down.

Imagine several young men in a sound physical condition, seated side by side at long desks in a large room in which there is no adequate ventilation, writing such phrases as "Steamship *Arlanza*; Manchester to Rio; cotton goods; five thousand pounds." If you wrote several such phrases in a day you would begin to feel somewhat envious of the cotton goods. I used to turn over the pages of an atlas in order to locate some obscure port in Scandinavia or China, and I would find myself entranced by the very shape of a country, its mountains, its rivers, its vegetation, all romantically coloured on the map. For a moment I could see myself on the turret-deck of an oil tanker, my face scarred with the mark of the sea winds; heaving tipsily in a whaler in the Bering Sea, or floating placidly in the deep blue waters of the Indian isles. Suddenly a bell would ring and I would be summoned to carry a pen to the Underwriter's desk.

The very nature of this work tempted us to activity, emphasizing more forcibly the fact that we were bound by four thick walls. What forlorn cargoes we carried in our minds were shipped, one fortnight in the year, to some crowded seaside resort. No wonder that as time went on, all the individuality and natural yearning for adventure died out of a youth, till with advancing years he degenerated to a querulous old dullard with a family of children for whom he could imagine no other fate than his own.

I worked in a room called the underwriting room, the place where the main business of the marine department was conducted. There were about twenty of us; I, the youngest, called junior-clerk. Amongst other duties I had to copy what were known as declaration policies into large registers. I cannot remember many details of that labour; I have a distinct impression, however, that practically all the arduous work I thus executed was of little or no advantage to the firm, and that my carefully written records were rarely, if ever, referred to. At first, sensible of my fortunate position—for a desk in the underwriting room was something in the nature of an honour—I was conscientious, making my entries with scrupulous care. Later, when I realized they were never looked at but only lodged away in some basement strong-room where, year in year out, they grew thick with dust—I grew reckless, wrote quickly and illegibly, and only entered half what I was supposed to. I had been to the strong-room one day. Discovering old records of the firm's transactions dating back nearly two hundred years and by now entirely useless even as antiques, I had been seized with a frenzy of impatience for such a shameful waste of youth's energy. I took bundle after bundle of ancient claims documents in long yellow envelopes, foreign registers from branches all over the world, account books, and ledgers—all written by hands long ago dead—and thrust them into the great furnace that heated the water-pipes all over the building. How vivid that scene is! I trembled at my temerity, standing over that deep, white-hot pit, tumbling stack after stack of mildewed papers into the heart of that clean flame. I have always felt that I did the firm a great service in thus ridding them of many of their unwanted records.

I shall not enter into much description of the men who worked with me in that underwriting room. I can recall one who was permanently under the drowsing influence of alcohol. In the afternoon he could be depended upon to sign any risk in the firm's name, however precarious it may have been. To him, brokers with doubtful slips (pieces of paper on which rough details of the merchant's risk were given) flocked assiduously. It was a source of endless enjoyment to us younger clerks to watch this blithe inebriate, his black, glossy head swaying over the desk, scrawl his initials across a slip he had not even seen. If the ship he had so guaranteed on the firm's behalf were to founder within five minutes of his signing his initials, the firm would have eventually to pay the amount stated as value of the ship or cargo. The bare initials constituted a promise.

They all seem much the same to me, those men of all ages from twenty to sixty, cooped like scrabbling hens in one room. I close my eyes. I see wads of policies dropped on a desk before me; I see at the end of the day, baskets full of waste paper; I see a row of impatient brokers waiting for the Underwriter who will not emerge from his private sanctum; I see a powerful, exquisitely manicured hand turning over the pages of a massive scarlet book known as Lloyd's Register, wherein the details of every ship in the world are entered; I see a slip of pale-green paper which bears the announcement that such and such a ship is stranded and a total wreck off the Land's End.

They were all the same, I said. And so they were; essentially inoffensive men whose youth had been trapped in the beginning as mine had been trapped.

But there is one, who even to this day stands out as a type of humanity from whom selfish ambition had squeezed every noble principle that might originally have been present. This is the Underwriter. I cannot remember his name. He was always simply, the Underwriter: a creature of power who controlled the whole department; whose word or gesture might lose a man his position; whose total earnings were more than the sum amount of all the other men in the room.

The Underwriter. . . .

Picture a small bow-legged man with a wrinkled epicene face in which two eyes seem to press inwards to a thin slot above a flat nose; a yellow wig ill-concealing a head hairless as an egg; lips that curve inwards to a dry mouth; a body which would appear to be composed of some substance neither bone nor muscle, yet resilient as rubber; hands dry and as inexpressive as pieces of leather. A man who reserves a succulent smile for brokers who have been known to bring him good business; a man who encourages men to grovel before him, then suddenly kicks them away with a snarl. A man whose knowledge of the world is confined to figures on a blue slip of paper; a man who is the quintessential type of that odious being who flourished in our day under the name of capitalist.

To me that man is conspicuous as a sort of monster; a bloodless leech, sucking youth dry and bloating himself with its sweated energy. He was loathed by us all, yet nobody dared to disobey him.

Such was the Underwriter, a man honoured by his high position as head of one of the oldest marine insurance firms in the City of London; a man with the mentality of a fly and the power of a spider whose web has been built for him. We could not breed such a type to-day; were he by chance to appear amongst us we should treat him with compassion.

I will draw one picture for you, then I will cease for to-day.

It is midday of a hot summer morning, and the heat in the underwriting room is grossly oppressive. The junior clerk as he deals with the queue of brokers' boys at his desk is borne up and refreshed in his task by the slight breath of fresh air which finds its way in from an area through a half-open window near him. The Underwriter, however, who is at the other end of the room, thinks very differently about this stimulating little breeze. A soot has blown in and settled on his clean blotting-paper. He rings his bell and the junior clerk runs immediately to his desk, thus delaying his own pressing work. "Shut that window," says the Underwriter, without looking up. The junior clerk goes to the window and, whether accidentally or deliberately he never knows, lets it down on its cord with a sharp bang that echoes jarringly through the sanctimonious silence of the room. The silence that follows this unexpected noise seems emphasized. The Underwriter again rings his bell and the junior clerk again attends. "Let that happen again," says the Underwriter, "and I will have you removed."

The junior clerk stumbles back to his desk in a blind rage, wondering whether it would not be better to be removed.

*

About a week after the birds had appeared in Trafalgar Square the newspapers brought them before us with increased animation. Previously their visits had been confined to London. They had disappeared as miraculously as they had appeared; the last that had been seen of them, a smoky patch in the sky over the North Sea.

Now suddenly we heard of them in the remote islands of the Outer Hebrides, attention first being called to their presence by the agitation of immense flocks of gulls and other sea-birds who one morning all flew inland, screeching and wailing most dismally, and herding on to the roofs of small fishing villages. Almost simultaneous with this report came a similar tale from the west, where several of the uninhabited isles of Scilly were invaded by the birds, who drove the gulls away over the sea and back to Cornwall. A man in the lonely Wolf Lighthouse saw, through a telescope, ranks of dark-coloured birds—more like crows he reported—who appeared to be breaking up and heading in different directions.

Everybody was in a fever of excitement. In the office we could talk of little else, and even the Underwriter found it hard to maintain his usual profound gravity when news came through to Lloyd's—the great centre of marine activity where news of all shipping was received—of a British ship in which we were interested, having caught fire and exploded to a total loss somewhere in the Pacific Ocean near the Dutch East Indies. I remember the first vague report of her having been sighted in difficulties miles out to sea, nothing more than a struggling speck from which, as it seemed, a thick line of smoke uncoiled into the sky. I was told to run to Lloyd's, a few yards from our office. In the centre of that magnificent room was a rostrum in which sat a uniformed messenger whose duty it was to call, in a loud voice, any broker who was required for business. To him I gave the name of the broker whom our Underwriter wished to see in order to reinsure, if possible, the sinking ship.

I remember that nobody would touch that particular risk, so we could not avoid the heavy claim, both for the hull and for her cargo of arms which she had been carrying to China. Within a few hours we read on the tape-machine at Lloyd's that she had gone down with all her crew. No further news was ever received of her, but it was supposed that the birds had in some way mastered the vessel, confused her crew, and brought about her disaster.

Within a few days the newspapers were crowded with news

of the birds' activities in all parts of the world. There was a story of the Pope who, travelling in all his gorgeous panoply from the Vatican to some church in another part of Rome for an ecclesiastical function, was considerably agitated by the sudden collapse of the sumptuously embroidered canopy under which he was always carried. Apparently a small band of perhaps a hundred birds suddenly swooped upon it, cramming it down upon the venerable prelate's head. The Swiss Guards, who were always in attendance upon the Holy Father, raised their rifles and shot without much aim or discrimination into the air. An aged cardinal was killed. The birds, however, escaped and flew away, carrying large shreds of the canopy in their beaks. The Pope with great diplomacy and tact adjusted his tall white hat, moved his ringed hand over the people in the authentic sign of the cross of Jesus, and restored order. The cardinal was hastily carried away.

I remember that incident—though I was not, of course, present—because of the fact that although it had been strictly ordered by the Pope that no photographs were to be taken of his procession, one of our English newspapers devoted its entire back page to a misty picture of the prelate seated in his swaying throne, looking a little uneasy under a tattered canopy, surrounded by an immense crowd of soldiers, cardinals, and members of various religious orders, all in quaint costumes.

About this time also, a detestable man who had sprung into great prominence in Germany was grievously plagued by the birds on the occasion of an important political gathering. He was prominent as persecutor of the Jews and oracle of the old imperial war-cry of his country. Every now and again he used to address great gatherings of his people, the subject of his discourse generally being concerned with his desire for peace with all nations. Nobody in our island took these ingenuous aspirations seriously, an attitude which was, of course, apt to make the little fellow angry.

Once, when he was addressing such a meeting, a small bird flew over his head, casting his load with a gentle plop on to the carefully brushed black hair. The reverent silence that had been maintained amongst his vast audience, broke gently to a shy murmur of laughter. Stern soldiers shouted for order. Almost immediately fifty or sixty birds pounced upon the flag that fluttered by the side of the speaker, tore it to pieces, and flew away with outrageous cries. The meeting continued with some difficulty, the Chancellor—as he was called—not wishing to draw attention to the streak of grey offal on his head by wiping it off, but continually embarrassed by its presence.

Such incidents as these were common to most of the great capital cities of the world. And it was not many hours before London saw the birds again. This time they came, not in one massive flock but in several smaller groups, fluttering round and round the City and never landing anywhere except on roofs and tall monuments. A swarm draped themselves over the figure of Justice which stood on the dome of a sinister building called Bailey, a place where criminals were judged and often sentenced to death. When the birds left it, the figure was so spattered with their odious droppings, that it had to be cleaned. This, however, seemed to annoy the birds, who were observed the next morning huddled around Justice in even greater numbers. They looked very cold, pressed tight against one another as though for warmth. Nobody dared fire at them for fear of disfiguring the statue, which was held in high esteem. When eventually, after several hours, they flew away, the same offensive mess was coated thick all over the unfortunate goddess, whose scales were loaded with quantities of this disgusting offal.

They came into the City several times, but did no more than circle round and round above the buildings, crying in thin mournful tones. One very remarkable thing about their appearance was that they were clearly larger than the birds who had first visited us. Their plumage too was gayer and more diverse, some having spotted breasts, some with larger ruffles than others, some with bright yellow tail-feathers. No doubt many that flew about the country escaped notice because of their resemblance to other birds, though I doubt myself whether they ever visited the open country; they seemed to prefer towns. Thus Manchester, Liverpool, Birmingham, and Sheffield—all had similar experiences to ours.

Many attempts were made to catch them in order to imprison them as curious specimens behind bars in a place called Zoological Gardens where every known animal was in captivity. But nobody so far had succeeded in enticing the birds anywhere near the various traps devised. They rarely, in those first days, alighted to the ground. A very brisk trade was exchanged between corn-chandlers and kindly old ladies who hoped to invite the birds to earth with seed. Pigeons were renowned for their courtesy in accepting this invitation. But these birds would not accept.

They were very strange days. We never knew where next we should see the birds, nor in what numbers. We grew less afraid of them when it seemed obvious that they intended no harm. We assumed that they were perplexed by the hard, treeless streets over which they flew in such bewilderment. They had come from some far country, we said, and could not find their way home again.

Meanwhile the drought continued, the sun seemed to burn a hole in the hard sky, no cloud appeared from dawn to evening, and at night the stars were brilliant in their splendour. In the suburbs, householders who rarely opened their windows, now never closed them. The seaside resorts were thronged with holidaymakers; a continual flow of people flocked in and out of the railway stations every Saturday and Sunday, seeking release from the heat in some cool shaded place by river or sea.

It is hard to remember the exact sequence of events. But I know that it was about this time, a few days before my holiday, that another aspect of the birds began to present itself to me.

I came home one evening and fell on my bed in a heavy lassitude. Lillian came and sat in my bedroom, for it was cooler there, and we talked in a desultory manner. We neither of us felt very well; the heat was driving the life out of us.

I found some maps and began to visualize the country I was soon to visit.

"Mother," I said, "you're not well. You need a change. Why don't you come with me?"

But no, she would not come. "It would shake me up too much to go all the way to Wales. Besides, you'd rather go alone."

She had spoken the truth, for I wanted to go alone. But I did not feel easy at leaving her in the care of Annie. I had a premonition of some danger I could not define.

While I thought this, idly turning over my maps, I heard a sudden tapping on the window-pane. I then realized that in spite of the heat, the window was closed tight. Outside, two grey, drab birds fluttered against the glass.

Lillian jumped to her feet, startled and frightened. "They're here," she cried. "They're here."

I crossed to the window. The birds rose and flew straight for the pane, dropping to the ground when they hit the glass. I made as though to open the window. If I could catch one of these creatures my name would be famous. So I thought. But in my heart I knew I should never catch one.

Lillian ran to me.

"What are you doing?" she cried.

"Why, letting them in," I said, forcing myself to laugh light-heartedly. "If we can catch one——"

I broke off, seeing she was really terror-stricken.

"What's the matter, Mother?" I asked, putting my arm round her shoulder. She turned on me in rage.

"You little fool," she cried. "If I hadn't closed all the windows they'd be here in this room now."

"Well, what would it matter," I argued, "if they did come in?"

"It means that both of us would die," she said. "Do you understand what I mean? We should die; both of us."

It was an old superstition that a bird in the house meant death. I was silent.

Suddenly she went to the kitchen and called our cat.

"Tibby, Tibby; come here, dear. Tibby——"

I stood by the window looking at the birds. They were sitting in the dried soil, miserably cocking their heads now and again at the window. They looked very tired.

I heard our old tom-cat bounding down the stairs from the bed where he had been sleeping. Then I realized my mother intended setting him on the birds.

I ran into the kitchen which adjoined my room. She had the cat in her arms and was holding him against the pane, showing him the birds.

An unreasonable rage seized me. I took her arms, released the cat, and drove it upstairs again. Then I flung open the window, my mother holding on to me, attempting to restrain me. Seeing, however, that she could do nothing, she left the room, slamming the door behind her.

"You will have to pay for it if you let them in!" she cried.

I ignored her, and throwing some bread out into the garden, waited to see what would happen.

The birds took no notice of the bread, but sat there and looked at me solemnly. Their eyes were deep and cold.

The window was open. There was nothing between me and these strange creatures.

Suddenly I was frightened. I could not face the thought that they might fly into the room, circling wildly round and round, smashing cups and plates, hitting my head and emitting that offensive odour which already I could smell. I would have to pay for it, my mother had said. Perhaps she was right.

I closed the window gently so that she could not hear. Almost immediately the birds flew away in a heavy, graceless flight.

We learnt next day, Anna, that many in our street and elsewhere had been disturbed by the presences of solitary birds around their windows. Most people were reluctant to say much about it.

*

What picture have I given of the youth who was me in those days? Serious, rebellious, self-centred, discontented, unromantic?

Let me at any rate cancel the last of those adjectives by telling you that he fell in love, not with one but with several persons, though he generally contrived that these passions should not overlap. What do I mean by "falling in love"? It is a phrase that has dropped out of use, since in these days we do not lapse into love as though it were a disease; we love, simply and naturally, without any of that consuming self-analysis which generally accompanied sexual passions in my youth. Falling in love was a complicated business. In young people it was regarded as comic, a subject for much hilarity amongst the elders who very soon forgot their own early days. Overt loving was not easy then. We

had not long emerged from an era in which the sexual passions
had been so obscured by a false cover of chivalry and maidenly
modesty; so robbed of their stamina by the honeyed phrases of
novelists who depicted their heroes and heroines as ignorant of
the most elementary functions of their bodies—that it was hard
to face the real truth in oneself; the unblushing truth that what
we needed and were often unable to get was sexual satisfaction.
The war, that I mentioned earlier, had broken down a great many
old conventions, for in times of stress the simplest passions of
men and women are laid bare and, faced with death, youth will
not be denied that which its blood demands. Those years forced
upon us almost savagely the fact that men and women were all
fundamentally the same, needing the same stimulus from each
other.

I was then a boy at school, and it was during those schooldays
that distortion of our sexual natures began to take place. Even
in adolescence, we possessed a most ambiguous conception of
the physiological structure of the male and female bodies. We
were never told anything about the body. We did not even know
the difference between our liver and our kidneys; to us they were
merely mysteries upon which from time to time a thing called
"chill" could settle. If we dared to show the smallest amount of
open interest in our genitals we were, even at a very early age,
most severely rebuked.

In such ignorance we were left to rake about as we liked in
the morbid dunghill of our undefined, and correspondingly
alarming, desires. All boys were much the same and, I dare say, all
girls. Schools were vicious places where children of one sex were
herded close together, rarely seeing children of the opposite sex.
And sex was a joke.

Yes, a joke; the most daring, most manly joke that could exist.
Only between members of the same sex was it openly mentioned. Our elders never made any attempt to untwist the rav-
elled cords within us. It was indeed impossible to associate one's
parents with the dreadful fleshly desires that so bewildered us.
How well I remember finding it distasteful, even impossible to
accept the fact—when I came to know the facts—that my father
had begotten me; that through his passion my mother had borne

me. And when I came ultimately to accept this, I remember looking upon my parents in a new light. They too were "wicked";
they too, guilty of a sin classed by the church as amongst all other
deadly sin. The picture grew, various eminent figures of the day
rose in my imagination; they too, the same as myself. Something
unseen, something shameful that every man and woman bore.

There is one phase of school life I must touch upon. That is
the development of homosexuality brought about by close contact of adolescents of the same sex.

The term "homosexual" which we do not use here, signified
that the victim was powerless to form any attachment with the
opposite sex. Being as human as anyone else, he therefore turned
his attention upon his own sex. You will notice I said "victim,"
and you may well ask why, when here it seems natural to allow
love to flower in any form—whether between youth and youth,
maid and maid, or youth and maid. But in our days the homosexual was held in such grave dishonour that any outward man-
ifestation of what were known as perverse passions, brought
him within the severest punishment of the law. Yet by reason of
the one-sexed atmosphere of our schools, these very disorders
were encouraged. At all schools, romantic friendships between
boy and boy, or girl and girl were prevalent. They often devel-
oped into physical relationships, though the authorities did their
utmost to disguise this. We all know here how natural it is for
a boy at puberty to turn towards his own sex, a girl likewise;
and how this desire ultimately develops into a new and stronger
passion for one of the opposite sex. If, as sometimes happens,
the homosexual stage maintains its way into adult life, we take
no more notice of it than we do of the ordinary mating of men
and women. There have always been natural homosexual persons; often of such high intellectual activity as to allow them an
honoured place in any community. There always will be such
persons. But in our days homosexuals were created by artificial
means; that is to say, by the prevailing influence of the one sex at
a time when the other sex should have been dominant.

I think it should now be more or less clear that the appalling
lack of candour with which our people faced their sexual desires,
led to a gross amount of secret perversions of so preposterous a

nature, that I cannot attempt to describe them. I can only indicate such perversions by telling you that frequent attacks were made by sexually demented old men upon young girls and boys who were not even of an age to be aware of their latent sexuality.

Here, then, very briefly, is my sexual world. For nine-tenths of us, our sexual natures were a bewildering mass of frustrated and distorted desires. We were taught by the Church that fornication was deadly sin. We were reminded harshly by the law that certain sexual activities would deprive us of our freedom and honour; we were taught to regard women as sacred mysteries incapable of emotions similar to and even stronger than our own. Our women—starved by men who preferred to keep their final ounce of power for the prostitute or established mistress—became neurotic and malicious; our men—starved of the complete enfolding of a woman's love, except the dominating love of their mothers—became obtuse and arrogant. If a man was tender, he was termed effeminate; if a woman was strong and capable, she was termed unwomanly.

In such a state of mind I began to notice young women, and to realize that they attracted me in a way I hardly dared to admit. In such a state of mind I noticed young men, and knew that what I felt for them was considered something shameful—never to be spoken of.

*

When I look back, I see that I and my contemporaries were consumed by a succession of intolerable sexual desires which the economic system forbade us to satisfy. At an age when the sexual impulse was strong in us we were forced back upon such makeshifts as literature, music, painting, and entertainments of a highly erotic nature. It may be that I exaggerate the importance of this in other people. It is sufficient to say that what I failed to capture in the various contacts I made with young men and women, I captured to some degree in literature, music, painting, and drama. With a feeling of gratitude, I remember the erotic revelations exposed to me in the pages of such writers as Shakespeare and Swinburne. I say with gratitude because although it was a shabby enough substitute for actual expression, I derived from these writers, and others, some emetic against the poisonous Thou-shalt-nots with which my religious education had been loaded. It consoled me to discover that the greatest poets had been afflicted with those disorders which the Church so acidly rejected as impurities. To turn to Shakespeare's Adonis was to find somebody in sympathy with myself, particularly as that tender youth found it hard to rise to the occasion.

It amuses me now to recollect my favourite passages in literature. The democratic trumpetings of an American poet who in uncontrolled verses seemed to desire the whole world to go to bed with him; the swaggering conduct of a Scandinavian hero who ran off with three wild mountain women, declaring that he could manage the lot; the voluptuous saturnalias of Petronius Arbiter; the deflowering of Chloe by the shy, eager lad, Daphnis; the revels of Apuleius; the astounding liberalism of Plato's Symposium; the gross and glorious ribaldries of Gargantua. These shadows loomed up the walls of my small bedroom many a night, when with a candle by my side I would read into the dawn, falling asleep to dream that I too could take three mountain women; possess myself with impunity following the decrees of the American democrat; or make a better bed-fellow for Alcibiades than the impassionate Socrates.

I still carried into my early manhood those shifty figures of adolescence; never quite sure what it was I wanted; never knowing how to set about obtaining it. My homosexual side played havoc with my heterosexual side. Falling between the two, I compelled myself to create a super-being with the characteristics of both sexes. I used to fall in love with a girl because she looked like a youth; with a youth, because he had the fair flushed face of a girl. Always, somewhere I imagined there must be the perfect creature, sexless yet the very apotheosis of sex. Every time I professed love for anybody I fully believed it was for the last time. I was an absurdly romantic youth and must have been a great plague to my lovers. Still lingering in me were those illusions of chivalry which placed woman on a lofty pedestal from where she could never condescend to the bestial desires shared by me and my poetic figures. In our middle-class society con-

summation seemed impossible without marriage, which in our
days was the inevitable consequence to any indiscreet coition,
since it was held that a young woman who bore a child without
having bound herself by stern vows to a husband, was a wanton
creature, disgraced, and her child deprived of all normal social
rights. Such children were called bastards, or love-children. One
might surmise that the offspring of marriage were hate-children.
I have a clear recollection of assuming at an early age, when I had
come to some naïve understanding of the obscure phrases used
by my elders, that since natural children were born of unmarried
people I myself must be an unnatural child. Perhaps, indeed, I
was. . . .

Consummation without marriage was forbidden, and marriage impossible on the small amount of money I was earning,
since it was always expected that a young man would "keep" his
wife; that is to say, pay for the clothes she wore, the food she ate,
and the roof she lived under. It is true that some women, where
money was short, used to go out to work and thus bring in a
double amount of money. But the arrangement was not satisfactory, since a conscientious woman would need much of her time
to attend to the cares of the home.

If marriage was impossible, there was the alternative course
of sowing wild oats in the west end of London, where women of
various ages waited every night to oblige me, suggesting, either
by word or gesture, that they were ready to be of service to me.
At such times I walked on as though I had never seen them.
Inside, something seemed to twist my heart.

Curious, touching women—their faces painted so that a natural smile seemed to crack upon them as would a pasteboard
mask if you attempted to twist it into any shape other than that
in which it was modelled. They were like dolls. I sometimes had
the feeling that they depended every night from the finger-tips
of an expert marionettist who dangled them over appropriate
places from long strings, drawing them up again as dawn came
and the hollow ghost of love had been buried till another night.

I remember walking round a place called Leicester Square
with that same friend I mentioned earlier who used to meet me
on Sunday evenings. We passed a number of these prostitutes,

many of whom he hailed with impudent good-humour; for that was his nature; he was more warm-hearted, less wrapped in muddled philosophy than I was. He accepted the prostitutes as part of the social system.

"In Heaven's name," I asked him, "why do they paint themselves?"

My friend informed me that it was a form of advertisement so that men might know whom to pick; a type of professional uniform.

"But this is no distinction," I said impatiently. "Almost all women look the same."

A succession of pictures comes before me—pictures of myself as I was then in those faraway days in the 'twenties'; pictures of myself with those whom I loved and those who, perhaps, loved me.

The picture I see first is that of myself and a girl walking over a wide heath in the south of London. We draw towards a silent lake on a still spring evening. The girl, who is named Jennie, is quick, capable, and strong, full of impetuous practical jokes, blended with a quieter poetic impulse which makes her express herself in verses which she brings to me for my criticism. We think we are both poets. I stand with her by the lake and kiss her clumsily. Some small animal scuttles through the bracken, startling us to break away from each other. Jennie runs wildly and climbs a tree; I pursue her, laughing and shouting. Then presently, exhausted, we fall down upon a bank and kiss again. We are lovers; we will live for each other; we will write great poetry, live in the open air. Even now the memory is sweet to me because she was my first love. For weeks she is my world. Then there comes an evening when I stand, stupid with misery, on an empty underground railway platform at midnight, waiting to catch a train back to Stroud Green. We have quarrelled and parted. And I can remember now the grand despair with which I dismissed all women from my life. The phase does not last long.

Winter comes, and snow is falling. I see myself waiting impatiently outside a playhall called Tivoli in west London. As though she had drifted from the sky on a snowflake, the new love emerges lightly towards me. She dusts the snow from her coat and greets me. She is small, chubby, with large, open eyes and a pretty voice. Everything about her is pretty and tinkling. I compare her again to the snow, and feel certain that as soon as I touch her, she will melt out of my grasp. We go to plays and entertainments together. I do not tell her that I write poetry; I know she will be dubious of such an achievement. Instead, I pretend that I am Man-of-the-world, thinking it will please her. But my strange preoccupation with poetry and art cannot long be concealed; I cannot continue for ever talking about motor-bicycles, clothes, and dancing. She is aware of an unusual streak in me. One evening she breaks her appointment, and I never see her again.

Now there is an interlude. I am tormented by the face and form of a lift-boy in the office where I work. He is red-cheeked with freckles and thick sandy hair. There is a grace about his movements. I speak to him going up and down in the lift; I use the lift upon every possible opportunity. He shows that he likes me—a revelation I cannot endure, it is so sweet and so bitter. His face comes to me in my dreams at night; I feel his hand as it had once touched mine in a casual contact. I imagine that everybody in the office is looking at me, suspicious of this delightful friendship. One day I speak abruptly to the boy; he blushes and bites his lip, wondering. I use the lift less and less. I banish him out of my mind.

Now it is a girl whom I meet at a dance in north London. She seems to me older and wiser than the others. I assure myself that she can show me much. Soon I have fallen deeply in love.

We spend long Saturdays in the country, walking many miles and returning late to the City. We kiss too often and it is never enough. I begin to be fearful of the only resolution left to us. Innumerable theatres, cafés, and cinemas we frequent together. I write poetry for her which she indiscriminately classifies as wonderful. She does not understand poetry and is therefore a superbly easy audience for my vanity.

In secret we spend two days together in the old cathedral town where I had been educated. I dare not tell my mother, for such behaviour is an unforgivable breach of convention. Hot and embarrassed, I enter the dark, antiquated hotel with my lover.

Before the manageress I try to pretend that I am in the habit of spending week-ends with young women; I blow out my cheeks and strut about as though I were a man of forty. We do not share the same room. We could only do so had she worn a circle of gold round her finger to signify that she is my wife. I have not enough audacity to pretend that she is, and give her a ring to wear for the occasion.

We do not share the same room. But later I go to her room, lie on the bed with her, and kiss her, till a moment comes when fear mounts in her. I leave her and go back to my own room. Sitting miserably on my bed I ask myself why I have spent all this money for the sake of a few kisses. I blame her for her modesty and do not think to examine my own sexual approach.

A few weeks later we meet for the last time. It is in August; in the middle of that summer in which the birds came. I remember the occasion well, because while I am with her I see the birds flying over the river.

We stand in the shadow of a monument—Cleopatra's Needle, overlooking the Thames. It is very late. In my heart I know that I can no longer feign interest in one who seems to me to have denied the obvious issue of love. I am oppressed and worried by the condition of the world; stifled by the intense heat; half fearful of the strange birds who daily grow more and more ubiquitous in the City.

She is light and talkative; she does not seem to sense my lack of response. We look over the river to the red lights of a huge advertisement, scattered and distorted in the shifting mirror of the water. A tram rattles past with a sound as though it were falling to pieces; a policeman's footsteps thud heavily on the pavement behind the monument. Huddled on seats lining the road are groups of silent, sleeping people, outcasts who have no homes to go to.

My companion talks. I do not know what she talks about; perhaps a new dress or a play that she would like to see. Her voice seems to me to break the very solemnity of the night.

While she is talking, suddenly I see the birds, a small flock of them floating like tattered black cloth above a police boat in the river.

"Did you see them?" I cry. "Did you see the birds?"

She reproaches me for my coldness. I tell her I have been watching the birds and did not hear what she was saying.

"Then," she cries petulantly, "you think more of the birds than you do of me."

I can no longer maintain pretence. I tell her there are more important things in life than a new hat or a new play. With melodramatic bitterness I quote the lines of an ancient sonnet at her:

> *"Since there's no help, come let us kiss and part;*
> *Nay, I have done; you get no more of me."*

We part bitterly. In utter gloom, with so strong a sense of impending tragedy that I can barely think of the lover I have so callously dismissed, I walk towards the station and so home. With a magnificent gesture of self-renunciation, I inform myself that love has no more place in my thoughts. And I count on my hand the people I have loved who now mean no more to me, nor I to them.

Tossing over and over, sleepless in my bed, I light my candle and turn to the trough of books beside me. . . .

*

Again and again to books; to a twilight world of shadows more pliable than living figures; to words printed on a page rather than words spoken by friend or lover. I reached a stage when a line of the poet Keats could give me more of the tranquil essence of autumn than the sight of red apples heavy on a bough, or Michaelmas daisies drooping through a garden hedge. I summoned art to supply me with that which I seemed unable to obtain from life itself.

We have discussed art often, and arrived at no very satisfactory conclusions concerning it. Let us see how it applied to the lives of ordinary people sixty years ago.

Art. How hard, how final the word sounds. And in a sense, how hard, how final is any excellent work of art. Into the creation of it a man puts all the love which he has ever felt for the natural world. It is to be an offering to the creative force that made him: A signature of his Being. The artist must work for himself; work solely to express himself, seeking for no reward other than the satisfaction of knowing that out of him has come a restatement of truth.

In those days it might be said that there were few artists, many craftsmen. Few men had enough belief in themselves, in God, or the universe, to produce a fine work of art. Because they did not represent that make-believe world for which many yearned, people despised and ignored the few art-creations of any real value. Yet men still cried for escape from reality. "Give us," they demanded, "a reason for being alive. Show us that there is something in this world—not in another—which is worth attaining. You artists have visions which we do not possess. Reveal them to us in the style that we like best."

The artists were quick to respond to this cry, seeing that people were very willing to pay well for what they wanted. It is significant that all popular art was concerned with morals; with virtue and its rewards, wickedness and its punishments, rather than with the elemental ingredients of life itself. Since Nature had nothing to do with morality, people mistrusted it. A sentimentalized picture of virtue was thrust before them so that they could sigh and say, "I cannot be good like that, but I do see how attractive goodness can be and how worth while it is, since it always achieves distinction." One of the most popular forms of fiction, for example, told in varying themes the story of a humble person who by a life of intensive virtue "won through" to an illustrious position in society.

Fed with this type of art, people ceased to attempt to reform their own conditions, in static contemplation of mythical figures. They identified themselves with these figures, saying, "I could be like that, if things were otherwise." And sham-artists were, to use an old expression, two-a-penny.

Literature was one of the chief mediums employed. There were magazines designed for all types wherein any one who wished could read about his own fate as it might have been, had things been otherwise. As well as journals there were books—so many, that very often the same tale was written over and over

again by many different writers. There were thousands of novelists in my day; I can now only remember the names of three
or four. Some had started with great aspirations of artistic excellence, only later to discover that the people cared nothing for
their truths, and that if they wished to prosper financially they
must answer those demands which I have already described to
you.

Music and painting suffered a similar fate to that of literature,
though perhaps not so obviously. A few years previously music
had been a pleasant diversion in the home. Then a thing called
wireless came. It was a remarkable method of capturing sound-
waves so that one could hear from hundreds of miles away a man
singing or speaking in another part of the world. So from every
house in the streets you would hear crippled sounds of borrowed
music. There was something essentially impure about the music
thus sent out; a casual listener, passing by, felt as though he had
unwittingly trespassed upon the privacy of an unseen world.
Satiated by the excess of it, few people consciously heard it, just
as few people consciously read books. It was, I think, the supreme
entertainment of our times, unless perhaps cinema came first. A
man had only to buy what was known as a "set" and he could
receive all this noise at any hour of the day. It was generally much
louder than the actual sound would be. If it was normal in tone
the listener would complain that it was too soft. Often, while listening to the music which poured out of their sets, people talked
and ate—the whole procedure being accompanied by the ceaseless rumble of traffic in the streets outside. Yet if the wind blew
a slight gale they complained; if cats howled in the night they
threw things at them.

What about cinema?

This was probably the most influential amusement offered to
men and women. Like wireless, it could be obtained at almost all
hours of the day, though, unlike wireless, it was not laid on to the
home. (I'm quite sure it soon would have been. In my day they
were heading in that direction.) A man had to go to special theatres to obtain this particular type of escape from reality.

Cinema consisted of stories recorded by a process called cin-
ematography. These pictures of men and women acting, were

flashed on to a large screen. They were, in short, moving pictures or plays: another wonderful invention of man. The voices of the actors were reproduced by a soundwave system which synchronized with their actions. When they spoke——

To this day I can hardly refrain from shuddering at the memory of those loud, hollow tones—the most hideous mockery of the human voice that was ever produced. I think that cinema, with all its spurious emotion, its travesty of life, its meretricious sentiment, brings us to the worst form of art with which our people struggled against actuality. Night after night, all over this island, you would find men and women of all ages and types herded together in darkness. What little air penetrated these places was foul with the smell of sweat-heavy clothes and artificial scents. Little pages walked up and down with chocolates and cigarettes; organs lent to the dim atmosphere a sense of religiosity which would have been curious to the stranger, who might easily imagine that all the people sitting there were devotees of some occult religious rite.

In the concealing darkness of these halls, lovers inclined towards one another whenever the characters on the screen did likewise. The "act of sex," as we called it, was not shown in detail on the screen, though there were signs that it probably would soon be considered quite proper to do so. The nearest they got to it in those baffling days was the kiss—and very prolonged it was, a grossly magnified clinging of lips to lips. Since, however, the hard-working actors on the screen never entered upon really serious clinical business the lovers in the audience were teased into a condition of intense sexual irritation.

The dramas shown were very like the magazine stories, generally depending for their success upon a similar display of virtue and its rewards. Some people went to these dark halls two or three times a week in a miserable attempt to build up a secret life of surmise.

I have told you what I can about the pantomime world which artists offered to men as an escape from reality. It is only a brief survey. But it may be sufficient to convey to you that art grew to dominate man to such an extent that, his faculties becoming blunted and starved, he could experience little that was not second-hand. There was nothing new under the sun, and the old things were not good enough. It was only when the birds came that I and others who escaped from the City at the end were enabled to see all that is for ever new under the sun; all that we see before us now.

... Will you ask Berin to come later in the evening when the moon rises? He tells me he has made some new songs, and although I have said so much to the detriment of art, I should like him to sing them to me....

*

In trying to detach myself as much as possible from the events, customs, and manners so far recorded, it occurs to me that a reader who knew nothing of the old world would assume from my narrative that it was so miserably governed, humanity so dense and apathetic, that I never spent a happy moment in their midst. Have I been unfair? I should be ungrateful if I pretended that the old civilization gave me nothing, if I pretended that there were not many moments of great happiness in the City life. The sun still shone as it shines now; it still made people smile, reminding us that there was warmth in humanity somewhere, had it but the chance to break through. The excesses of civilization had not been able to rob spring of its power; a single budding plane tree in a courtyard of the City could change the atmosphere of a season. In the parks there were flowers; I can remember banks dappled with crocuses.

Sometimes in the lunch-hour I would take an omnibus to a different part of London, beyond the Cathedral. Here there were cobbled yards; ancient rows of houses; trees and alleyways where old shops, buried away out of time, sold judges' clothes, wigs and legal paraphernalia. These pleasant places were known as the Inns of Court, and were mostly the residences and offices of barristers, solicitors, and others who had to do with the intricate machinery of organized justice. They had changed little, these Inns, in the past two hundred years. On spring days I would buy sandwiches, go to one of the Inns and, sitting on the side of a fountain circle, forget myself in the composition of verses or in vague memory of things I had never seen. I related these courts to scenes in old books I had read. I can still clearly recall the naïve thrill which ran over me when I discovered a house with the letters P.J.T. carved above the doorway; I had read about the house and those actual letters in a book by a famous Victorian novelist.

Some days in this lunch-hour, I would eat quickly at a café, then with a friend who worked near me, visit one of the many bookshops which were scattered about the City. Behind the Lord Mayor's vast house, stacked against a small domed church which had been designed by the same artist who designed the Cathedral, was a shop where books of all types were displayed in troughs outside. My friend and I would gradually push our way through the people already gathered there, and spend a half-hour reading at random from volumes that we seldom bought. He was, I remember, very fond of literature and used to write poetry under cover of a massive ledger. I remember the delight with which I made this discovery one day and his immediate embarrassment, for poetry-writing was considered an unmanly occupation. However, when he found that I too wrote verses, we became very friendly, and used to talk for hours about books, criticizing the poems that we wrote. I think, in that wooden box of mine upstairs, you will still find some notes in his handwriting about a poem I had written.

I remember an old bookshop we discovered, grimy and derelict in appearance, buried in some side street near the Tower of London. This bookshop sold nothing but old books, and they were piled so high up to the roof you felt always that there was some rare treasure at the top which was too far away for you to reach. Somewhere, shovelled away in this incipient avalanche, was a little whiskered man with a green baize apron, who knew nothing about books and simply bought them by the hundreds from old libraries as one might buy sacks of coal. My friend and I felt we were in another world. Carts rumbled outside; the wheel of commerce never ceased to revolve. Inside, it was only words of ancient men that tumbled and muttered around us. And the little old man in the green apron would puff his clay pipe, never moving; all you saw of him, like a spider in some dark corner, a bald head and a cloud of blue smoke. He used to read a journal called *Poultryman*, all about hens, eggs, and the profits to be made from them. How comic that seems, with all those books around him. Perhaps he contemplated a new line of business, for I dare say books were hardly profitable.

There were short days in winter when the City seemed to glitter with half-revealed secrets. Days when it rained steadily; when lights were lit early in shops and offices; when the shining streets were domed by the humps of glossy umbrellas. On such days a common goodwill seemed to fall naturally from harassed people, hurrying here and there to catch bus, train, or tram. In face of discomfort, a vision of home, with firelight, tabby-cats, and rich cups of mellow tea, seemed to buoy up men and women. Some days a yellow fog shrouded the streets in gloom, so that every vehicle travelled at a snail's pace with its lights full on. Then the City was unreal and ghostly. Suddenly in the muddy light you would collide with a newsboy standing at the corner of a street. Down in the smoky underground cafés at four in the afternoon, you would find young men playing dice and chess silently. One forgot the clamour for business in the fog; figures glided past like barges up the river at night.

There was one day in the month which stands out in my memory: a magic day known as pay-day, when all of us received little envelopes containing the notes which were our wages. In that hour one realized why people worked, and how foolish it was to imagine that anyone had chosen this sort of life because he liked it. From highest to lowest, all seemed the same in that moment.

I remember the excitement on Christmas Eve in the City. Christmas, as you know, was a religious feast which celebrated the birth of Jesus. On the vigil of Christmas the offices closed early, there was only a pretence of work throughout the day. Girls would bustle in and out with parcels of presents they had bought; people would come round with raffle-lists. Later, as soon as the taverns were opened, you would find them full of men laughing and joking with the barmaids, drinking one another's health, wishing all a Merry Christmas. Then, in the long sawdust-sprinkled avenues of Leadenhall Market, merchants sold the last of their stock at low prices, anxious to get it off their hands. There you would find husbands in search of cheap turkeys to take home to their wives for the Christmas feast. Travelling home in the train there always seemed to be less room than usual; everybody carried parcels, everybody laughed; many were drunk, nobody cared.

Our people were discovered at their best and simplest, whenever any special occasion called them to unanimity. One of the last of such occasions I can recall was that of the death and funeral procession of our King, called George. In bitter winter weather a million people waited in the streets of London in order to see the bleak gun-carriage upon which rested a box containing the body of a pious and simple gentleman whom everybody had loved. Behind the box walked a slight boyish figure—the son of the dead man—the King of England. A week before, men and women had been stirred by a sentence which, cast in the nobility of our beautiful language, recalled everybody to the fact that his own death could not be far off. *"The King's life is moving peacefully towards its close."* Hearing these words, the people forgot material disputes and pondered upon the great mystery of life and its shortness upon this earth. In a moving solemnity they assembled around a man who, in his dying, emphasized the littleness of their own lives.

I remember . . . yes, I remember much, much that was pleasant. Many cafés where I talked and ate with my friends; many churches where in summer it was cool and quiet; many alleys where in winter I could search for books. And away from the City I have a picture of myself standing outside the door of Three-hundred-and-ninety-six, listening to my mother playing and singing to herself. She would rarely sing if she knew she had an audience. She had a deep voice—more powerful than one might have expected from her small body. Through the window I caught the glow of the firelight; in the street, men on bicycles with long poles were lighting the gas lamps. An autumn evening with rich sunlight falling down the sky and firing the windows of the Alexandra Palace. Then home was precious.

Another aspect of that northern suburb is a summer scene; a morning when I rise early, and ride my bicycle to an artificial pool somewhere near the Palace, where it is possible to swim. Here I often went. At that early hour men were different. It was so strange to reflect that those white, naked bodies would in an hour or so be padded with thick clothing, packed in a train and carried to the City. Here, early in the morning, with the fresh sun over them, they were alive, naked, and free, swimming, diving, and lying in the sun as though they had no care in the world. It was a place with a character all of its own, that swimming-pool; and it is bound up in my memory with a morning, the last I ever spent there, which I must presently describe in greater detail. Let me not break these retrospective pictures now. Let me cease. I am conscious that however much I try I shall but thinly convey the happiness of those days. It is easy to condemn; harder to praise. When I close my eyes I can hear and almost long for the roar of an underground train; the babble of humanity crowding in the refreshment-room of a theatre; the rustling of old books in some dark shop; the patter of rain upon a thousand umbrellas. I can smell the peculiar hot fragrance of coffee and buns in a tea-shop; the rotten fruit and fish around the London monument; the acid of new print on a newspaper; the scent and sweat of humanity clustered together in a lift. Trains, telephones, cinemas, umbrellas, musty bookshops, tobacco pipes; badly cooked food, heavy clothes, lamps yellow as melons in foggy streets; shrieking of newsboys, clash of iron lift gates, stamping of feet along an underground passage; pelicans, solemnly critical in the park; soldiers with gleaming breast-plates; wrinkled old women selling violets under a statue of the god of love; summer mornings in a pool near a network of railway lines; autumn evenings with my mother singing; the phantoms of figures from a hundred books, mounting up my bedroom wall; friends, lovers——

All this seems incomparable to the rise of that field, the hedge of meadowsweet and vetch below us, the flight of the lark, or the yellow corn stacked there in sheaves.

Yet suddenly nothing of what I see before me seems real. For a moment I wanted the old life back, whether lies or truth; hypocrisy or candour; cowardice or bravery.

Whatever it contained it gave me much.

*

The events of the last few days had drawn the life out of me so that lately I had been unable to rise early and go to swim in the pool. I would wake early enough. Then turning over again I would mumble petulantly, "What's the use? What's it all for?" I did not know what anything was for. When I woke every morning I felt that I could not endure London and Leadenhall any longer. How long would I have endured it, I wonder, had not the birds brought an end to it all?

One morning, however, only a day or so after my mother and I had been disturbed by the two birds in the garden, I awoke with more consciousness than usual. I suddenly saw that if I succumbed to this spiritlessness, I should rapidly sink into a slough from which there would be no escape. Acting on this thought, I jumped out of bed and quickly put on old trousers and a shirt. I felt stirred by something inside myself which I could not define.

I went out, got my bicycle, and started to ride. It was not very far, perhaps three miles. A thin bell struck seven from the tower-clock in a shopping centre called Crouch End.

I rode along a street where there were dingy shops, not yet open for the day's business. Newspaper boys ran from door to door, thrusting their journals impatiently under knockers and into door-slots. There were men with milk-carts leaving bottles of milk by each door.

I passed a police station, a fire station, and a public library. The library was the institution where I had first discovered the existence of fine literature. To that singularly barren-looking building I probably owed a great deal more than I ever acknowledged.

I came down a hill to an older part of the suburb. Back from the road was a solitary old church tower. Every Sunday, bells clashed from it to summon people to the new church which stood close by. Gravestones tumbled in the weedy churchyard. Elder trees, may bushes, and brambles were tangled round stone epitaphs that declined like sinking ships deep into the ground.

There was a feeling of stagnation about the place. The road was lined by houses all of the same bleak piety; the blinds were drawn, the gates closed. It still bore the title Church Lane, a title reminiscent of a time when there had been trees and fields here, and a wooden bridge over a little stream by the church. All changed, yet resenting the change. There was something melancholy about it in that clear morning light. I felt as though the sun had revealed some ancient grudge which for ever lingered about the place. The houses were so silent it was hard to believe that in an hour or so the doors of most of them would open to release upon the target of London the rapid shot of driven clerks.

Inscribed upon little white discs on some of the gates were the words "*No hawkers; no canvassers; no circulars.*" For the first time in my life I noticed them consciously. "Leave me alone," they seemed to cry. "Leave me in peace. Remind me not of the world's misfortune. Leave me to my memories of a time when life seemed sweet, when I was young and full of courage."

In a few moments I had left Church Lane and reached a wider road where tram-lines marked a route towards London. The scene grew dingier, the scattered shops cheaper. Nothing seemed to be sold here but cast-off clothes, penny magazines, bottles of bright liquid called mineral water, and rickety furniture. I turned off into a street of houses yellower and leaner than those in Church Lane. It seemed as though the very houses themselves were starved and cracking with lack of sustenance. Every window was draped with threadbare yellow curtains; it was a colour identical with that of a London fog. High above ran the railway lines; somewhere, smudging this meagre scene with smoke, were the two enormous stacks of chimneys.

I came presently to another main road with more tram-lines. On one side was a chain of dirty red-brick buildings. This was a sweet factory. A sick, burnt smell rose up from it; a smell like sugar and sulphur frizzling together in a coke fire. It was a singular place, sourly gay in some queer manner. Hundreds of girls were employed here, all in the making of an edible substance which nobody in the world required, but which most—because of the power of advertisement—consumed. The smoke that greasily stained the blue sky had this acrid, sweet smell. If you were possessed of a grim imagination you might surmise that here, day by day, people were immolated before some greedy God and burnt; that the smoke rose from the fuel of their sweet flesh.

I passed the place, my vision quickened; my eyes noticing a hundred things I had never before remarked. It was as though the whole grimy suburb had been concentrated for me under a great glass dome, and that through this cover the eager morning sun shot his rays into every detail.

I rode up a hill towards a railway station. I was getting near to the eastern gate of the lofty grounds of the Alexandra Palace. There were stringy meadows of withered yellow grass on one side of me, surrounded by low palings and marked by long uncomfortable seats. On the other side were more houses, slightly cleaner than those I had just left. I dismounted at the railway station in order to wheel my machine along a passage above the railway line; it was a short cut which soon brought me to the tarred door of a narrow cinder track which led down to the swimming-pool. The track was protected by a black fence with jagged pieces of tin stuck along the top to prevent people from climbing over to the racecourse on one side, the railway embankments and reservoirs on the other.

On my left were little thin patches of sun-baked earth, called allotments, where men reared flowers and vegetables. There were papery sweet peas climbing weakly up string supports; tall yellow daisies; and a few pink-white gladioli with dried leaves falling back from them, the colour and texture of an onion's outer skin. Nothing looked as though it had any more strength to live. On my right, farther away under some trees, I noticed a hayrick which seemed curiously lonely standing there on the fringe of the racecourse. A few yards in front of me, sunk in a hollow, was the wooden fence surrounding the swimming-pool.

. . . I suddenly inclined my head. I had heard something. A chattering, a harsh croaking, a sound which seemed to scrape along the quiet morning air like a blunt knife drawn over a slate.

A man passed me, also on a bicycle, a towel wound about his neck.

"You'll never swim this morning," he called.

"Are they changing the water?" I asked him.

"Oh no," he chuckled. But his amusement was forced. "The place has been turned into a first-class aviary overnight."

I heard the chattering sounds again, nearer now. It was like the thin spasmodic laughter of very old people. But no, it was a harsher sound than that; full of a secret glee which I did not like.

"You mean the birds are there?" I asked the man.

Yes, he said, the birds were there. They were drinking the water.

I laughed; so did he. It seemed funny.

I forgot my disappointment at not being able to swim, and rode quickly to the door, which swung open with its habitual creaking as I pushed it.

A small knot of men stood talking by the little pay-office to the attendant, a stout broad man whose humour made him very popular. I believe he was an old sailor.

He turned to me as I pushed the door open.

"Like a load of dove-dung for the garden?" he shouted with a laugh. "You can come and scrape up a cart-load if you like when these little beggars have done messing around."

"How long have they been here?" I asked.

"All night, for what I know," replied the attendant. "They was here when I come this morning, and here they're going to stay, ask me. They're proper soaks. Lord knows what'll happen when they find their way into a brewery."

I went nearer to the edge of the bath. Lined along one side were little cubicles, each with a cracked mirror advertising some disinfectant. Here, the modest swimmer could disrobe. Few people, however, used them. On the other side were sun-scarred benches and pegs where most people undressed. At the deep end was a long spring diving-board covered by coarse matting. There were steps down to the water at various stages along the sides of the bath.

But I did not see any water that morning. From end to end of the bath, the surface of the water was thickly obscured by the birds. They barely moved except to dip their heads and drink. A few chattered and croaked. About half-way along a number of them appeared to be quarrelling over one stray bird who hovered above, attempting to penetrate into the solid thicket of wet feathers below him, and find a place in the water. Some of them seemed to want to make room for this outcast; some seemed to resent him. Suddenly he swooped down angrily, pouncing on the softly swaying shapes and forcing a way through with his beak. There was a frenzied screaming and a fluttering of wet feathers.

"That's a proper lady," said somebody.

"You'd better put up a notice, Joe," remarked another, "saying as how this is bird's day and no men won't be admitted."

Some one called me. "Hey, sonny, don't you fall in! No one'll ever be able to drag you out of that mess."

"Can't we make them go?" I asked stupidly. "Throw something into the middle of them. . . ."

There was a life-belt hanging on the fence.

"What about this?" I suggested.

"Oh no, you don't!" A small pale fellow came up and pulled the belt from my hand. "Suppose you make those birds wild? Have you ever thought what they could do?"

I had often thought what they could do. Yet I wanted to tempt them.

One or two birds rose from the water and flew on to the diving-board where already a long row was assembled. The sudden movement scared me. The little pale man had turned to the door; the others, whistling casually, were drifting slowly in the same direction. Only Joe remained and seemed unmoved.

"You won't disturb that old crowd with a life-belt," he declared, "It'd take a gun to get through that lot, then you'd have the whole bloody bath blown to bits. Throw your belt, sonny; let's see what they do. It's my mind they won't stir, not a bloody inch."

"I think you're right, Joe," I said. "Not really much use in throwing it, is there?"

More birds had assembled in the sky. I saw indeed that there were a great many flying about which I had not before noticed. Those above cried as though to attract the attention of those below; but they would not move. The birds in the air seemed to want to entice the others away so that they could enter the water themselves. But the birds already in the water dipped their heads and drank almost without ceasing, bringing their heads up again and shaking them with prim regularity. They were big birds, nearly as large as rooks, gleaming green and blue, their feathers glittering with drops of water. The same pretty expression was in their sharp faces; the same bright little eyes. But something more; something mean and cunning.

I drew away from the edge as one or two fluttered out on to

the concrete path a yard or so from my foot. I suddenly realized how I dreaded that one of them might touch me. There was a sour smell in the air.

I turned to the door.

"Well, so long, Joe," I said casually. And I told him he ought to start a trade in bird-baths. It was the type of feeble joke for ever upon our lips in those uneasy days.

I mounted my machine and rode away quickly, looking back once or twice. A man passed me on his way to swim.

"You'll never swim this morning," I called out, glad to find somebody to whom to break my news. And I told him about the birds.

Then I raced on, past the withered meadows; past the scorched factory; the dingy shops and the railway arch; the old church tower, the gravestones, and the truculent houses; the library, the fire station, and the police station. I raced on, never seeing anything now. For I was possessed of that vitality which drives all carriers of critical news quicker to their destination.

*

My mother had got up and was in the kitchen making herself tea. She spoke a little irritably, saying I was rather earlier than usual. There were heavy lines under her eyes; I saw she had slept badly.

I told her about the birds.

"They were drinking the water," I emphasized.

"Well, dear," was all she said as she poured hot water into the pot, "I expect they were very thirsty, like us."

"Yes, but don't you see," I cried impatiently, "if they go on being thirsty, where shall we all be? The reservoirs are only a few yards away. They'll start on those next."

"Oh, what nonsense! They won't allow that to happen."

"Who's going to stop them?"

"I don't want to talk about them," she snapped in sudden anger. "There's quite enough to worry about without birds."

She went out of the room, and presently we sat down to a sullen breakfast together.

But I was right. By midday more and more birds had gathered over the north of London and had swarmed to the reservoirs. Distracted local councillors came and surveyed the strange scene, but they did not like to venture too near. The smell was appalling; in a few hours the water was foul with their dung.

I told my friends in the office how I had seen the birds that morning, but they seemed as little interested as my mother. Lassitude had overcome everybody. It was more than heat sickness; people seemed entirely dazed, stupid.

Various stories about the birds were brought to us by brokers. It was rumoured that a number of them were hovering around Battersea Power Station. Again, a swarm had surged on to the vast drum of a gas-container adjoining a cricket field in south London, where an important county match was then in progress. They had stayed there motionless, making no noise, yet so disturbing the players by their very presence as to put them entirely off their stroke. Nobody had been able to attend to the game; a famous and popular batsman had been bowled out with the first ball.

More serious was the news, later confirmed in the evening papers, that a famous English aviator demonstrating a new and supposedly "silent" type of monoplane over Hyde Park in the west of London, had been pounced on by the birds, who, screaming and croaking in evident rage, had attacked him with such fury that he lost control of the machine and crashed to the ground. He was not killed; but he was blinded and terribly maimed. This incident stirred people a good deal from their apathy, for the aviator had been a popular hero. The public indignation was revealed in a multitude of letters which poured into the Press. All these complained of the birds, and emphasized that "something ought to be done."

But what? Nobody knew. There seemed to be no end to the number of the birds. Thus, although the reservoirs in Hornsey were entirely submerged by them, various swarms were located in all parts of England and other countries. People went about, however, saying petulantly, "the Government ought to take the matter in hand." They had a profound and pathetic faith in the ability of this Government at Westminster to deal with any unforeseen circumstances, however extraordinary. At that time, however, most of the gentlemen who composed the Government were away; either at a place called Geneva, discussing peace treaties; or playing golf, dancing, and swimming in the south of France and other fashionable places of amusement.

The King was in one of his country homes, hoping for a rest. Every hour, however, he was bothered by politicians who kept on sending him notes about the warlike situation in Africa. The politicians must have regarded the birds as a great nuisance, coming at a time when they were all so busy having holidays or parleying about peace. The newspapers were daily informing the public that the situation was as grave as that of another August twenty years previously. For once they spoke the truth though they did not know it.

August was the silly month. And this year the whole world seemed to have lost its head; nobody knew which way to turn. The half-whimsical, half-sinister behaviour of the birds for ever hovering about us and, as it seemed, contemplating fresh mischief, added greatly to the universal inability to think clearly. Yet few people could take the birds seriously. It was outside the English temperament to take anything seriously, except sport.

The evening of the day I had seen the birds in the swimming-bath I went to the west of London with my old school friend. It was two days before my holiday. I did not feel I could go home to Stroud Green, sit about in the house doing nothing, sticky in the burning evening heat. So I told my mother I should be home late. She was not well, but she did not push any claim upon me to come home early and stay with her. She was quiet, afflicted also with the universal apathy. I was selfish, and did not think much about her.

Early in the evening I met my friend in Leicester Square. We had some food at a sandwich bar in a side street by Charing Cross Station, a cheap street named after a romantic English aristocrat of another century. When we came out, we walked towards the river embankment.

My friend was in high, almost nervous spirits. We talked wildly about war, the birds, and our individual affairs. I tried to give a reason for the presence of the birds, saying they had been sent by some insulted God to teach men a lesson. But my friend would have none of that. He did not believe in God; everything, he said, must follow a natural law.

"Yes, but whose natural law?" I demanded.

"They have a biological reason for existence," he maintained. As we argued, the evening slowly grew darker. We had walked along the Thames Embankment and stood looking across the river in the same spot where I had parted a few nights ago from my lover. The memory of it saddened me suddenly, and I urged my friend on. We came to Westminster and along a wide street of Government offices called Whitehall. In the middle of the road was a chunk of stone called Cenotaph; it was a memorial to the men who had been killed in the last war.

We came to Trafalgar Square. It was nearly dark now; the flashing advertisements began to trace the shapes of twinkling coloured words, urging the spectator to use this fountain-pen and no other; to drink that beverage if he wished to be a happy man. Lies pricked into the darkness—yet how beautiful they seemed! We walked past the colonnade of an old theatre which seemed to mutter a dusty rhetoric to itself. So eventually to Piccadilly, that centre of London, that warm heart of the great many-limbed beast, for which exiles in other countries had nostalgic dreams. Poised delicately in the centre was a statue of young Eros, loosing his arrows into the vulnerable hearts of men. I never discovered whether the presence of this innocent God in a part of London where love was commercialized, was a conscious satire or not. Sitting on steps at the base of the statue were some shawled old women selling flowers; they were familiar figures, as permanent a tradition in Piccadilly as Eros and the prostitutes. In defiance of darkness, electric advertisements sputtered and shone from every building. They were like elaborate pyrotechnical constructions. It was difficult to believe in the actual solidity of the buildings upon which these electric signs so flamboyantly quivered.

A thick crowd of people walked slowly along the pavements; interrogative glances were exchanged between strangers. The entire atmosphere of this neighbourhood was totally different from that of the City, where people hurried and pushed, never caring who passed them. In Piccadilly one was made aware of every individual. The people, who with such impeccable dignity worked in the sober City, were different creatures if one met them in the west of London. Here, people seemed to be creeping after pleasure, not with any manifestations of joy, but with a stale furtive air as though they knew well enough that all the pleasures had been discovered and sampled long ago.

My friend and I went into a café which had a reputation for attracting artists, musicians, poets, actors. We sat at a marble table and ordered pale, tepid beer in tall glasses. A ceaseless chatter of quick conversation echoed through the room. We looked around us. One could not go into this café without expecting to see somebody "interesting"; and by that I mean either famous or infamous. There were women with red finger-nails, sleek, stringy hair, and sad, sharp faces; women with pasty, spectacled faces and rough tweed suits. Men who looked like women, with long hair, powdered faces, and scented silk shirts; women who looked like men, with neckties, flat bosoms, and cropped hair. Often it was difficult to distinguish between the sexes.

Behind me was a man with a mop of hair falling over his shoulders. He was dressed in an open white shirt, knee-breeches of dark green velveteen, and he carried an umbrella. He was an ubiquitous curiosity. I had already seen him in a concert hall, an underground lavatory, and a Catholic church. I never discovered who he was. That evening I remember he was talking to a small audience of three or four persons, about some esoteric point in the art of magic and divination.

A tall, handsome young man with a carnation stuck in the jacket of his loud blue check suit, carrying a pair of scarlet gloves made of wool, came in at the door and was immediately hailed by a party of pale youths with high squealing voices and narrow waists, who made a place for him and showed the greatest interest in his gloves.

My friend and I began to talk about the people, comparing types, judging their worth, who were artificial, who were not. We wrote verses on the back of a list of foods and drinks. It grew later—towards eleven. More and more people drifted in: some alone, some in groups.

Then a strange thing happened. The door burst open noisily and a large man entered. He stood there, swaying a little, glaring insolently round the room. He laughed loudly and people looked up. There was a sudden murmur of astonishment, followed by an uneasy silence.

He was an exceptional figure, very tall, with a keen, angular, somewhat blotchy face, and a thick golden beard. His hair was the same colour, thrown back from his head in a careless sweep. He was dressed in a bright yellow shirt with a long blue tie; a tweed jacket bulging with a variety of articles he had in his pockets; and grey trousers.

But it was not the man who caused that little gasp of astonishment to go round the room. It was the small gray bird on his shoulder.

He stood there, swaying and hiccuping, with this small bird gently rubbing its beak into his neck.

A waiter passing, stopped, stared, and dropped the empty tray he had been carrying. The metallic clang broke the silence; people began to talk excitedly.

"I wonder how he caught it," said my friend casually.

"And if he did catch it," I replied, "why doesn't it fly away?"

But I did not believe he had captured it. It was so quiet, so timid—it did not look as though it had the power to fly away. Faced with the crowd of staring, chattering people, it seemed to shrink close up to the man as though for shelter. Its feathers were not very bright, but subtle in colouring: a sort of grey which concealed all other colours. The eyes blinked as though the sudden bright light blinded them.

The man did not stand there long. He appeared to be looking for somebody. He was clearly drunk and could not easily distinguish one figure from another.

He called out, "Does anybody want to buy a unique bird?"

Nobody responded. Then he laughed and shouted in some language I could not understand. Suddenly he saw somebody over in a far corner, sitting alone. I followed his eyes and saw a woman, sitting gravely, studying him. He called with a raucous shout, pushed his way carelessly past chairs and tables, and sat down heavily opposite the woman.

I looked across at her. She was dressed in quiet simple clothes with no adornment anywhere upon her person. This lack of colour compelled one's attention to her face, which was grave and as colourless as the cream-coloured blouse that she wore. In this serene countenance her eyes glowed with almost fierce richness. They were beautiful eyes, so full of light in their depths, that they seemed to cast a radiance over her face. Looking back at her face after having seen her eyes was as though you had looked on a death-mask that suddenly smiled. I felt that the lids of those eyes, when they fell, would draw a curtain over the entire face.

Her hair was black, with here and there a greying streak; it lay thick and smooth, brushed back from her ivory-cool forehead. She was rather tall and thin, but well-proportioned. I could not tell her age. If I said twenty-five, I noticed the line of grey in her hair which seemed to contradict that. Yet the eyes were young and full of vigour.

When I looked at her I was instantly stirred. She sat with a slight frown on her face, tapping her teeth with a pencil. Against the clatter of the café the only sound I could hear was this critical tapping of wood upon a row of small white teeth.

"Interesting female," said my friend.

I nodded without speaking. The man with the bird leant over the table towards her. She appeared to accept his drunkenness as inevitable; neither did she take any interest in the bird who crouched low on the man's shoulders, its head tucked away into its feathers, as though asleep. I was fascinated, as everybody was, by the bird; but I was fascinated more by the critical intensity of the woman's gaze, her clear distaste and yet tolerance of her companion.

We stayed watching this curious trio. My friend said he had seen the man somewhere, but could not recollect where. To me also the face seemed familiar.

He drank a great deal and grew incoherent and louder in his talk. Once he took the woman's arm roughly, with a gesture of possession. She tried to push him aside, but he insisted on fondling her. He was urging her to come away with him. She would not stir. They were quarrelling. He, brutally loud; she, colder than ice, her lips pressed tight in her white face. Two people sitting at the same table hurriedly left the room.

The man's voice rose. "—tired of me, Olga. Sleep with any damn man who'll pay you enough . . . tired of me——"

I jumped suddenly to my feet. I felt as though something had attacked me also.

But she, too, at that moment, had risen, and managing to elude his grasp walked quickly, but with great dignity and command, away from the table.

The bird screamed suddenly and the man tried to push it away from his shoulder. I stood watching Olga as she went towards the door. She passed a few inches from our table. I glanced at her, my heart pounding in an excitement I had never felt before. For a moment she caught my glance. Then she was gone.

I sat down. There was a commotion at the other end of the room where the man, attempting to check the thin, ragged screaming of the bird, grew furious, rose, and knocked over some glasses. The bird had fixed its claws tight into the man's shoulder. Its cries were most melancholy, pitiful, wailing sounds, the saddest sounds I have ever heard.

An attempt was now made to remove the man, as he struggled wildly to shake the bird away from his shoulder. Three or four waiters came up and seized hold of him. Suddenly the drunkard relaxed and went limp in their grasp, so that they had to drag him to the door like a sack of oats. A heavy silence hung over the room. The drunkard made no sound except a heavy breathing; he seemed almost insensible. The bird still clung to his shoulders.

They passed our table and I drew aside. I was afraid, not of the drunkard, but of some extraordinary quality to this scene which I could not understand. I saw the bird pressed so firmly into the man's shoulders that it looked almost as though it were part of the substance of his tweed coat. I drew aside, feeling there was something here I should not see. I did not understand, and the memory of it was to trouble me for a long time until I did understand. In the thick, misty eyes of the drunkard was a futile agony which made me aware of a similar agony somewhere in myself, deep down. If I looked at him, the more I was conscious of this agony in myself. I dared not look.

My friend was talking, but I could not respond. All the time, carved into my mind above this feeling of distress, was the image of that coldly passionate woman's face—a face clear in my memory as no face had ever been. Olga....

There is little more to tell of that strange evening—a lovely and a terrible evening. They got the drunkard out; I saw the last of him as they carried him through the door. Then the waiters came back, laughing nervously and pretending that the incident was all part of the day's work. My friend and I left very soon. It was past midnight. I caught a late omnibus and walked part of the way home. The night was burning and still; yet as I passed along the dreary suburban streets most of the windows were closed firm, with blinds drawn. I crept into the house without disturbing my mother, though I saw that a candle was alight in her room. She had closed my windows; I did not open them.

One word was on my lips; one face carved into my mind. I could not sleep.

The end of this story was revealed in the newspapers. I saw next day a photograph of a well-known poet called Paul Weaver whom I immediately recognized as the drunkard of the previous night. He had killed himself. The case attracted a certain amount of attention because of the fact that he was a poet whose early sensitive lyrics had been lately superseded by a number of violent erotic verses which some critics deplored, some admired. He had thrown himself before a fast-moving bus shortly after his eviction from the café, and had been instantly killed. The bird—as in the case of the old woman in the telephone-box of whom I told you earlier—had apparently escaped.

No mention was made of the woman who had been with him—she whom he had addressed as Olga.

*

The next day was the last before my holiday.

That Friday, as all such days which are a vigil of some unusual event, seemed interminable. How I worked I do not know. Often my pen dribbled along the paper in a chain of lethargic noughts, so that where I should have written five hundred I more often wrote fifty thousand.

I lunched alone in an underground café some way from the office; my literary friend was away on his holiday, and I did not want to meet anybody else. There, I read for the third or fourth time the account of the poet's suicide which was given in the newspaper. His portrait revealed a fine and sensitive face which seemed the antithesis to the coarse, lined face which I had seen last night. Yet it was the same man.

He had been a great scholar of mediæval poetry; his early work had resembled the lyrics of the Elizabethans and was rare in our days, when sharp spasmodic verses with little rhythm and less sense were the fashion. The paper said that the poet was an interesting example of a man born out of his period; he had no sympathy whatever with any contemporary movements. As a youth he had worked in obscurity, nobody but a few friends— amongst them an old classical poet of accepted integrity—recognizing his unique talent. He had been very poor. Then suddenly he had changed his style completely, with it his name and, so it seemed, his very identity. He wrote furiously passionate verses, archaic drinking songs, and vagabond love poems. Then he was honoured by critics and became popular; he was published and quoted as the most representative of our younger poets. His later life had been eccentric and savage in the extreme. He was compared favourably to Marlowe, a great Elizabethan poet whose violent young life had been cut short in a drunken quarrel.

I read my paper and sipped my coffee, re-creating the incidents of last night and trying to find a reasonable explanation for it all. I wondered whether the poet and Olga had been lovers; what sort of a woman she was; where she lived and what she did. Chiefly I wondered how I could contrive to see her again.

A clock struck the half after two; I hurried up, paid my bill, and dashed out. I was forty minutes late. The Underwriter had been inquiring for me; he had wanted somebody to go to Lloyd's, and in my absence he had had to send an older man who was already very busy.

"You're for the carpet," said a colleague as I came into the room.

I was summoned into the private room. It was a close, airless place, surrounded by panels of frosted glass, with a thick carpet on the floor and a large desk in the middle. Hanging on the wall was a painting of a sailing ship tossing in a heavy sea. It was the nearest the Underwriter had ever got to peril on the high seas.

He was sitting at his desk, alone in the room. For several seconds he did not look up as I came in. Then, still without looking at me, he asked me whether I imagined this was an office or a club for my amusement. I did not answer, knowing I could not trust myself to speak calmly. His yellow wig was bent over a docket of claims papers. The massive scarlet tome, Lloyd's Register, lay at his elbow. He went on talking, telling me that I must remember my position as junior clerk; reminding me how many there were ready to step into my position.

My fingers clenched and unclenched. I had an impulse to tear his wig from his head and pour ink over his bald pate. Never had I wanted so badly to hurt a man. I think he knew it, for he looked up suddenly and must have seen tears of vindictive passion brimming in my eyes.

"Get out," he said, "and think over what I have said to you."

I stumbled out without saying I was sorry, which was clearly what he had expected. The rest of the day he purposely tempted me to open rebellion; ringing his abominable little bell at every conceivable opportunity; sending me here for a pen, there for his spectacles; to the fourth floor for information that he never glanced at; to the basement storeroom for foreign registers that he threw aside.

Going down to the storeroom later in the afternoon to return one of these registers, I felt so sick and tired I did not care any more what the Underwriter might do. I stayed talking to the old fellow who had charge of the place. He was a curiously romantic figure, old and shabby, yet with a fund of antiquarian information which amused me. He would tell me stories about London in the Victorian days when he had been a dashing youth; about music-halls in the 'nineties; about his early travels with a concert party up and down the coast towns of England. All that had gone. Now he had to spend his days in an artificially lit room under the earth, honoured by nobody, surrounded by volumes and papers caked with dust, hemmed in by hot-water pipes. I liked him. He had a certain warmth, and a contempt for his superiors which he made no attempt to conceal.

I told him about my adventures the previous night. Then suddenly, in a burst of confidence—for I had told nobody else—about the face I had fallen in love with.

He said he knew; he knew what it was to fall in love with a face and never see it again. His eyes grew sad. He looked comical, his little tufts of yellow-white hair sprouting haphazardly from his nearly bald head. I remember there was a large pimple nestling in the hollow between his nose and upper lip.

"Why don't you get out of here before you're old and it's too late?" he said. "You're a foolish young fellow if you stay here."

Then the house telephone rang; somebody in the claims department wanted a foreign register file. I hurried upstairs, conscious I had stayed here a long time and might be called for another and more serious homily.

But nothing happened. It was a Friday, and the Underwriter, who generally went down to his country house for the weekend, left early. He sent me out to summon a taxi. It was the only command of his that I ever executed with any willingness, since it meant getting rid of him. I watched him as he passed my desk on his way out; a ridiculous hard black hat on his head; the inevitable umbrella, even in this heat, hanging on his wrist, a fat newspaper folded under his arm. I had a sudden desire to strip him of his clothes; to witness his shame at the revelation of his pot-belly. Naked, I knew he would be comic and I should cease to hate him, only laugh at him.

I could not get away very early. There were many things to be put in order before I went. Old declaration policies to be entered; a basket of letters and documents to be filed away; and other small matters which all occupied me some time. I felt strangely conscientious about it all. I had a curiously tidy mind which could never bear to leave things in a state of disorder.

A little after five I was left alone in the room with one irritable man who always stayed late in a feverish attempt to catch up with his work. My friends had said good-bye and wished me an enjoyable holiday. I went on entering policies with no sound in the room save the scratch of the other man's pen. Morose and surly, he sat some feet away from me. We did not speak.

Now it was quiet I did not mind the place. I even derived a certain satisfaction from the knowledge that I should not see it again for two long weeks.

I worked quietly. I did not want to go home; I wanted to go to the café on the chance that I might see the woman again. Once I walked to the telephone box thinking I would call my friend and ask him to meet me. But I checked the impulse. I knew I must spend this last evening with my mother. I drove the haunting face from my mind, remembering what the old clerk had said about faces seen once and never again. It was inevitable, I told myself, that I should never see her again.

So I worked in the forsaken room, till about half after six. Then I put away the last policy and went upstairs, six floors, to wash my hands. The liftman had gone home and there were few left in the building. I washed, came down again, found my hat and a book I was trying in vain to read, bade good-night to the other man, and left the room.

By the lift gate I met the old filing-clerk coming laboriously up the stairs from below. He also had been kept late. I felt suddenly affectionate towards him and invited him to come and drink with me. He accepted.

"I'm going to Wales to-morrow," I told him as we sat on high stools in a tavern opposite, drinking beer.

"So you told me," he said. "You're a lucky young fellow. Never seem to get farther than Southend myself."

I told him I was going to think things out.

"That's right," he said. "The best thing you can do is to get work on a farm and never return to London again. You ought to do that. You've got guts—— But I—I'm played out, done for."

I reassured him uncomfortably, knowing that what he said was true. He was only a wreck; nothing could launch him again.

"Whatever you do," he said solemnly, "don't take a wife, not you. Have your fun, but don't you marry. That's the only thing that saved me from——"

I never discovered what bachelordom had saved him from. For from outside we suddenly heard the loud chattering of the birds, a sound as yet unfamiliar enough to compel attention.

We ran out with others in the bar, and were in time to see them flying low over Leadenhall towards London Bridge. Something dropped to the ground from amongst them. It was a black bowler hat, similar to that worn by the Underwriter. I ran to pick it up, but already a policeman had it, and was examining it while he scratched his head half humorously. It was dented, battered, and covered with dung. Nobody knew to whom it belonged.

"Whose is it?" I asked the policeman.

"Don't know. Like to see if it fits?"

We all laughed. The old clerk came up behind me and wrinkled his eyes over the hat.

"Looks like his, don't it?"

"You mean the Underwriter?"

"Ah," he said. "That's right. The Underwriter, God blast his soul."

He spat and looked up into the sky. The birds had flown out of sight.

"Anyhow," I said, "somebody lost their dignity when they lost that."

"Yes," he agreed gloomily. "And it won't be long, ask me, before we all lose it."

*

I spent that evening with my mother. We sat in the garden and later walked up to the ridge. I wanted to talk to her about last night, but something prevented me. I found it hard to speak to anybody about what had happened in the café.

Lillian was in one of her sweetest moods, very quiet, sad at my going away from her, but wanting me to have a good holiday.

"For you don't like London, do you, son?" she asked me, with a slow smile. Then she sighed and said she wished we could live in the country.

"How lovely it would be to see a field again, or a cow, or a wild flower."

I tried to urge her to come with me to Wales, but she dismissed the idea as impossible. I think she knew that I wanted to go alone.

"I expect you will find a new girl," she said, "a milkmaid or something. And then you will have to speak in Welsh."

We were sitting on one of the seats above the tennis-courts. The sky was shadowy towards the City, with a rosy mist that softened the rigid outlines of buildings.

"I wish we could have rain, and I wish the birds would go away," sighed my mother.

"They won't go away yet," I murmured.

She asked me what I thought "they" would do about them. I said, what could anybody "do" about them?

"You can't do anything about the stars," I added. "You can't move them about."

"Oh, but they're different," she laughed. "They don't come and drink up half our water or drop their business all over our back gardens."

"They might," I said. "They might, if somebody wanted them to." And I asked her, did she really believe in God?

"So you think God sent the birds?" she said quickly. "Well, perhaps he did. After all, he used to send boils and frogs and plagues. Perhaps he did send the birds, son. There's no knowing."

She sighed again and said, "What's it all for?"

It was late. The tennis players had left the courts.

"How quickly time goes," said Lillian. "We used to say when I was a little girl, 'Time flies; I cannot.' Now what does that mean, do you think?"

I said I supposed it meant that time rushed on and we had no power to arrest its progress.

"Whatever we do we can't alter our fate. We can't put the clock back and do it all over again in a better way. We've just got to go on making mistakes till we're too old to make any more. I wish I was your age, Mother."

She told me I was a funny boy. "Mad, like my father, who went gadding about all over Europe and never found anywhere to rest for long."

So we came home, and I made her sing to me, watching her hands over the keys, listening to her familiar tunes. She sang an old hymn:

"Now the day is over, night is drawing nigh;
Shadows of the evening steal across the sky."

I kissed her and we went to our rooms. My bag lay packed with clothes and books by my bedside. I lingered, putting in a few more things and taking others out. I wrote a note to Annie, which I should give to her in the morning, asking her to look after Lillian and write to me should anything trouble her.

The windows of my room were closed. I opened them with sudden impatience, not caring then whether a bird flew in or not. But no bird came; only moths fluttered in and blundered against the lamp.

I could see the light through the yellow blinds of my mother's room; her shadow as she combed out her hair before the mirror on her dressing-table. I turned over the pages of the few books I was taking with me. There was one about wild flowers, for I knew nothing of flowers and wanted to learn about them in the country. On a sudden impulse I added the poetry of Keats to my collection.

I was happy yet unhappy; a strange mixture of emotions flowed in me. My mother seemed to have sung a valediction to many things. The day was gone. There would never be another Friday similar to this.

The next morning, struggling with my heavy bag, I got to one of the London stations and caught my train for Shrewsbury. There was a great crowd, and I had difficulty in obtaining a seat. We were packed close together, and I thought I would never endure the heat. But when the train moved out, a slight breeze broke the stillness.

I had newspapers and journals to read on the way, but for a long time I did not touch them. The news seemed the same every day. I watched London moving away from me. Warehouses, factories, ranks of massive chimneys like dirty fingers pressed upon the sky; rows of dark little houses with back alleys where children waved their hands to the passing train. Then suburban towns, many miles of them, all alike. Cricket-fields, tennis-courts, a nursery for seedlings. More hedges, a field or two, rows of straw-coloured houses and industrious little gardens; trees and wild flowers in the banks; river, cornfield, village church, cart-track, cow, horse, harvester; apple trees, dahlias, hayricks; old men leaning over gates; young men driving the reapers over corn.

So I left London behind me for awhile and came to this country which is now our home.

The evening comes; rain is swelling those clouds at the end of the valley. The year is changing; long, dark evenings will soon be here. When I continue my story, I think most likely it will be in the corner by our fireside, with candlelight to help you guide your pen.

What were the words? . . . "*Now the day is over*———" Well, yes—and so it is. I must try to remember the tune.

II

THE MOUNTAIN

It is Autumn, the Fall.

When I look out of this window and see the Michaelmas daisies locked close together as though to try to resist the wind that beats them; when I see leaves like crinkled bits of charred paper clinging weakly to knuckled boughs; when I see the stream from the mountain bursting angrily down the valley, bearing leaves and branches with it; when I see these things I am tempted to ask what is the purpose of all this Life when we too, no longer strong enough to withstand the stream, must suffer ourselves to be carried away upon it?

Then I am reminded of another Fall, more than half a century ago, when I first looked upon this country and saw as I had never seen before that I too was a part of the endless stream of Life which flowed around me; that I too was governed by the same law which governs seed, flower, and fruit.

Sixty years ago. I left London, impatient to discover some harmony within myself that might constitute a surer foundation to my life. My last thoughts had been of my mother; her song, with its fatalistic words, was ringing in my mind: "*Now the day is over*." I had a premonition that more than a day was passing.

I thought of my mother with a feeling of guilt as though I owed her something I had made no effort to pay. But I could not keep her image with me for long. The farther the train penetrated into the heart of the country, the harder I found it to concentrate upon one who, I knew, belonged to the past. Another face belonged to the future. "Olga, Olga . . ." I murmured the word over and over again to myself until it merged into the metrical drumming of the train over the rails.

I stayed at a small village not far from Cader Idris. I had taken a room in the house of the local schoolmaster and his wife. From my window I could see the fast, cold waters of the river and mountainous hills on the other side. It was all new and magical to me; so quiet, so detached from the tumult of the life I had left, I could hardly believe it to be in the same world.

I took my meals with the family. The schoolmaster was an amiable man with a thirst for controversy. He would seek to engage me in long discussions about the political state of the world, discussions which I tried to avoid. He was eager to hear all about the birds. They had seen nothing of them in this part of the island, though they had once or twice flown over Aberystwyth. I told him what I could, but I was happier when we forgot these things and he chose to sing some of his native songs, while his son—a youth of seventeen—improvised accompaniments on the violin. Then something old and forgotten came out of these two, father and son. They were Celts, belonging to that strange race of men whose ancestry is lost in legend. They allowed something to speak through them without restraint. The boy drew from his violin a quality of savage tenderness which was almost a brazen echo of the deepest thoughts of the mind; he somehow fused the physical yearnings of man into a spiritual reality, held firm in the intangible quality of one drawn-out note. When he played, his face burnt with a subtle joy he could never have explained. He had rich yellow hair, long and loose, and full, liquid eyes. I loved him.

Some evenings Ivor, the boy, would drive me round the countryside in an old-fashioned car that the family possessed. I remember it well, and had cause to, as you will see. It was pale blue, with seats for five or six, and a threadbare black hood. Ivor studied at Aberystwyth during the day, so that he never found time to explore the country with me, on foot, as I did. He had lived there all his life and now he longed to see other places. And although I used to say that only in walking could you discover the heart of a country, I so enjoyed those evening drives that I induced him to teach me also how to handle a car. He would let me drive along the country roads and then, when we came to a town, take the steering-wheel himself. Once or twice we went thus to Aberystwyth, and he showed me the buildings where he studied. He was to be a schoolmaster like his father; but he had higher ambitions than a village school. In a soft, rich voice he used to talk and ask me questions about London which I never wanted to answer; I preferred to hear him talk about his own country. They were happy evenings. In his presence, intent upon learning to drive the car, I forgot London and the birds entirely.

The weather remained cloudless and I would go out with my flower-book learning the names of flowers and seeing them all as new and mysterious things. I remember with what ingenuous delight I came upon a bank of meadowsweet; how I found heartsease on the lofty hills. It was all new to me. The black, distant mountains; the sheep, driven by their lean, grey dogs; the dark lakes; the dense ranks of larches and firs; all the grave countenance of this beautiful country stirred me deeply.

"You should climb Cader Idris," the schoolmaster would urge me every evening when I returned to give an account of my walks. And even his wife said once, "Look, you cannot go back to London without having been up a mountain."

I laughed and said yes, I would climb it eventually. But there were so many other places to see, that it was not until two or three days before the end of my visit that I decided to make the climb. I started off early one morning with elaborate instructions from the family as to the best path to take, and with some food in a haversack.

A little more than half-way to the summit I stopped by a lake. The sunlight was soft and grave with an autumnal remoteness about it. The lake frightened me, it was so silent and deep, as though its waters covered a whole dead world unknown to me. Not a flicker of wind touched the hard surface; it lay perfectly still, like a closed eye, reflecting nothing. I felt as though I had shrivelled to the size of a pebble on its shores.

Then, as I looked, I saw that slowly the whole apparently unmoving surface rocked like a metal disc suspended in the air, from one side of its shore to the other. I heard the laboured washing of its waters drawn slowly over the stones.

It was alive, moving.

I drew away from the lake, uneasily quick in my movements,

and began to climb higher, gaining zest from the cold mountain air. I forced my way to the summit, driving thoughts out of my mind and attempting to concentrate upon the scene that grew around me as I ascended.

At the top I stopped by a little travellers' shelter, a stone shed where a man brewed pots of tea for climbers. Then I surveyed the scene I had come so far to view.

The splendour of the hills, valleys, rivers, lakes, trees, and fields, all assembled below me and spreading away as far as the eye could reach to the mouth of the open sea, moved me so that I felt tears of joy come into my eyes. I have told you how I had been moved by the sight of the distant City from the ridge above Stroud Green. Now the City seemed like a child's toy model in my mind. One blow of man's breath, I said, could have crumbled it to dust. But here was something man could not easily displace.

Suddenly I saw—and the realization was overwhelming—all that man had inherited and all that he had striven to distort. I saw that art, which struggled to reproduce those things which man had lost, gave but a pennyworth of the sum-total. I had been moved by great music, by a beautiful building, by a poem or a play. But I saw now that all these emotions had been borrowed; that they were never mine in the fullest sense; that ultimately they had to be returned to the artist who had but lent me, for a passing moment, eyes with which to see.

The wind whistled around me, flattening my stupid trousers against my thin legs. I opened my mouth; I did what that old Hebrew poet had done, "*I opened my mouth and drew in my breath.*" Consciously, I breathed.

I breathed again, in and out, deeper. There was a taste of life on my tongue, a sweet, cleansing taste I had never known before. And the more I breathed, consciously receiving and giving out waves of life, the calmer became my spirit. An extraordinary certainty of my own being possessed me. It seemed to me that this enormous world was mine, given to me, and that it wanted me, wanted the union with me without which it was not complete.

Oh, the arrogance of that moment when I saw that men could be gods if they would cease to remember that they had once been apes! Gods, because they possessed this great quality of awareness of Life.

It seemed to me that with this awareness we had the power to detach ourselves; like a bird, to float in the air at our side and see ourselves. "Like a bird," I said, "like a bird, for ever hovering about us and directing and feeling." I felt then that I was no longer in my physical body, that I was in the cold air above, watching, prompting, and feeling. From this detached vantage-point it was my business to regulate my physical body, encouraging it to plunge into the ever-moving stream of life; eating, drinking, breathing, loving, and being.

This was the power of the Soul, for ever to be *aware* of the activity and behaviour of the physical substance. For if this material frame lapsed into insensible activity, its perfect mechanism was abused. It would begin to hammer like an engine driven to action with no oil. Anything done without the awareness of the Soul was energy wasted. If I touched a stone with my finger, my Soul should know the sensation of contact with another body; if I drank cold water, my Soul should record the sacramental excellence of that experience.

It then appeared to me that we in our time had accustomed ourselves to the habit of unconscious experience. We ate, drank, breathed in a semi-comatose condition. Half of our physical life was passed in a twilight state of unrealized activity. A word often on our lips was "subconscious." "My subconscious mind," we might say, "led me to do that." We were very proud of this naïve discovery of our subconscious, because, we affirmed, it was an ungovernable force, a primitive urge; it was useful to possess a quality which might excuse certain of our meaner actions.

Yet, indeed, the subconscious was merely the conscious Soul making utterances and curious signs like a man gone dumb. To talk of body, soul, and spirit was a confusion. There was only body and Soul, with a bridge existing between the two that made communion possible. This was the bridge termed by the Church, Holy Ghost. When a man looked through his physical eyes upon a tree and suddenly felt some extraordinary energy within himself to reach out and embrace the tree, he travelled along the path of the Holy Ghost to the timeless country of his Soul which for ever mingled with the tree. The nature of existence was twofold, not threefold, as the doctrine of the Christian Trinity seemed to imply.

On every side was there evidence of this truth. Here, on the mountain.

I breathed in; I breathed out. And in that simple action I felt the twofold purpose of existence, the dual movement which turns life ceaselessly upon its course. In the very act of breathing, the pulse of the whole order of creation was shown to me. I took that breath; I gave it out. I could not give without taking, nor take without giving. In the same way the seed was given to the earth, and the earth gave the flower; the moisture was given to the clouds, and the clouds gave back rain; the man gave to the woman, and the woman gave man to the earth. There was not anything alone or unrelated in the universe. Even the lake that lay cupped below me moved in unbreakable communion with the wind that drew the water's calm sheet from side to side of the mountain hollow. When I breathed out there was a quality to my breath which the earth required; I could sustain the earth even as the earth sustained me. When I breathed, and knew I breathed, I created; I placed myself in the circumference of creation, was no longer a tangent touching creation then darting away from it. While I knew the Soul's inexhaustible powers of creation I need never fear death, for death was a word invented by one whose body had lost its Soul. When this matter decayed it would make the final act of giving to the Soul, and the Soul, thus for ever strengthened, would become identified with the other-universe from which it sprung. To nourish the Soul against this final charge I must ever keep before me the truth of its powers of creation.

Create—— Creation——

The word pleased me as though I had never heard it before. And there suddenly, as I stopped short in my thinking, the word irritated me. Was it enough to create by breathing and similar acts? Was it permanent enough?

I saw then why man created art, because there before him was something which he could leave behind as a record of his physical life. Was I then to make such things—poems, pictures, music?

No, I cried; no. For what poem can ever sustain me as the breath of Life up here can sustain me?

I was no artist, I told myself. There were some who were driven to record the life they knew so keenly; their art sustained them. Yet in the long-run, whom else could it sustain? I dared not belittle the great works of men. And yet, I thought how the form of death clung alone to man's works of art. These beautiful things, perhaps a church spire seen through a network of dark winter trees; a great piece of music; the sculpture of a lovely body—what pathetic solemnity, what unutterable sadness and longing hung around such things! Contemplation of a great work of art was also contemplation of an end from which there seemed no escape; contemplation of a tree in winter, or a bare field, filled one with the knowledge of unending life. No life was possible without communion with life. And who could have communion with a church spire or a sculpted frieze? You could only take from these things; you could give nothing.

"You are virtually dead," I muttered angrily, "until you can establish tactual relation with life. Your conscious Soul must know that you are breathing, eating, drinking, loving——"

Loving. There was no escape. What a commonplace conclusion to approach from so tortuous a route!

I came away then; walking quickly because of my burning thoughts, down the narrow stony path which led towards the lake. With all my being I longed to press against me the form of another human person, young, beautiful, and desirable, who found me also desirable, that we could derive from each other the twofold act of creation, taking and giving. And the thought of Olga's face tormented me almost beyond endurance.

I remember how quickly I walked, almost ran past the lake and thus homewards. There was a young shepherd herding sheep on the hills some way past the lake. He was beautiful, totally unconscious of me. I hurried past, muttering a greeting, hardly looking at him. For it was a body I wanted, some human body to hold close to mine. My feeling, my entire powers of sensation seemed then to have passed to the centre of my body; to my stomach, my bowels, my genitals. There seemed nothing now but this veritable pit of yearning to be at one with somebody.

I came back to the schoolmaster's black little house and there was Ivor waiting to show me a paragraph in the newspaper which told of some new activity of the birds in London. I cannot remember what it was. For all the time, sitting over the table in the stuffy room with the paper outstretched before us, while he read aloud and commented, his head and mine nodded close, his fingers met mine as he turned the page.

"Goodness to me," he said, "look at this——"

"Yes," I murmured, "yes"—never hearing a word he said.

"I think I must come back to London with you and see those birds." He turned and smiled at me, his lips half open, his white teeth gleaming. I saw him through a mist as though I was stupid with drink.

"Would you like to?"

"I should love to see those birds, goodness to gracious I should."

"You would hate London," I told him. "You'd much better stay here."

"Oh, but do you think so? I want to see life."

Suddenly I made a decision. I had two days yet to spend here.

"I must leave you to-morrow," I said.

Then his father came, his mother summoned us to a meal, and I told them again that I must go the next day, making as my excuse that I wished to see a certain old town on my way back. They were sorry.

"And you have not really learnt to drive properly," said the schoolmaster. "It is a great shame you must go."

I thought of the evenings in the car.

"Never mind," said Ivor. "I shall come to London one day; then I can drive you round and you shall show me the sights."

They tried to induce me to stay, but I was firm. So they gave up urging me, and later I asked them to sing and play to me for the last time. I looked at Ivor as he drew that old sweetness from his violin, and I wondered what it was in him which prompted a desire to go to London and see life.

We said good-bye. I pressed Ivor by the hand, for he would be up early in the morning to Aberystwyth.

"I will see you in London one day," he paused on the stairs

with a lighted candle in his hand. He laughed softly and the light flickered round his face.

"Yes," I echoed, "in London."

The next morning I departed, with many messages of good-will from the schoolmaster. Even his dour wife presented me with a packet of sandwiches and some cake. Perhaps she was impressed by the fact that I had paid her for a fortnight's lodging and had only stayed eleven days.

"Come again," they said, "you must come again."

I said I would, but I did not mean it.

Blow up the fire, light the candles. This dark afternoon assaults my spirit. To-morrow I will take this youth of ours, this romantic metaphysician back to London.

III

THE COLLAPSE

On my return to London, all those thoughts which had so refreshed me on the mountain were swept away. On Cader it had been possible to forget the distressed condition of the world; in London it was not.

In a fortnight it seemed to me that people's faces had grown haggard, their eyes thin with suspicion and fear. The City was foul with the stench of dried ordure, for the shortage of water was now so serious that the streets could not be washed at night. A lurking stillness had settled over everything; the pavements were like shallow lids made tender by a furnace that raged beneath. Trees were dead, flowers withered long before their time.

Newsboys vied with each other shouting such phrases as "France leaves the League!" "Villagers dying of thirst!" and— perhaps the smallest voice—"Birds interrupt Welfare Society!" I snatched a paper and read angrily, not wanting to learn anything of the confusion which was beginning to shake mankind, yet knowing I could not avoid it. The usual "features" in the evening paper were absent, crowded out by a spate of sensational reports which poured over the pages.

But the affairs of the world are outside the scope of my story, and I do not intend to deal with them. It will be your business to augment from my personal history, so that you have some picture of what, so far as I know, happened to the entire machinery of civilization. Certain dreadful things I witnessed; certain terrors I, in common with millions, endured. But of what went on in other parts of the world I can tell you no more than what I gathered from a study of the newspapers, from listening to wireless reports, or from hurrying to and from Lloyd's, where a chain of casualties and the anxiety of merchants and shipowners to insure their properties against perils of war, and "Pests of the Air," kept my colleagues and myself in a fever of excitement.

"Pests of the Air." This was now the official designation of the birds. People spoke of them contemptuously and declared that the Government was soon to take the matter in hand. Exactly how they were to take it in hand was not known. But while there was still a Government and a King, how could any loyal Englishman worry himself about such trifles as "Pests of the Air"?

The prestige of the Royal House, at all times well maintained, was strengthened by the calm and semi-humorous behaviour of King Edward, who was one day followed by a bird of particularly extravagant plumage. The King was driving to an exhibition of Empire products in which he always took great interest. As he alighted from his car a large bird swooped down from above and followed him into the hall where the exhibits were being shown. Its brilliant feathers and shrill voice contrasted strangely with the severe, dark clothes of King Edward and his gentlemen, several of whom made vague attempts to beat the creature away. They were unsuccessful, however, for the bird still hovered about the group when they were inside the hall. Policemen were summoned to deal with this uninvited retainer, and a silent scuffle took place behind the King's back, in the course of which a statesman called Baldwin was bitten on the nose and cried out in pain and rage. This disturbance apparently annoyed the King, who so far had made no remark. He turned irritably, "I am sorry you should have been bitten, but really, I imagine we came here to study more important things than birds." Then he smiled and added, "Besides, it is probably from the Colonies and should not be attacked." It was felt that the King had set a fashion in his attitude to the birds. They were pests, and must not be allowed to interrupt ordinary business. The King had clearly shown his people how to behave. In acknowledgment of this lead, a considerable demonstration took place outside his large house that night. Great crowds gathered, and many people even went so far as to swarm irreverently half-way up a sprawling statue of King Edward's great-grandmother which stood before the Palace. The crowd would not leave until, late at night, the King appeared on the balcony and bowed to the public amidst great shouts and cheers. It was observed that the bird still circled around him; but he took no notice. His calm behaviour, his apparent determination to dismiss the birds as unimportant nuisances, was commented upon in all the papers. If the King cared so little for these disgusting and unorthodox denizens of the air, these impertinent *mistakes* of the Almighty—then so would his people. The Royal House had stood firm; England would stand firm. It is a curious fact, however, that from that day, the King was not seen again in public.

A new view, then, was taken of the birds. They were pests, like locusts, black-beetles or wasps. They must be "dealt with." Yes, certainly. But how?

This was the question which the sorely tried grey-beards in the House at Westminster one day decided, after a good deal of pressure, to discuss. It seemed to be within the province of the Home Secretary, or possibly the Minister of Health; or should it be dealt with by the Minister of Transport, the Admiralty, or War Office——?

The House dispersed, having reached no conclusions. Then the newspaper proprietors, anxious as usual to show their power, began to tell the Government what to do. Shoot them down! screamed one paper. Entice them by means of tasty foods into gas-laden pockets in the air, snapped another. Lure them to a park previously cleared of people, release an army of hungry cats, and hope for the best. Offer a pound for every bird slain whose corpse can be produced.

Yes, yes, certainly. But one fact stood out. Nobody had yet been able to kill or capture one of these pests. On the contrary, a considerable number of people engaged in conflict with them had died. And in all these mortal conflicts, no bird, not even a feather, had ever been found.

About this time we realized that the sparrows, starlings, pigeons, and gulls which usually frequented London in such great numbers were now hardly ever seen. Whether they emigrated to quieter parts of the country was never discovered. They were certainly absent from the City. Whenever we saw birds we knew they were the pests. And this absence of normal bird-noises seemed to close London into a box; as though the sky were a vault through which all birds, except the pests, had flown to freedom.

What did they eat? It was a question on many people's lips in those days. Nobody had ever seen them eating. In earlier days when good-natured ladies had tried to cosset them, they had affected the utmost contempt for the traditional seed which pampered pigeons were known to devour in quantities. The brisk trade in bird-seed that for a week or so had gladdened the hearts of chandlers, had entirely declined. People had no desire to buy seed purely in order to have the pleasure of seeing it swept into a dust-cart at the end of the day.

There was very little doubt, the common voice expressed it on all sides, these unreasonable and ungrateful creatures—so unlike the popular conception of what a good bird should be, from a cockatoo to a canary—were impertinent, offensive. A few pigeons, yes; people were fond of pigeons so long as they refrained from depositing their loads on the newly whitened façade of the Royal Exchange. A few seagulls, yes; they were a considerable diversion in the lunch hour on London Bridge, gracious enough to accept any scraps that were offered them; a sparrow or two, yes; so long as they did not twitter too early in the morning. Owls, yes; they were romantic and macabre. Thrushes and blackbirds, oh yes, yes, yes; they were so very useful to poets. Nightingales, of course; they had been the means of revealing to us the amazing virtuosity of the wireless. Peacocks, indeed yes; their feathers were invaluable, and the air of prestige they gave to a country house was not to be underrated. Hens, ducks, geese, turkeys, with their gastronomic corollaries: omelettes, green peas, sage stuffing, truffles, Michaelmas and Christmas—certainly these admirable creatures, so long as they are always kept in the farmyard. Canaries, cockatoos, budgerigars—as many as you like; so amusing when they use words that father only uses when he is alone; so pretty in a drawing-room; such admirable exponents of the virtues of a cage; such a constant and piquant source of irritation to the cat. Yes, yes, by all means—almost feverishly we hasten to assure the feathered world—all these species, by the million if you wish it. We understand these things; we understand they were called into the world to divert us in their several capacities.

But birds that never look the same two days running; birds that grow in the night; that drive other birds away from our midst; that have no respect for our national statues; that offend our King; that hold up our Government when it has serious things like war to discuss; that rob us of our water when we are short enough already; that refuse to eat the delicious seed we scatter for them; that emit a most unpleasant odour; that scream in harsh voices; that invade our private lives—these we will *not* endure.

Such was the common voice. No single voice raised above the crowd was ever heard to ask the question, "Are these birds natural? Can a materialist view ever explain their presence amongst us?" The birds were an abomination; this was agreed. But the drought—the unprecedented hardness of the hot cavern of the sky—this was not an abomination. On no account could this be termed an abomination. For it was an act of God, and acts of God, though embarrassing, were to be respected. And the war in Africa—this was not an abomination. No, this was a state in human affairs which could all be easily explained by a study of economics. It was certainly annoying; but it was perfectly natural. Supernatural and natural calamities—these were inevitable and explainable. But the birds; they were simply an abomination.

It was not to be expected that religion should fail to apply its dusty theology to these natural and supernatural calamities. The Archbishops of Canterbury and York met and discussed the attitude of the Church. They were tired, possibly, of having had little contact with human affairs since the jubilee thanksgiving in honour of our late King a year or so ago. Time was ripe for the Church to show its gloved hand; to lead its own particular short-cut to the throne of God; to call the attention of its children to their sins. Hence, a special form of religious intercession was ordered and printed, and a day set apart when from every church in the country prayers for rain and peace would rail at Heaven's gate. At the same time a great massed company of choirs and dignitaries would gather in St. Paul's Cathedral and do their utmost to gain the confidence of the omnipotent ear.

But the birds were left out of the programme. It was not considered within the dignity of State religion to mention these trifling annoyances.

"O Lord, send rain upon the earth." Yes. Most seemly.

"Grant us thy peace, O Lord." Eminently suitable.

"O Lord, deliver us from the birds." No. Most certainly, no.

*

On my return I heard various stories about the activities of the pests. I recollect that an elaborate military ritual known as changing-of-the-guard had one day been completely disorganized. This quaint custom took place in Whitehall, and was always witnessed by a group of interested spectators from the country. Soldiers, magnificently dressed, performed on horseback a sarabande in a courtyard while others took their places. What were they guarding? I'm afraid I don't know. Probably their own dignity. It was not preserved that particular day, however. A stream of filthy birds, who had apparently just flown from a mound of horse manure, charged down upon the soldiers, threw most of the men off their horses, and sent one horse scampering wildly down Whitehall. Great consternation was caused to hundreds of people when the horse finally charged straight into the window of a teashop near Westminster.

The birds now seldom appeared over the City in great massed swarms such as had first been their habit. The scene in Trafalgar Square was never repeated. It was now their pleasure to fly about in smaller groups of, perhaps, five or six hundred. They no longer disappeared into the sky; they were always about us—chattering, croaking, screaming. By night they roosted in and about famous monuments; they did not seem to care so much for trees. They took evident delight in disfiguring our most important buildings with their offal. Hundreds were always to be seen in the scaffolding of the Houses at Westminster, where some sort of renovation work was continually in progress. I remember also how they delayed the augmentation of the Bank of England. The Old Lady was undergoing considerable extension. Amidst the skeleton of the new construction, retreating behind massive cranes, concrete slabs, and iron girders, the birds found a thousand comfortable nooks. They never attacked the workmen; they merely made it difficult for them to continue their work.

A marked feature of the birds, one that I have already mentioned and which was now noticed with some concern, was their remarkable power of growth. They were no longer the pretty little birds we had first seen, though some, curiously enough, remained small. The great majority were larger than crows, with long beaks and sharp, mischievous eyes. Their smell was most obnoxious. I can best describe it by saying that it was the sort of smell which hangs around old damp plaster walls and cupboards that have not been opened for many years; but it was a hundred times more sickening. The noise they made if anyone attempted to obstruct them was atrociously harsh and strident. Their legs grew longer, their claws more crooked and firm. Their flight was very ungainly, wings flapping as they rose, with a dull clicking noise not unlike a nightjar.

In those days the colloquial phrase, "So-and-so has got the bird," was commonly employed when speaking of a person who had been rebuked by his employer or dismissed from his position. Now this phrase could no longer be thus used. For it became true. And it was a truth that nobody dared to admit. Of all the devilish wickedness wrought by the birds, there was none so disturbing as their growing habit of detaching themselves from the swarm and solitarily pursuing, from place to place, some particular person. As time went on, more and more were singled out for this unwelcome attention, often so subtly, that they were at first unaware of it. It was always the same bird; with some a large creature; with others, a small. And so acutely sensitive were people to this ordeal that hardly a soul would refer to it. You could therefore no longer say that So-and-so had "got the bird." I cannot tell you why people were so sensitive. But I can relate my own experience and tell you of the ordeal which I, in common with everybody else, had to suffer. I have already given you a hint in this direction in my account of the two detached birds who one evening disturbed my mother and myself at Stroud Green.

When I came home I saw at once that my mother and Annie were concealing some secret from me. It was not only that my mother was worried about the general condition of the world; there was something more personal in her mind. Thinking I could raise her out of her dejection, I gave her a long account of my holiday. She was hardly interested. I told her that I had been driving a car and suggested that we should buy one. But she made little response.

Later in the evening I spoke to Annie and asked her why my mother was so depressed.

"Why, you ought to know," said Annie, "it's the birds."

"Birds——" I began stupidly, thinking she meant the great mass of birds that flew about the City.

"Birds," she repeated sharply, "what tap and tap on the windows every night and give us no peace."

I began to understand. "Oh!" I said slowly. "Oh—I see——" Then I turned on Annie angrily. "Why didn't you write and tell me about this?"

But there was a wild, half-furtive look in her eyes, and she would not answer me. Suddenly I felt frightened.

I went to my mother. She was sitting in her chair attempting to read.

"Why didn't you tell me, Mother?" I held her hands and looked into her eyes.

She tried not to meet my eyes and caught her hands away.

"Did Annie tell you?"

"Yes——"

"I told her not to," she cried.

"But why? Why shouldn't I know, Mother?"

"Oh, I don't know. I don't know. Don't worry me."

She would not look at me. I saw there was terror in her eyes and the same half-furtive expression I had seen in Annie. I entreated her to be frank with me, but she broke away and rose to her feet.

"Every night——" she began, with her back to me, fumbling at the cupboard where she kept her wine, reaching for a glass.

I took her hands and led her back to her chair.

"Sit down and tell me the truth. Annie says that this bird taps on your window every night. Is that true?"

"Yes, every night." She spoke quickly. "And it's killing me—I tell you, it's killing me. I can't eat, rest, or go out anywhere. Annie will tell you, I can't eat."

"Is it a big bird?"

"No, no; it isn't big."

"Do you see it in the day?"

"If I go out, it's always there. I feel it always above me, and I can't get at it, can't even see it properly. I daren't go out any more. I have to stay in and keep the windows shut. Don't ever open them, son; don't ever open them. It's like—like a blot somewhere. Something I can't—get at."

She began to cry. "Oh, son, why ever should it happen to me? I haven't done any harm to any one."

She hadn't done any harm. . . . The words carried me back to an old woman screaming in a crowd; she also, she had assured every one, had done no harm.

"What do you think it's going to do to you?" I demanded angrily.

"It's going to kill me."

"You're just naturally upset by all this bother, the drought and everything. The best thing you can do, Mother, is to get away somewhere—into the country where it's quiet. You should have come to Wales with me."

"It isn't so easy as all that," she said.

"It *is* easy—if you make it so," I argued.

"You're young. You don't think. You've got your own affairs, you don't think of me any longer."

I denied it, but I knew it was half true.

"You're wrong," I said. "I do think of you, a great deal. Only—"

"——you think of your life, your future more? Oh, it's right you should, son. Don't take any notice of me. I'm only a silly old woman who might just as well be out of it. What's it all for, anyhow? You've got a hard enough future before you."

She seemed to divine the future and the feelings in my mind. Nevertheless I urged her to change her life.

"Mother, we can make a fresh start, somewhere away from here. You can, if you try."

"What about your work then? Is that nothing?"

"Work!" I laughed. "I have a feeling I shan't stand much more of that."

Then I launched into a diatribe against London and Leadenhall; told her how intolerable the City was in these days; how determined I was to get away from it. Very soon I forgot her troubles and lost myself in my own affairs. She said very little; the old apathy seemed to have settled over her. But nothing would induce her to consider any scheme whereby we might alter the routine of our lives.

Suddenly, in an angry, selfish mood I left her, and went out.

The sun had nearly set, and the sky, in which no shape of cloud had risen for so many weeks, oppressed me. I felt that I never wanted to see the sun again.

I found myself by the gates of the Alexandra Palace, perceiving, without reading, its notices of motor-cycle races, horse-races, exhibitions, and band-concerts. I went up the path by the side of a little rail-track where the tram-car ran, and so to the top, to a terrace of gravel spread out before the sprawling corpse of the gross building. From here there was a view of northern London similar to that from the ridge at Stroud Green.

Immediately below I saw the racing trades and the stand from which onlookers watched the races. To the left was a long wooden fence which surrounded the public bath where I had so often swum. The place was closed now, for shortage of water prevented its use. I looked at it mournfully; something told me I had swum there for the last time. My eyes wandered to the reservoirs, five or six flat basins. Only one contained any water, and that was but half full; the others were hollow cavities of sand. Running near them were the railway lines, stacked with trucks and disused carriages. Towering above this darkening scene were three or four enormous chimneys; from one of them, a straight line of black smoke pierced into the sky. Clustered around on every side was a thick network of streets, dense with little houses, red, brown, and yellow. There were a few puny trees, and somewhere, I am sure, the inevitable gasometer. Set in the middle, small and grey, like a stone lying in a confectioner's shop, was the detached old church tower which I have before described to you. It was singularly conspicuous.

I surveyed all this. Then I turned to look at the frowning shade of the Alexandra Palace. The whole building seemed to have been thrown out of proportion, because of the fact that one of its four main towers had been lopped off in order to enable scientific engineers to make experiments in a new invention called television: an invention which would enable people to witness current events from a great distance. It was similar to wireless, but it applied to the visual sense, as the word implies.

I looked at the building and I began to feel something like regard for it. It was so insignificant, so clumsy, so pathetic. After all, I felt, it means no harm. Inside was the monster organ, squatting silently above two files of peeling coloured statues of the kings of England. From the decapitated slate tower came sounds of hammering: thud, thud, thud on the heavy, windless air. Some one was working there, late as it was; working in order that people might have their jaded tastes stimulated with a new wonder—crying, before the freshness wore off, "Isn't this television wonderful!"

I turned again to survey the scene before me. Little twinkling lights by railway and street began to trace the shape of the suburb like pins stuck round a design and the design then blotted out. I sat on the balustrade by a stone urn, with dead geraniums rising thinly out of earth dry as bone. The distant sounds of the streets below were crystallized and unreal. I remembered another view from a mountain-top. And then I said, "Oh yes, you may have a vision on a mountain; you may grow philosophic wings, but when all is said and done, *this* is your home, these are your streets. Here, within the very shadow of this meandering building, you were born, and on these parched slopes you played with your nurse as a little boy. Something, always, you must leave here, forswear and forsake it as you will."

I was moved. This world—so different from what I had just left—had nourished and bred me. All my young dreams had risen from those streets; I knew every turning in the tangle of houses beneath me.

Then, almost feebly, another voice cried, "It is stupid, meaningless, stifling. Here is no freedom, no spirit, no peace." I told myself it was ephemeral, whereas the scene from Cader was eternal. I reminded myself of the conclusions I had reached on the mountain; of the great dreams I had made of my future, away from the City, with a lover. Yet within a day of my returning to London a deadly apathy seemed to have made all movement impossible. I forced my thoughts upon Olga. To-morrow, I decided, I would go to the café on the chance of seeing her again. I would make myself talk to her, then I would know whether she was really the person for whom I sought. I deliberately made up my mind. "You must go to the café to-morrow," I said.

I looked at the scene again, and I saw that it was dead. Nothing moved; there were no rivers, no fields, few trees. I was looking upon the work of man, and my thoughts stopped still at the word death.

"Olga, Olga," I murmured, as though I could send my voice away to summon her to fuse new life into me.

Thud, thud—answered the hollow neck of the headless tower. Thud, thud——

As I turned to go, in the darkening air above me I was vaguely aware of a small shape, fluttering sharply from angle to angle, like a bat. But it was larger than a bat. I remember quite clearly saying to myself with a cynical little laugh, *"You're nothing, you're nothing; you're nothing but a nothing."* The words stay in my mind. They were associated with a little cinema fantasy: a story of a mouse who wanted to fly. But when his wish was granted and wings sprouted from his shoulders, he became a bat. Then a company of large and hideous bats bawled these derisive words in his frightened face: *"You're not a thing at all."*

A strange hopelessness overcame me. On the mountain I had been a bird; here I was a bat, foul and blind.

And while I thought all this, above me fluttered the hovering creature like, as my mother had said, a dark blot in the air. I was hardly aware of it. Though deep down I must have known it, I would not admit the fact that my turn had come; that there was no longer any escape.

I came to the Palace gates. It was dark now, the lights in the semicircle of shops were lit, and loud voices and drunken laughter sounded from the tavern across the road. A tram waited, slung its trolley-arm over in the opposite direction, and jangled away towards Tottenham. Four roads converged here to an open space where, in the middle, a small patch of railed grass forlornly spoke of a time when this had been a quiet village. One of the roads on my right was a very steep hill lined by heavy old-fashioned houses. It was a dangerous hill for traffic. But the driver of the car which suddenly came flying wildly down the hill, swaying uncertainly from side to side, did not seem to know that. It passed me in a flash, nearly mounting the pavement in a great swerve and a hollow rattle of ill-driven gears and brakes. Something clung to the black hood, but I could not catch sight of it clearly before the car vanished in the same direction as that taken by the tram.

Somebody shouted, the usual policeman appeared.

"He had no lights," cried a fellow selling matches outside the tavern. "No lights I say, no lights."

I ran home. I wanted to be indoors behind a closed window.

*

From that night I was oppressed and haunted by the form of a bird which seemed to have the power at any moment to materialize in the air around me. I never saw it as a clear solid figure like the other birds who flew about the City; to me it was always a phantom, more felt than seen. It was something that I possessed and could not shake off; in my very efforts to rid myself of it I was aware that it wanted to become a part of me. I thought again and again of the small bird crouching on the poet's shoulders; of the old woman who had been carried away from the telephone-box; and of hundreds who had met their deaths through attempting to destroy the birds. Remembering these cases, I did not try to beat it away. But I could not, I dared not face it. I was filled with terror at the thought of ever meeting it face to face. I tried desperately to disregard it. The heavy sense of dread and anguish with which its presence filled me, was appalling. I could not sleep in a room with open windows, for I had a terror of waking to find it flying round the room in the darkness, or worse, sitting on my chest, looking at me with inhuman penetrating eyes.

Every day now I saw horrible and savage tragedies. Slowly,

man by man, the world was going mad. "A wave of suicides," commented the papers. And it was the truest thing they ever wrote, though they did not realize the full meaning of it.

I saw a fat old man pressed face downwards over a drain in a gutter near Stroud Green Station; he was writhing and screaming in anguish, his fingers clawed into the hard pavement as though he were trying to burrow into the ground, his knuckles torn and bleeding. I hurried on, away from the sickened crowd that gathered.

I saw a priest in his cassock running down a moving staircase with such violent agitation that he crashed face downwards on to the ground at the bottom. A bird swooped on to him; a bird that seemed to be nothing but scraggy wings, covering him in a network of black gauze. The priest's cries were lost; he shuddered and died.

Face downwards . . . face downwards. Always I have a picture of people lying on the ground with their faces buried away from the terror above them. Yes, the world was going mad. Yet—how strange it seems—the Press still bore us news of the fighting in Africa. People used to talk about the war almost eagerly, using it as a blanket to cover up the inmost dread of their minds. And in spite of so much horror, there was much to laugh at. How curious, for example, was the placid, epicene bird—not unlike a drab dove—who attached himself gently to the chasuble of a Catholic priest saying Mass in a church I visited one Sunday. The creature blended so perfectly with the cream silk of the vestment that nobody realized his presence, until at the words *"et in Spiritum Sanctum"*—which occurred in a table of Christian belief—the soft little thing cooed succulently and flew round and round above the vessels on the altar, to the consternation of priest, people, and acolytes.

They were very subtle creatures. Once they assembled and waited for hours on the steps of a famous club in the west end of London. Inside, whiskered old lords, military celebrities, bishops, judges, and other important persons, fumed petulantly all day, unable to leave the place. Having kept them there well into the night, the birds flew away at three o'clock in the morning without having done any damage whatever.

Often they were playful. They seized fruit and eggs from shops and dropped them over the streets. I shall never forget the rain of hen's eggs and oranges that pelted down over the City one afternoon. Silk hats, fashionable toques, bald pates, shampooed hair—hardly a hat or a head escaped this bombardment.

One of their most effective attacks was launched upon a number of shops held in some disrepute. They entirely overpowered the assistants behind the counters and carried away a great load of contraceptives and surgical instruments. Holding these articles between their beaks, they made an organized invasion upon a place called Ritz, where persons of importance were eating dinner. The birds did nothing more than drop their unwelcome missives upon the tables of the diners. Having executed this errand they departed quietly, without attacking any one. There was, of course, a panic in the room. But the panic was hardly commensurate with the shocking embarrassment of an old roué of the highest aristocracy who was left gazing with horror upon a number of tablets supposed to rejuvenate sexual power, which lay scattered blatantly over the spotless tablecloth.

The pests showed a remarkable capacity for embarrassing people of all types and classes. I saw a small bird sit for several minutes on the legs of a supposed paralytic who wheeled himself about in a chair and sold matches by a place called Change Alley in the City. The old cripple had sat there for years. I remember his unvaried call, always delivered in a thin, piping voice: "Kind friends, buy a box o' lights f'r the po—or maimed." Nobody had ever doubted the impotency of his hunched legs, swathed in rugs, until this impudent bird, after ten minutes' playful jabbing with his beak, shot the paralytic out of his chair, upset his matches over the pavement, and sent him scuttling as fast as his legs could carry him, along Cornhill. That was the last we saw of him.

On the evening of the day after I had first become aware of my familiar attendant, upon the terrace of the Alexandra Palace, I walked up Cheapside, hemmed in by crowds of people hurrying on to buses and making for underground railways. About two or three hundred birds flew in a direct line for the ball and cross that capped the dome of the Cathedral. They did not attract very much attention. I stopped to read the announcement on a board in the churchyard of the service of intercession which was to take place in a few days. The Archbishop of Canterbury himself was to be present; the Lord Mayor and the Corporation of London were to help in sending their weighty words up to the heavenly throne; a chosen selection of choirs was to sing hymns and psalms under the leadership of a renowned church musician. Evidently it was to be a national approach to God. All the best that we could produce was to be paraded in the hope that he could not fail to be touched by the sight of so much collective piety.

As I studied the notice, more and more birds flew, with a harsh sniggering sound, high up on to the dome. Then one detached himself and flew low over the narrow street by the side of the Cathedral. A big bird; bright green with glittering tail-feathers, very small eyes, and a curved, predacious beak. Several people cried and shouted as he came lower and flew amongst them. Somebody struck at him. He disregarded this assault, and as though he had found his destination, flew straight into the open doorway of a large shop where women's hats and other articles of apparel were sold. I waited, curious, slightly amused; for the moment lifted out of my own black thoughts. It was not long before a number of women emerged from the shop. They came running out like frightened hens, some with their hats torn off and hair dishevelled, gabbling and gesticulating wildly. Last of all to come out was a woman who had apparently been buying coloured ribbon, since she was entirely swathed in twisted strands of the material. She looked strangely like a richly embalmed corpse who had come to life. Yards of the ribbon trailed behind her, dragging with it a various assortment of pins, brooches, hooks, buttons, and decorative clasps. She was a large woman with a soaring bosom, a heavily powdered face, and masses of orange-coloured hair which flowed about her head and was almost indistinguishable from the ribbon.

With a scream of rage she leapt to the door of a fat slug-like car which stood by the pavement, and cried to the chauffeur to drive off. The man, however, unused to this sort of behaviour from his mistress, and as yet unaware of the bird who pursued her, failed to start his engine in time.

The group of gabbling women in the doorway parted aside with piercing shrieks. I heard a swish of horny wings and a high scream of devilish merriment. The bird, large as a raven with ribbons streaming away from its hooked talons, flapped violently through the window of the car and pounced with outspread wings upon the woman who had just entered.

Not until then did the panic-stricken driver start the car, in his agitation pressing the accelerator much too forcibly. The machine lurched forward. Inside, all I could see were twisted strands of coloured ribbon, a fluttering canopy of long green wings, a vast swaying form. Then the car hurtled towards Cheapside at a furious pace, scattering people right and left.

Above, the birds from the dome flew round and round; shrieking, whistling, croaking. Revolted by what I had just seen, heavy with apprehension, I moved away from the Cathedral, walked down Ludgate Hill and thus towards the west of London, hardly daring to raise my head to the sky.

Last night I struggled inside this young man I have tried to present to you. This young man who, so many years ago, saw the end of his civilization. I suffered the same misery as he did, my spirit departing from me as I contemplated a day so black with despair that the memory of it almost caused me to abandon his story.

To-day, I am with him still. He has little connection with the old man who sits here speaking these words; yet, he is always in me. And I feel again the burden of his misery. I am with him as he wanders on like a lonely ghost, trying to find his home. I am with him. I cannot help him, cannot guide him. But perhaps his presence can guide me, has something to tell me, the old man who now speaks this history to you.

He is in a café, somewhere in the heart of London, very near the statue of young Eros. As the evening advances he knows that he must go into the other café, there to wait upon the slender chance of seeing a woman with black hair and deep eyes whose name is Olga. The thought of this possible meeting fills him with trepidation. He is nervous to the point of stupidity.

For the last ten minutes he has been studying a menu.

Although he is hungry he is unable to decide what he shall eat. But the question of what he shall drink is even more insoluble. Because drink is expensive, and by what a man drinks shall a waiter judge him.

The café is below the streets. A large room with small tables placed in a long line down the centre. At one side is a bar over which alcoholic drinks may be obtained. The opposite side a similar counter displays a variety of cooked and uncooked foods: hams, joints of beef, pies, dishes of fruit and much else. An individual called "chef" can be seen bobbing about in the back near the stoves. This is one of the cooks. He wears a tall white hat and a white costume, and often grows to resemble the food he cooks, becoming, as years go on, a sort of apotheosis of roast pork. There is a little platform in a corner where four men produce with an air of indifference a dreadful sound called music. One man snaps his hands over a piano; another plucks the strings of a guitar; another would be seeming to tear his talonous fingernails on a banjo; and a fourth—most curious of all—shakes peas in a drum. The four sounds combine to produce a most melancholy noise.

In order to hear themselves speak, the people eating and drinking have to shout above the din of this music. The room is full and so thick with the smoke of tobacco that a blue haze clings high up around the lights. Our young man is wedged at a table between two others, one of the long line that runs between the bar and the food counter.

As we noticed before, he seems anxious about his drink. Several times the waiter has come to take his order. Suddenly a decision is reached.

"Bring me," he says, with an air of nonchalance that only partially conceals an evident self-consciousness, "half a bottle of Liebfraumilch. Nothing to eat."

The waiter hurries and returns presently with a fine thin bottle of German wine which is examined carefully and ignorantly by our youth. Pouring some out, he drinks languidly, holding the glass high and studying the clear yellow liquid through the light. His attitude is that of a person who wishes to impress his immediate neighbours.

Now and again he lifts his head with a thoughtful expression and writes in a book. He is alone at the table. One would hardly remark him. He is dressed in the same quiet manner as all the other males, though there is a certain negligence about his shirt-cuffs, a slight air of arrogant individuality about the white hand-kerchief which splashes conspicuously from his breast pocket, which would cause the acute observer to study him more closely. He would then find, however, nothing more than a well-featured face, thick, rather curly hair, a slight, slim body, and well-shaped hands. The brow is frowning. He laughs and dashes down something in his notebook. He drinks more eagerly; runs his fingers through his hair.

Presently the young man pays his bill, and walks slowly to a leather upholstered seat. There is a precision in his movements which we would not have noticed an hour previously when he entered the café. He stops on his way to look at some one who interests him. Then he sits down on the seat, takes out his note-book, and appears to fall asleep.

A sudden crash of music-noise awakes him, if indeed he ever was asleep. He becomes interested in the man shaking peas in a drum. Waiters carrying trays pass in front of him, sometimes tripping over the legs that cross their path. But he does not change his attitude. As he writes again in his book, bites his pencil, and chuckles loudly, he is conspicuous.

He watches the man shaking peas in a drum. He is dressed in a blue silk blouse, with long full sleeves; baggy knickerbockers of the same material, with a red sash round the waist; red boots reaching to the knees.

A splendid costume. He shakes peas in a drum.

This fact would appear to excite our young man who, scrib-bling furiously, looks up with a twinkling smile in his eyes.

Suddenly his manner changes to one of gloom. Almost fur-tively he rises, puts on his hat, and dodging between tables with an unnatural skill, makes for the staircase out. He looks quickly up to the roof and down again. About his walk there is a light-ness, an unconsciousness, which is quite foreign to him. He col-lides with somebody and does not even murmur his regrets. By the top of the stairs he stops, looking down. The noise of the peas—a shuffling, a shaking, a clattering—drives insistently in his ears.

He runs out to the brilliantly lit and crowded street, blinking stupidly as he faces the electric-blue lettering on a theatre opposite. A slight, swaying shape mounts from behind him and flaps uneasily in the air. He does not look at it although he knows it is there. It is so hot on the pavement he wonders whether he has come out of the café or not. He lurches a little, feeling sick.

"Oh, my God," he mutters, "I'll get outside that drum. Oh, my God!"

The uniformed attendant by his side coughs and draws attention to the fact that he is standing in the middle of the doorway, thus blocking the exit of two people behind him. He moves rapidly away and crosses the streets.

Follow him with me into the other café.

He is sitting at a marble table, drinking beer. His head falls forward into his hands, and he remains thus with eyes closed for some minutes. It is not yet ten o'clock and the room is only half full. A tall, thin man who enters the room presently notices him and sits opposite him at the same table. This man has an angular nose and jaw. His colourless eyes blink through a pair of thick spectacles; they are like the vacant eyes of a fish seen through muddy water. He is dressed quietly.

The young man raises his head and only half sees the thin man before him. He is looking for some one else, a girl with black hair, smooth, pale skin, and deep eyes; but she is not in the room. He orders more beer, and as he drinks splashes some on the table.

The thin man has been studying him closely for some time. Suddenly he speaks, leaning over the table and touching the younger man's arm with a secret and confidential gesture.

"Would you like to see some photographs?" he asks quietly. He smiles.

The young man frowns; his head shakes uncertainly. "Photographs? What should I want to see them for?"

But his mind whirls round; he catches an obscene leer from the thin man.

"I thought," says the man, "you would be interested in my pictures."

"Why?"

He looks the thin man straight in the face, and the sharp angles of that sly smile cut deep into him.

"Why should you select me—of all people in this room—to show your pictures to?"

He drinks again. More and more people come in, but he does not see amongst them the person he came to seek. She, the woman called Olga, has entered and taken a table some yards away from him. She is alone and he does not see her.

The thin man is speaking.

"I saw you, sitting here alone—lonely, like me. I'm up from the country, you know. Came up for a little spree and to see these birds everybody's talking about. And when I saw you there, I said to myself you were the very person who would enjoy my pictures. I said, there's a person who appreciates beauty, like me."

He brings out a small pocket wallet and lays it on the table.

"You can take them elsewhere," snarls the young man.

"I have a little cottage in the country," the voice dribbles over the table, "where it's quiet, quiet, you know. And then, I come up here sometimes to see a bit of life. You'd like my cottage, you would."

"Go away and leave me alone."

Several people look up, hearing his voice. The woman, Olga, looks again at him, wrinkles her brow and then, with chin leaning on palm, watches him thoughtfully.

The thin man has opened the wallet and drawn out an inch of postcard.

"You will really enjoy these," he insists.

Suddenly the thin man spills six or seven postcards flat on the table. The young man raises his hand to sweep them on to the floor.

Through a thick mist he sees pictures on the table. A rose-covered country cottage; a summer garden border; a cocker spaniel——

"My little place——" sounds the voice.

The young man is aware of a sharp, triumphant face burning into his.

"Now don't you think these lupins are nice? Raised them from seed, too! Not many——"

Some people in the doorway draw aside as the young man pushes wildly towards them. He stands there for a moment looking round the room. He catches sight of Olga looking at him with her deep, thoughtful eyes. She smiles slightly. He gives a curious cry, and forces his way through a group of people out into the lounge.

Something is fluttering over his head. He hurls himself furiously through the revolving door and stands, swaying from side to side, on the pavement. His gorge rises in him; he is sick. The fluttering shape brushes his cheek as he stands with drooping head by the gutter.

A flashily dressed man calls out to him, "Look out, sonny! You got something flying round you."

But he hardly hears. For now he is running across the road towards the steps of the underground railway, running frantically to escape from the bird that flutters and squeaks like a bat above him. He struggles down the moving staircase, pushing people aside in his panic.

A train is waiting and he jumps in, a moment before the doors crash to. Like a person walking in a dream he leaves the train at Finsbury Park, mounts an omnibus, and reaches the street where he lives. He walks quickly down the long hill, opens the front door, and staggers in, shaking, drenched with sweat.

His mother comes out from the front room and sees him standing stupidly in the passage, gasping and trembling.

"Why, son," she cries, "you're ill——"

"No, no—it's all right, Mother. You leave me alone. I'm all right."

But she follows him to his room, uneasy in her heart. She finds him lying face downwards on his bed, sobbing like a child, making spasmodic little sounds of drunken grief.

"Oh, son, what have you been doing?"

"I'm drunk. I'm drunk. Leave alone, Mother—please— leave me alone——"

"But, son, don't worry so. I understand——"

"No, you don't, Mother. There was a girl—I went to see—a man with some pictures——"

"Yes, son, of course. Do you think your mother doesn't know all that? Keep quiet, son; keep quiet."

She holds him while he cries. Upstairs, Annie opens a door and listens carefully to their voices.

"I understand, son," Lillian keeps saying. "I understand. You'll be better in the morning. Shall I get you something to eat?"

But he begs to be left, and presently she leaves him.

The young man lies in his bed twitching convulsively. The windows of his room are closed. All night long there is a tapping on the pane, a metallic sound of bone upon glass. Under the bed-clothes he hears it, louder and louder, until the sound seems like a knuckle rapping on the hollow curve of his skull.

*

I sat at the breakfast-table waiting for my mother. She came in presently in a faded pink dressing-gown.

"I can't eat," she said. "I can't eat anything."

I stared at the food on my plate. "I'm sorry, Mother," I muttered. "I'm sorry about last night."

"Yes, son, I understand," she said. "Don't think anything more about it. Eat your breakfast, there's a good boy. I don't expect you feel like it any more than I do."

"No, I don't," I said. And for a second I glanced up and smiled at her.

For the next five minutes we tried to coax one another to eat. "Mother, you're ill," I said.

"No, I'm all right. It's this dreadful heat; that's all it is."

"Yes," I echoed. "It is hot——" Speech failed me. I did not even like to look at her. I knew she had not slept all night.

"You'll come home early to-night, won't you," she said.

"Yes, early." And again I muttered that I was sorry. I felt ashamed. Not that I had done anything particularly shameful in coming home drunk. What really drove at my conscience was the fact that I had seen Olga and had been too drunk to talk to her. It was infinitely worse than not having tried to see her at all.

My mother did not ask me any questions, for she seemed to know that I did not want to talk. The kindest side of her nature was revealed in her capacity for remaining silent at such times as these, content to wait until I should speak to her voluntarily. She came to the door with me, kissed me, and again told me to come home early.

"I'll take you out for a walk," I said.

But she shook her head. "No, no. It's too hot for walking."

In the train at Stroud Green four men were playing cards on a newspaper stretched over their knees. "Nap," one of them called; "Misère," cried another. The cards, dirty and crinkled at the edges, slid along the paper as the train swayed. I sat in a corner trying to read a book, but I could not concentrate on it. The mechanical gestures of the four men playing cards seemed to emphasize the utter futility of existence. They played cards and the world was shaking around them. They themselves were as powerless to move independently as the cards they dealt to each other. And they did not know it. "Have you heard about old Smithers?" asked one. "No," replied the others. And they leant over while he whispered something to them.

The train drew into a station. I was seized with impatience. Pushing past the group I scattered their cards to the floor without apology, and got into another carriage.

Again I tried to read my book, and failed. I drew a pencil and a notebook from my pocket and began to write.

"I saw you at the café last night and I wanted to speak to you. I was drunk. I was——" My eye caught sight of something over the page that I had written the night before, some lines which seemed to have been written by another hand, the writing was so scrawly and uneven.

"*How you shake, you man with peas. How little you know why you shake, you man with peas. Shaking, shaking. Like bears who once danced to man's encouragement, you, man with peas, are driven; and men drive you as they did the bear. When man, tired of driving bears, has driven man, who then will be left to drive? Who, but himself? He will shake like a pea in a drum.*"

I looked up to the rack opposite; something had stirred there. I saw it, crouched low, a shapeless grey figure like a bundle of dirty old rags with two gleaming buttons set in the middle. I wanted to leave the carriage but I could not. The other people seemed unaware of the spectre in the rack. Was I dreaming? I put my hand to my brow; it was sticky with sweat and my head drummed with a sullen pain. Was I dreaming? Was that thing in the rack real?

I could not look up there again. When the train came into Broad Street I jumped out quickly, forgetting my book, and ran along the platform without looking back.

In the office I signed my name in the attendance book and sat down to sort out the casualties from Lloyd's List. I was early, not many people had arrived. The list was very long and the more I studied it, the more the words danced crazily before my eyes, so that I had to come back over and over again to re-read a paragraph. Eventually I made a list of casualties serious enough to notice, and went upstairs to another department where records of all our interests were kept. When I came down more people were in the room, and I saw by the shadow through the frosted glass of the private room that the Underwriter had arrived. His bell rang and I went in. His black hat was standing on the table, and as I looked at it, suddenly I laughed madly.

He looked up and began to speak. "What do you mean——" He was incoherent with rage. Then he saw me looking at his hat; his lips drew to a thin purple line in his face.

"Are you mad?" he said. He rang his bell again to summon some one else. Then I stopped laughing.

"I'm sorry, sir," I said. "I'm very sorry." I paused, aware that I had gone too far. What could I say? For every time I looked at his hat I was filled with this mad desire to laugh. It was a new hat, and one side of it was streaked by a long, dirty white dribble.

"I have given you several warnings," he said. "This is the last time I speak to you."

I looked at him and for a moment our eyes met. Then I left the room quickly, banging the door behind me.

The morning passed and I went to lunch at a cheap café called ABC. Again I pulled out my pencil and notebook and started to write to Olga. Then I stopped. What was the use of writing to a person whose full name and address I did not even know? How could I find out where she lived?

Stored somewhere in the office was a file of all the recent copies of a newspaper called *Times*. To these I referred, searching back to the issue that gave an account of the inquest on Paul

Weaver some weeks ago. I found it, and my heart thumped with nervous excitement as I came to the words I wanted. "A witness who gave evidence. Miss Olga Mironovna, of Heath Street, Hampstead." I rested my elbows on the pile of newspapers. Olga Mironovna, Olga——

The name was like wind sighing over quiet water. I thought of the lake in the mountains. Olga Mironovna. I could write to her now; it was so much easier. Why had I not thought of this before?

I was called back to my desk where three or four brokers waited. For the rest of the afternoon I was kept busy, and there was no time to think of anything but risks and perils of sea.

A young broker with a chubby red face leaned over the desk, dangling cover notes before me. "Got your gas-mask?" he asked.

"What do you mean?"

"Why, haven't you heard? We're all to be given gas-masks next week. Good opportunity to test their efficiency. Then they're going to rout these bloody birds with poison gas——"

I did not believe him. "Where did you make that up?"

"Why, it's in the papers," he exclaimed. "Don't you read the papers?"

High up in the ceiling I knew there was something swaying to and fro, as though it waited to drop lightly on my desk. I forced my hand to write and assured myself there was nothing there.

Then I gave him back his slips and looked up quickly. There was nothing. Had there ever been anything? I went on with my work, my hand shaking, sweat pricking through my forehead.

It was nearly five o'clock before there was any lull in work. Then I found paper and started again to write my note. "Dear Miss Mironovna." It sounded silly. "Dear Olga Mironovna." But that sounded too familiar. I wrote a dozen notes and tore them up dissatisfied. Finally, I managed to write a brief note in which I said that I wanted to meet her, and that I could not easily explain why in a letter; would she consent to meet me for a few minutes?

I put the note in an envelope, sealed and posted it. On the way home I thought of nothing else. I imagined her receiving it, her look of surprise, perhaps vexation, as she threw it away; or an expression of curiosity and amusement as she took up her pen to reply. Most likely, I told myself gloomily, she will never answer.

And deadly apathy seized on this; it will be a good thing if she doesn't answer. You will have done all you can, then you can go no further.

In the house we had one of those wireless machines which we generally used in the evenings to listen to the latest news. That evening I was particularly interested to hear whether the broker's story of the proposed gas attack was true or not. So after supper we switched on the machine and sat listening.

We sat in the front room. It was very hot and almost dusk. In spite of this, only one window was open a little at the top. I sat near it, looking out and listening to the brisk, calculated voice of the announcer as it came through the loud-speaker. My mother sat away from the window near an old deal bureau upon which were two empty silver candlesticks. I noticed them and reflected, as I had hundreds of times, that I must buy some long candles to go in the sticks.

"Mother," I said, "I must buy some long candles for those sticks." But she made no reply, probably because she was tired of hearing me say it.

Then I thought, what is the use of buying candles now? The world may last no longer than their light would last. And yet, in a curious way it seemed to me that so slight a thing as two new candles, standing up there in the dusty gloom of that corner, might impart a new spirit of confidence into this room. Yes, I determined, I must buy the candles and put them there; it will be a sort of declaration of independence, a challenge to fate: "Do what you will; I will buy candles." The announcer's voice droned on dutifully. Then he came to the information I wanted to hear. He announcer repeated what the broker had told me that afternoon. In a few days, gas-masks were to be distributed to the people; they would also be instructed to stay in their homes with doors and windows barred tight. Sirens would sound when the attack began. At noon fleets of aeroplanes were to scour over the City, emitting jets of poisonous gas whenever they came upon companies of birds. When the attack was finished and the atmosphere pure again, sirens would sound an "all-clear" signal. "It is to be hoped," said the announcer, "that many volunteers will come forward to assist in the distribution of gas-masks and——"

—The voice ceased suddenly on a sharp, choking sound. Above it we heard a snapping as of some bony substance against the microphone; a rustling as of half-burnt paper. Then the connection was broken, we heard no more.

My mother had risen at these unexpected sounds and was standing in the middle of the room, wringing her hands together. We did not speak for a moment.

"What—has happened?" she asked.

I did not answer, for my thoughts had turned again to the empty candlesticks. I felt strangely unmoved by the sudden cessation of the announcer's voice, though I knew well enough what it meant.

"Mother," I said, "come over here. There's a lovely moon rising."

She came over to me at the window and I put my arm round her shoulders. She was shaking with fear.

"Mother, Mother," I said, "oh, let us get away from here——"

She made as though to leave me and put on the light.

"No, don't turn on the light," I said. "Stay in the darkness here a moment. Listen to me. We must leave London; we must get away soon. I've been thinking—thinking of another country where there are flowers and it is cool. It will kill us if we stay here much longer. What have we to stay for?"

"I can't go away, I can't," she muttered.

"Oh, why, Mother? Why must you always say that?"

"I'm too old for changes now. You go, son, and leave me."

"Suppose I did, Mother?" I spoke with sudden harshness.

Then she cried, "No, no—I couldn't bear it. I've nothing to live for here, alone. I didn't mean it, son. You mustn't go. Promise me you'll never leave me—never, never——"

"I won't leave you," I said. "I only want to take you away somewhere, where we can both get back our faith in life. If we don't go away from here soon—I don't know, I believe something awful will happen to all of us. We're mad if we wait for it to happen."

"Wherever we go," she said, with that sudden prescience with which she was gifted—"wherever we go it might happen. Do you suppose we shall escape by running away?"

She would not change her decision. Should I then leave her, I thought, and go alone? There was Olga. I must at least wait and see if she answered my note.

My mother turned away from me and switched on the light. We drew the blinds. Night was come. Annie came in with cups of cocoa that she often made for us before we retired to bed. We sipped it slowly, prolonging it and stirring it unnecessarily. Because we knew that the sooner we finished the cocoa, the more difficult it would be to avoid going to bed.

The room was stifling; the whole aspect of it cheerless and barren. Every colour was a faded colour as though an eternal autumn had settled over the place. The empty candlesticks mocked me, emphasizing this faded air. I had finished my cocoa; it was after eleven. There was nothing to do but go to bed.

"Mother," I said, "you must make me buy some candles for that corner. Not coloured ones, plain white. Don't let me forget."

Two days passed. They were miserable, apprehensive days in which every incident passed slowly with the unreality of a hated dream that keeps recurring to a sick man. I had no sleep by night, no security by day. Every footstep I took seemed a dangerous one. I dreaded the night because I had to shut myself into an unventilated room and suffer hours of sleeplessness; I dreaded the day because I had to go outside where there was no shelter to protect me.

On the third day a letter in unfamiliar writing was dropped through the letter-box. I took it eagerly and read. It was a brief note and to this day I can remember every word of it.

"I will be at a café called Samovar, in St. Martin's Lane, to-morrow evening at 6.30, if you would like to come there."

There was no address, even no signature to it. I folded it in my pocket-book and took it out a hundred times during the day, trying to weigh the value of every word. 6.30 to-morrow evening. It seemed to me that I had to pass through a lifetime before then. Why not this evening, I complained, why not this evening?

*

I dreaded that meeting, even though I desired it so greatly. I did

not know what I had to say to her. I did not even know whether
upon closer acquaintance she would attract me at all. I thought it
extremely probable that she would find me dull. Summing up my
virtues I found them grossly overbalanced by my defects. I was a
clerk amongst a thousand others; an English youth, neither original nor particularly virile. She came from a country of which I had
but the vaguest understanding; a half-sinister place to my knowledge, where revolution lurked, the machine thrived, and megalo-
maniacs wrote exuberantly pessimistic books. She had been the
friend, perhaps the lover, of a great poet; she probably moved in a
circle of intellectual and artistic people. I moved in no circle, but
lay stuck firm in the middle of one so vast that I was a mere speck;
my few friends were very ordinary people like myself.

If my mind was commonplace, then what of my body?
I looked at my face in the mirror above my dressing-table. I
thought it meretricious, like a face you might meet in a magazine
illustration, entirely without meaning. My body seemed flimsy
and frail, my arms thin as sticks, my legs white and scraggy. As
for muscles, they did not seem to exist.

My glance fell to the books on the table, the handful of erotic
classics with which I had tried to gratify my sensual thoughts.
There was no erudition here, no culture. What could I talk about
with authority? What particular subject had my intellect ever
handled? Had I any intellect?

She would despise me, I said, when she found that I had
a magazine face and no mind. With this thought, I stood outside the half-curtained window of the small café where she had
arranged to meet me. Inside, I could see her sitting in a basket-
chair, her back to me, calmly reading an evening paper. How
could she sit there, unperturbed, like that? I asked myself, when
I was in such turmoil only a few yards away from her. Didn't she
realize I was there? Didn't she know how I felt, or could nothing
move her to turn round and acknowledge me? "Come," I said,
"life is wretched enough; this can't make it worse and it may
make it better."

So I drove my unwilling legs towards the door, my stomach
like a hollow cavity, my heart pounding.

Clumsily I sat down beside her, nearly knocking over the

small table in my agitation. She perceived at once that I was in a nervous state, for she smiled—that slow smile of her closed lips which made her eyes quiver with amusement. You remember? How often, when others were laughing, she would smile quietly like that, half to herself, as though she alone had found the real secret of humour and would impart it to nobody.

What were my first words? Perhaps, "Good evening, it was good of you to come." I know, whatever I said, she took no notice, but only looked at me steadily for several seconds.

(Do you remember her eyes? How, with all their blackness, they were so fresh and clear? When I looked at her that first evening I knew that she saw all my thoughts from the half-agitated, half-ashamed expression of my face. In that long glance she made me aware of my own individuality. She would not presume to enter the solitary world which was mine. It seemed to me that for the first time I had met a person who saw exactly what I was and accepted me without question.

She spoke. "I wondered. I thought it would be you, but I was not quite sure. That is why I didn't sign my name. I hoped it would be you." When she spoke, my nervousness seemed to go, I felt easy and confident with her.

"Then you're glad it's me?" I said quietly.

"Glad?" she said. "Yes—perhaps I am. You interested me on the two occasions I saw you."

"The last time you saw me, I'm afraid——" I began.

She smiled and interrupted me. "Were you going to say you are afraid you were drunk?"

I nodded. "I meant to speak to you," I said. "I went there for that. And then—I couldn't. It's difficult to go over and speak to a stranger there isn't it?"

She half laughed. "Why, yes, I'm sure it is, when you are as tipsy as you were."

"But even if one was sober," I argued, "it wouldn't be easy in a place like that."

She disagreed. "I think it would be easier than in many places. You see, there are all those people laughing and talking and drinking. Nobody takes any notice. It would be easy to talk to anybody you liked with so much noise going on around."

"Do you often go there?"

"I went there a lot with Paul Weaver," she said. "He was an old friend."

For the moment I was embarrassed and murmured something unintelligibly sympathetic.

"How did you find out my address?" she asked. I told her, and we were silent for a moment, both thinking of that first evening in the café. I wanted to ask her whether she had been the poet's lover and many other things which could not yet be asked.

We ordered something to eat, and while we ate she told me a little about her life and I about mine. She had come over from Russia at the time of a great revolution, when she had been a little girl. Of the dreadful hardships she had had to endure, she spoke calmly, as though they had not touched her. She had come over with an old aunt who had later died. Her parents and her brothers were all killed in the revolution, and when her aunt died she had no money. She had taken many jobs.

"For three or four months," she said, "I wore coloured trousers and a silly sailor hat."

I did not understand.

"Do you know the Plaza cinema?"

I nodded.

"I was one of the attendants there. It was a strange life; so closed in, so soft and scented. I didn't dislike it in a way, though when I came out every night it was good to walk on a hard pavement after so much walking on carpets as thick as lamb's-wool."

"You couldn't endure it for long? You left there?"

"No, I had to leave. You see, I was Russian, and your English girls—they are very nice and they were kind. Men used to take them out and give them a nice time. They wanted to take me out, and sometimes I let them. But they also said, she is Russian, she will understand what a man takes a girl out for—do you see? They thought I was so much easier. English people are very nice, but they always think that Russian people live like animals. Then the other girls got jealous. You see? They used to talk about the Russian whore. So I went. I had to."

An absurd desire to exclude myself from this unpleasant category of English people, prompted me to say, "They're not all like that. There are better people than you would meet in a cinema."

"Ah yes, of course," she said, looking at me. "You mean that you are not like that?"

I blushed very red. "Did you think I was?"

"No, I didn't think so. But I should so like to know why you wanted to see me."

I remember thinking it unreasonable of her to ask this. I had not yet attuned myself to her frankness.

"I can't—tell you that easily," I stammered. "It's—it seemed fate that I should meet you. I couldn't stop thinking of you ever since the first evening I saw you. You were just different from anybody else I'd ever seen——"

A waitress fussed round the table, and a number of people had gathered by now in the small room. It was unbearably hot, and I felt it was impossible to speak here.

"Let's go," I said, "somewhere where it's quieter and we can talk more easily."

She was agreeable to this, and we took a train up to Hampstead, where she lived. Walking up a street towards an open heath, she pointed to a little dressmaker's shop.

"That is where I work now," she said, "making dresses for ladies who like to be thought rich and artistic. Do you know the sort of ladies I mean? They come in with haughty expressions and ask for a material to match this or that. They must always have everything to match. They think they are aristocratic, but they are not. No, not quite."

I laughed. She had summed up a certain type of English female very well, and for a time we discussed them.

"They are very solid," she said, "and they like to be thought unsolid. You know them best when you see their husbands, nice men always, who play golf."

"You've studied us very well," I said.

"Ah, when you are a foreigner in another country you see people much clearer. I dare say were you in Russia, you would see how stupid we are."

"How do you sum me up?" I asked.

But she shook her head and laughed. "No, I will not tell you."

I begged her to speak what was in her mind.

Then she said, "I believe you are very moral and like examining your conscience."

This was a shock to me; I had never thought myself moral. "I'm not," I declared. "Not a bit moral."

"But you like examining your conscience?" she insisted.

"Well, yes," I admitted. "I suppose I do."

"Then you are moral," she said, with a smile. "Since before you ever do anything you want to do, you have to ask yourself whether it is right to do it."

I felt mortified. "What makes you say that?" I asked.

"Well, this evening, you meet me and you are so frightened, you nearly knock over a table. You wonder whether I will think you a coarse man; you think it is not quite right to meet a girl like that. Why is it not quite right if you wish to? I do not mind how I meet people if I like them."

I explained to her that I was bound by a network of conventions which she would never understand, and that it was hard to break them. But even here she disagreed with me.

"No, no. I know your conventions very well. My country was so conventional that only a revolution could break it. Now they are even more conventional. No, no. Some are born conventional; some are not. And you——"

"I wasn't born conventional," I declared. "I swear I wasn't."

"No, I think you were not," she said. "But you have a passion for doing the correct thing according to your standards. I expect you have a tidy mind and a large, untidy heart, haven't you?"

We were standing by a pond on a plateau above the undulating heath, with trees and bushes in the hollow beyond us. Opposite the pond was a large tavern full of people, with many cars outside. A number of people sat on iron seats near the pond; children were sailing toy boats on the water, and dogs were barking. Yet in spite of these sounds, it seemed very quiet and still. I felt that Olga and I moved in a world of our own. In the half-light she seemed like a carved figure standing over the pond and conjuring pictures from the oily water. I felt like a child. She suddenly turned and smiled, opening her mouth. Then I knew that I loved her and that she loved me. "Olga——" I said. But she pointed to the pond and spoke.

"What a lot of things one sees in water," she said. "It is like being in a hot room and looking out of a cloudy window-pane to a country you can never reach."

Her voice was sad.

"Do you often think of your own country?" I asked.

"I was very young," she said, "when we came over. I was a little girl, thin and miserable-looking. I remember crying when we came over in the boat in your English Channel. 'Look, look, Olga,' said my aunt, who had been crying as much as I had; 'there is England, child, where they will treat us kindly.' I saw your white cliffs and—no, I did not want them. And though I do not think very much of Russia because it seems so long ago, I do not want this town."

"Neither do I," I said.

"No, you are unhappy," she said. "When I looked at you for a moment that first night, I said, there is somebody unhappy in the same way that I am unhappy, because he yearns for a freer life as I do."

"Olga," I said, "there are lovelier parts of England than here. I could take you to mountains and lakes where you would be free again."

"Perhaps," she murmured. And for the moment she would say no more.

I was filled with a great warmth towards life. Do you know that moment in winter when suddenly, on the bleakest day, your spirit leaps because you seem to sense a feeling of spring in the hard air? It is as though you smelt the warm sap in the bare, wind-driven trees. That is how I felt suddenly that evening.

As though these thoughts had been snatched from some sphere which was not yet mine to enter, a dark shape veered and fluttered a few yards above my head. When I saw it my spirits sank and I felt cold again. Now it was Olga who seemed unreal and the people around who seemed real. In a second I had been forced back to that dreary world I had struggled to leave. I shivered.

Olga knew. "Why—what is the matter?" she asked.

Her voice was so calm, I suddenly hated it for being able to keep its tones level.

"There's nothing the matter," I said; "nothing."

I felt desperate. How long was I to be thus tormented? An impotent anger with fate took hold of me.

Over the road an old woman was selling balloons in the shapes of fantastic faces with long, quivering noses and painted eyes. We heard a series of little explosions and saw the inflated faces vanish one by one, like lights suddenly pricked out. Then a small bird rose from the old woman's tray and flew into the air. The woman screamed in fury and shook her fist in the air. Several people laughed.

"What a shame he should do that to her," said Olga.

But my anger would allow no sympathy for the old woman.

"She probably deserves it," I said. "And anyhow, nobody ought to sell mockeries of the human face."

Olga turned and laughed in my face.

"Oh," she said, "so that is what you think?"

She walked over to the old woman and I followed her. Why should she take any interest in a withered old crone who would be better dead?

Olga was speaking to her and I stood beside, fuming inwardly, not speaking.

"You should make balloons like birds, with long beaks," Olga was saying. "That would make them so cross."

The old woman looked surprised, then she laughed. "Why yes, lady, that's right enough."

She still had a number of flat balloons in her tray. "Now won't you buy one, lady," she said, "and blow it up and see if that dratted hen comes for you as he did for me. If he does I'll twist his neck, that I will."

"Shall we buy one?" Olga asked me.

"As you like," I said.

She gave the woman some money and took a balloon from the tray.

"Now blow it up, dearie," said the woman.

One or two amused people had gathered round. I was less and less comfortable and wondered how Olga could behave like this;

it seemed so flippant to me. Did she not understand anything about the birds?

Quietly and calmly she placed the nozzle to her lips and began to blow, managing to invest that absurd action with a dignity which gave it an almost ceremonial quality. When it was blown up she tied the string round the nozzle and dangled a clown's orange face in the air. It bobbed up and down in her hand, grinning with yellow-painted teeth, its long, spherical nose shaking as though it were alive; its glazed eyes reminding you it was dead.

"There," said Olga, "there."

She released it and it flew lazily away over the trees till it disappeared.

"Well, lady," said the old woman, "that'll make them mad when they see that floating about in the sky. The horrid things they are." She cocked her little head on one side suddenly and looked at us both. "Your gentleman's looking very glum and sore," she said. "You take him off, lady, and have a little fun."

She burst into a cackle of laughter and hobbled away.

"Well," said Olga, when she had gone, "you heard what she said?"

"Yes, I heard."

"But you're not sure, are you—you're not sure whether we ought to have a little fun?"

"What did she mean," I asked stubbornly, "by a little fun?"

Olga smiled. "Oh," she said, "you are a dull boy, but perhaps you are right."

We walked away and came down into the vale where there were trees and fewer people.

"I think you are a flirt," I said maliciously.

"I—a flirt?" she cried. "Oh no!" And she pressed her lips tight in anger. "It is just that you are moral," she said, "that is all."

We stood under a hawthorn tree, she with her back to it, leaning against the trunk with her hands behind her. "I am not moral," I said, and to my dismay I realized that I had almost shouted the words. I was by now entirely beside myself. She stirred me so deeply I could not speak calmly. And it was not her with whom I was angry; it was with the menace that, even as I spoke, rustled above in the dry branches of the tree. Rather than succumb to its deadly influence I worked myself into a fury with Olga. It should be a challenge, I thought; the thing should see that I was alive, that it had no power to assault my spirit. And all the time I was shaking—shaking with fear and dread.

Suddenly Olga said, "You are not raving at me; you are raving at yourself because you are afraid of yourself."

"It is not true," I said savagely.

"It is true. You are afraid of yourself."

"No—not of myself, Olga——"

"—of—yourself——"

In the tree, branches rustled and shook. I broke down.

"Olga, Olga," I cried, "don't you understand? I am marked—like everybody else."

I did not look at her nor hear her walk towards me. But I felt my head caught in her hands and pressed against her till I wanted to fall to the ground for shame that I was so weak, and she, in a way that I could not understand, so strong.

"Oh!" I said, "oh!" and my words died away as she kissed me, and slowly I recovered control of my trembling body.

With nobody else had I felt so humiliated and glad to be humiliated as in that moment. She was so warm and alive to me; her touch seemed to draw me over to another country.

"Listen," she said, "I will tell you something. You do not want to speak about it, nobody does. I know that you are haunted. But you must let me speak, because I was the same as you a few days ago until I found out that it had no power to kill me if I let it come to me, unresisting. Do you remember Paul Weaver?"

Yes, I remembered him, I said.

"He resisted it, and he killed himself. He was my lover, and then something went wrong in him; he thought he could be another person. He was gentle and sensitive; he thought he could be a large-voiced man, loving many women and filling himself with drink. I could not love him any more then. He killed himself because he could not face himself as he really was. When he died, I thought I should die too, for there was nobody else I loved. I saw you, and there was something in your eyes which I knew was true. Only—only it isn't true until you see yourself."

She was struggling to tell me something which was hard to put into words.

"You are frightened," she said, "of the bird in that tree—yes? It is so—isn't it?"

"It wants to kill me," I muttered. "I daren't think of it or even admit its existence. I shall go mad——"

Again there was that dry, crackling sound from the tree, and I felt I could bear it no longer. I took my stick, ran from Olga and began wildly slashing in the low branches. She ran to me and dragged me away, gripping my arms with a force I did not know she possessed. She was terribly distressed.

"No, no," she cried, "oh—why don't you see? That all you have to do is to let it come to you, to look it in the face and accept it as part of you——"

"Look it in the face—no, how can I do that?" I said. "How do I know what dreadful thing I shall see?"

"I was like you," she said. "For days I was haunted till I thought I should die—oh, it was so terrible. But I knew, I knew, you see, that I should have to acknowledge its claim over me—its right to pursue me, if I wanted to live. It was something I had driven away and it had to come back, thwarted and twisted out of shape, so ugly. Oh, terrible, terrible—I only know you must do the same as I did; that if you try to kill it, you will only kill yourself."

Suddenly she let go of my hands and walked away a few yards. When she turned, the moonlight struck on her face, giving her a thin, ghostly appearance.

"I cannot help you," she said. Her words seemed to sound from afar off. I felt as though I were choking, struggling to breathe. There was a barrier between us, like a rank mist, which I could not break through. My head swayed; my body did not seem to be in my own control.

From that distance came her voice, grave and measured. "I cannot help you any more, for nobody can help. It is your own struggle. I have told you—all I can."

I tried to move towards her, but I had no power to stir. I tried to speak, but my lips were dumb. Mounting over me from the tree I felt as though a deep cloud of thick blackness enveloped me, that I was being slowly sucked into a world where I should be alone with nothing but myself to know and touch. As through a tiny chink in a dungeon cell, I saw Olga move and walk away. As she walked, the light of the moon seemed to wane, and the living darkness to rise and suffocate me.

A sense that she was perhaps for ever leaving me, drove me to action, and I called in a throttled voice, "Olga, Olga!"

The word loosed my limbs and I stumbled over to her, catching at her dress and gasping.

"You mustn't go," I cried. "You mustn't go———"

She turned for a second to face me and there seemed to be a hesitant expression about her face.

"Oh, my God," she said. "Oh, my God." Then she touched my forehead, turned quickly, and disappeared into the darkness.

I was alone. She had gone and taken with her the light of the moon. I was alone with my Demon in a dead world.

*

A moving darkness seemed to have dragged me from the outer world into the coils of itself so that I could hardly breathe or move. My limbs ached, my whole body seemed to be the prey of some obscene atrophy. I felt a surging revulsion against the foul atmosphere which engulfed me; the air I breathed was corrupt. Yet I could make no effort to escape. Olga had gone and all the new life that she represented had gone with her. There seemed no life left in anything. The senseless evening heat dried up the blood in my veins till I felt I was no more than a dry leaf clinging to a dead bough. Far away I heard the sound of a dog barking, cars running, some drunkard singing; I thought they were the last sounds I should ever hear, that they belonged to a world which I was leaving.

I had never before had so appalling a sense of the earth's boundaries; there seemed to be no place where I could go to breathe pure air again. I longed for a jet of icy water suddenly to spurt out of the ground; I longed for tongues of flame to lick the dry trees and consume them to ashes; I longed for a fierce wind to lash the brittle leaves to powder and scatter them over the earth. I longed for movement, for anything but this relentless corrosion of life.

Streaming out beyond the stars and the moon, I felt there was a sap of life, and that for ever now we should be denied of its vital flow into the encrusted veins of our world.

In a great wave of passionate despair—identifying the whole misery of the decaying earth with the wretchedness of myself, I raised my head to the sky and cried, "How long, O Lord, how long?"

There was no answer to this cry; no sign from the deity to whom I still maintained a half-hearted adherence. There was only a thin, squealing sound, melancholy and wintry, like the falling note of a curlew under a low, misty sky. But it was a far more despairing sound than that. Something full of mournfulness, the echo of all those heavy thoughts that oppressed me. Again it cried, the downward, shuddering note of something doomed to die yet wanting to live. It was a cry forced out of a soul that had lost all hope, like the lament of an exile who sees his native shores across a great expanse of water and can never reach them.

I saw then what I dreaded most to see; a grey bird flying in aimless circles round the branches of the tree, flying as though disturbed out of a long sleep. By the way that it flew I knew that it was blind. Suddenly I dropped my head away from it, for it had settled on a low branch and was looking at me. It was too much to bear. Because, with misty caverns where eyes should be, it looked down and saw nothing. Its vacant stare denied my existence; I was nothing.

I heard it fluttering again, lower, nearer my head. The sound of its wings was like the rustling of dead leaves over a stone courtyard. It cried again, so near me, that I thought I had uttered the sound myself. I could not move.

My stick was in my hand. Olga's words came back to me: "If you try to kill it, you will only kill yourself." And why not? I thought suddenly. What was there left to live for? The memory of Olga's white face broke the darkness. She had told me a truth; she had shown me how to recover my freedom. Then I knew that with all my strength I must guard my hand. With an almost involuntary movement I threw the stick away, far down the hill. Now I could not strike. But how long could I stay here, waiting?

Something touched my hair and whistled past me. Then I lost

my control, ran blindly, wildly down the tussocky heath, in and out amongst trees, tearing at my collar. Anywhere, anywhere, to escape. I hurled myself down on the grass in a sweat of terror, as though I could burrow into the ground like a mole. Behind, I heard the beating of wings. Pictures flooded my vision: of an old man lying face downwards in the gutter, of a priest lying face downwards at the bottom of an escalator—face downwards, face downwards. Do not look, do not look! screamed my mind; you will die if you look into those sightless eyes; it will tear your face to shreds and leave pits in your forehead so that you too will not be able to see.

With a superhuman effort I dragged myself to my feet, intending to turn and face it. But the touch of its claws on my shoulders drove me to violence. I struck out with my hands. Then it cried malignantly and came at my face. I held my hands before my face and began to run again—I did not know where. I heard a woman shriek as I tore past her. The horror close behind me, for ever wailing in that lost and malicious note, mounted in my brain till I thought my forehead would burst open. And the thought of my brain bursting out, tempted me to hurl my body against a tree trunk, to smash my face on the rough bark so that I could no longer see nor hear anything. A few yards down the hill I saw the dark shape of a tree. You must gather all your force together, I said, and fling yourself upon that trunk; then all will go, all will be blotted out, you will be released.

The tree, the tree! I cried. And as it grew nearer I tore my hands down my face as though to blind myself to what I must do. I felt again the touch on my head and threw up my hands to beat it away. And this compelled me to open my eyes; I saw I was within a few inches of the tree.

The knowledge of physical pain assaulted me. Reason returned. I thought of my face streaming with blood, my features disfigured. The impact might not kill me; I might only suffer terribly.

With all the force I could summon I swerved aside, stumbled over a gnarled root, lost my balance, and rolled many yards down the incline. I could not rise. I lay on my back, moaning. Suddenly it seemed that the sky and the stars were shrouded by a dense grey pall which drew itself over life like the coverlet drawn over a dead body. I could no longer resist; I had to suffer what was intended.

The creature, larger now than myself, came upon my face, its wings outstretched till I was choking for breath; its talons pressed into my chin; its eyes—those void chasms—close to mine.

In one dreadful second, which seemed like all eternity, I saw all that was me, all that had shrivelled to waste in me. Deep in the pits of those two dead eyes I saw the soul that I had driven out from me so long ago. And it was hideous.

—I cannot tell you more about that. Because to speak of what I saw then is to betray the living Soul which from that moment came to life in me, and still lives. I saw—and this is all I can tell you—I saw the corrupt emanation of the Soul of a man whom, as a great poet had said, *"God hath made to mar himself."*

I saw and I lived. Had I not seen, my Demon would have destroyed me. But I saw and I lived. Suddenly I realized that there was no longer a grey pall laid out upon me; I was looking up into the shining arch of the clear sky, speckled with a line of stars like dust along a sunbeam in autumn. Slowly coursing through my body I felt that sap of life for which I had cried so desperately. For a while I was content to lie there, rejoicing in the beauty of the world as though I had seen it all for the first time.

I stood up. My ankles ached, my limbs were bruised, blood was dripping from my chin. But there was so delicate a lightness in my body that I could not think of these small pains. The air was pure again. I breathed in and out slowly, as I had done upon Cader. I saw that I had not to go to a mountain to fill my lungs with life. I was regenerate, a new being. I was the exile who had found his way back to his native country.

I knew in a way that I had never before accepted, that I stood alone, that nobody could invade my Soul. Neither could I intrude upon the privacy of any other Soul. I could tell nobody of what had happened to me, though I might warn them—as Olga had—not to resist their Demons. I could save nobody, for nobody had the power to save a man but himself.

I thought of Olga, and though my instinct was to go at once to her and make her leave the City with me, I knew that the time was not yet ripe for this. Now that I lived as she lived and could never again feel ashamed before her, I felt no impatience for the life that I knew we should find together. Another figure rose in my mind. I could not leave my mother, I must make another attempt to reason with her.

So I left the heath; came up again to the pond at the top. The tavern had closed. It was late, and only a few people passed me as I walked towards the station. The heat was intense, yet it did not oppress me; the silence heavy, yet it did not sadden me. I no longer wanted wind or fire or water to force movement out of the earth.

In the empty carriage of the underground train I found a woman's bag and the torn pages of a book scattered about. Somebody had sprinkled sawdust on the floor. There was a copy of the evening paper. Details were given of the proposed gas-attack upon the birds in two days' time. Proposed gas-attack—— I laughed. Did nobody *know*? I went on to read about the Intercession Service which was shortly to be held in the Cathedral. I decided I would go. It should be the last event I would witness before I left London.

My eyes fell upon the patch of wet sawdust on the floor; on the bag lying idle and unclaimed upon a seat. How sad it looked; how futile.

I reached home, letting myself in quietly. The house was in darkness, for my mother and Annie had gone to bed. The windows downstairs were closed. I opened them. I went up and paused outside Lillian's door. A nightlight was burning inside. I wanted to talk to her, and I knew she would not be asleep. I knocked gently.

"Is that you, son?"

"Yes, Mother. Can I come in to say good-night?"

She paused.

"Yes, come in."

*

The room was dimly lit by a small wax light on the washing-table. The windows were closed and the curtains of heavy black velvet were drawn. It was very hot. On a table by my mother's bed were bottles of medicine, a wine-glass, and a silver lozenge-box in which she kept sugar for the cup of tea that she made for herself in the early morning. There was also a novel which she had been reading.

I sat on the edge of her bed and picked up the book.

"Any good?" I asked her.

"No, dear. The usual thing. Silly girl runs away from home and has a baby she doesn't want."

I laughed. This was one of popular fiction's inexhaustible themes. "It's sure to turn out all right in the end," I said.

"No. I looked at the end. It all comes out wrong. She kills her son—throws him over a cliff."

"Oh, that's too bad. You shouldn't read such horrors, Mother. They only upset you."

I looked at the tired head caught in tangled grey hair on the pillow. The clothes were drawn close round her neck, her knees were hunched up. She looked so much smaller and frailer than in the daytime. I felt very moved when I saw her lying there. There was something I had to say and I did not know how to say it.

"You look more comfortable in bed," I said, avoiding what was in my mind, "than any person I know."

"When you were a little thing," she said, "with long curls, like that picture up there which you hate so, you were lovely in bed asleep. I used to stand over you and wonder that you were mine. I suppose all foolish mothers do."

I looked up to the wall above her bed where there was a framed picture of myself as a small child of three, holding toy-bricks, long ringlets falling round my fat, sullen face.

"I don't hate the picture," I said. "I suppose I was better then than I have ever been since."

"Oh no, you're a good boy. Only you're too much like me and always were. Never know your own mind."

I always got irritated when Lillian remarked that I was "too much like her," as though it were unfortunate for any one to resemble her.

Suddenly she noticed that my tie was hanging loose, my collar open. "You look as though you've been fighting," she said, "or making love. Which, son?"

I hesitated. Fighting? Yes, I had certainly been fighting. But when it came to telling her about the nature of that struggle, I could not. There was Olga; I could talk about her.

"I got so hot," I said, "I took off my tie. As for making love— yes, Mother, you're right. I was up on Hampstead Heath. Mother—do you remember the other night when I came in late? I wanted to tell you that evening, I went to out to see—somebody, and I was too drunk to talk to her. To-night I have seen her. And it's all right—it's all right."

"You're badly in love, aren't you, dear?"

"I've never felt so happy in my life."

"Well, tell me her name then."

"Olga."

My mother repeated the word carefully. "Olga? Yes, I like that. But it's Russian, isn't it?"

"Yes, she's Russian."

I told her all I knew about Olga. At the end I said, "I want to take her away from London, Mother. She's unhappy here. And so are you. I want us all three to get away, far from London." As I spoke I laid my hand on her forehead. But now her mood changed and she made no answer.

"We can't stay here any longer," I spoke eagerly and quickly as though I could capture her with the strength of my words; "we've got to get away. It isn't safe for you here. You've got to come."

"Who says I've got to come?" Her voice was sullen.

"I only want your good."

"Don't argue about it now, son. It's not the time. It's very late, and you ought to be in bed."

I walked over to the windows, wondering how I could ever convince her of the truth.

"Mother, this room is so hot. It isn't good for you. Why don't you open the window?"

She turned sharply and raised herself. "No, no! Leave the windows alone; go to bed."

I drew the curtains a few inches.

"Leave them alone," she cried. "Who are you to interfere with me and tell me what I shall do?"

"I only know you ought to have these windows open——"

As I spoke I saw a pale, spectral shadow, like a withered hand, rise towards the window-pane. It had no power to touch me, I knew that. But what dreadful power had it over my mother? Hastily I drew the curtain back again before she should see what I had seen.

"Yes, you're right, Mother," I said. "I'm sorry. I have no business to interfere with you or anybody."

I bent over and kissed her good night. She held my head in her hands and looked at me.

"What's happened to you?" she whispered. "You're different. Is it—that girl?"

"No, it isn't only that, it——"

"Well, what is it? Tell your mother. She has a right to know."

"Mother, do you want me to help you?"

"How can you help me?"

"You're unhappy and I can help you to be happy."

"I don't care about myself," she muttered. "I don't care any more. It's you—you I think about. When I think about you, I can forget myself. Now you don't want me any more. You're changed."

"Yes, I am changed," I said. "But it isn't true, to say I don't want you any more. I am changed. I've found something."

"Well, tell me. Don't speak so strangely."

The tapping came at the window; she fell back into the pillow. "I can't easily tell you what I have found, Mother. You must trust me. I can only tell you with all my soul that if you want that tapping to stop, you must open the window and let it in——"

"You're mad—mad to speak to me like that!"

I saw it was impossible to thrust the truth upon her like this. As Olga had done to me, I could only indicate where her path should lie. Acceptance of her fate must come out of herself, not be driven in by me.

I argued no more but went to my room, opened the windows, took off my clothes, and lay naked on the bed, rejoicing in the feeling of ease and contentment that flowed over my body.

I put my hand to my chin and felt the dried blood where the wound from the bird's talons had already begun to heal. I looked

at the scar in the mirror. Here, on my chin, some malignant creature had pressed his claws, taking blood from me. This was the
only evidence I had of a fact that seemed like a dreadful night-
mare. To this day I carry that scar on my chin to remind me, if I
ever need reminding, of something that fought its way back into
me all those years ago.

*

What I now have left to relate are the events of the three days
that followed upon my meeting with Olga and my experience
on the heath. Each of those days stands clear before me, perhaps
because they were so sharply contrasted; perhaps because they
were so much more lived than the days which preceded them. It
has not always been easy to describe my behaviour and activities
in those evil days when I was haunted by my Demon, as thousands were haunted. The mind does not so easily retain grief as
joy. And because—in spite of the final collapse—I was happier
in those three days than I had been for months, I can remember
almost every detail of them. Although I saw death and tragedy
around me, I was filled with a conviction that the eternal things
could never be touched; that, whatever was to happen, I could
return again to some such place as Cader, and still see the essential world alive and joyous before me.

The morning of the first of those three days, I came out of
the house with a light heart. There was a new world given to me,
which I could learn to enjoy.

Then I stopped in my path up the hill, driven out of these
blithe thoughts by one of the most preposterous sights I had ever
seen.

A number of men were walking towards the station. I recognized most of them, for they went that way every morning. In
the wake of each one was a large bird, flying a few feet behind
and above their heads. Nor was this all. For outside the doors of
many of the houses, solitary birds were standing, as patient and
melancholy as herons, waiting for the inmates to emerge and
walk up the hill. By one house there were two birds. As I passed,
the door opened furtively and two men, one old, one young—

perhaps father and son—came out and closed the door quickly behind them. Like obedient clockwork figures, the two birds immediately rose and followed them. The whole ritual was conducted quietly, the birds making no attempt to attack or disturb the pedestrians. Thus they went up the hill towards the City, men and birds, the men with their faces inclined to the ground, walking heavily.

There seemed to be an unspoken conspiracy to take no notice whatever of the birds. Nobody looked up or spoke about them. The more I studied this curious procession, the more I noticed that in a most subtle way each bird seemed to mimic, by its flight, the actions of the person it followed. One bird, for example, following a red-faced, corpulent old gentleman, flew in lethargic downward and upward swoops as though it were a hollow feathered bag, swaying in the air, and having no power over its movements. Another, close behind a dapper little man with tight spectacles pinching into a almost bridgeless nose, flew in spasmodic jerks in a perfectly straight line, stopping for a second regularly, every few feet, then propelling itself forward again with the tethered impatience of a cork released on a string from a child's pop-gun. In various ways each bird flew differently, although their appearance was identical in almost every other respect.

I reached the station and the train came in. Although the roofs of the carriages were dotted with birds, nobody showed surprise. The birds which had followed the pedestrians made no attempt to enter the carriages. They seemed perfectly content to join the others on the roof. So this singular train-load steamed out. Not a word was spoken in the carriage in which three or four men sat with me. Newspapers were solemnly read, pipes and cigarettes smoked. I felt as though I were the only person who had seen the birds.

In the City, exactly the same sort of thing was to be observed. No omnibus passed without its sullen roof-load of birds who would not leave until the passengers left.

I passed a few who were not thus attended. I remember a nun with a bewildered expression on her face. Stark and severe, she moved like a wraith along Broad Street, her lips twitching with repeating some religious devotion. No bird hovered over her. In a curious way this seemed to have robbed her of life. She looked unutterably miserable. And nuns, though often empty of coun-tenance, were seldom miserable. Poor woman. She was so alone in that crowd of harassed humanity. I believe she prayed for a bird, for no incipient saint had ever been known to resist a chance of trial or temptation.

It was very quiet in the underwriting-room. I did not talk much to the others. I was embarrassed by the contrast between the elation of my spirit and the apathy of my friends. It was hard to know how to talk to them.

The Underwriter arrived very late, driving up to the office in a taxi from which he stepped with a furtive and almost hopeless air. I saw him hurry to his room and quickly close his door. He hardly came out of the room for more than an hour during the day.

I phoned Olga at the dress-making shop where she worked. She knew at once from my tone of voice what had happened to me.

"You are—not frightened any more?" she asked.

"No. I did what you told me, Olga."

I said she had saved my life.

"No," she said. "You saved your own life."

And she began to laugh—gentle, low laughter, beautiful to hear. I asked her when we could meet again; there was so much now that I wanted to talk about. To-morrow?

She could not come out to-morrow, she had special work which would occupy her all the evening.

"But, Olga, what does work matter now?"

"It is extra money, and money is useful. No; it must be the next day."

She told me to come to the shop about five-thirty. And because I felt annoyed with her for not putting her work aside for me, I said I doubted whether I could get away as early as that, knowing, of course, that I would.

She laughed again. "Very well," she said, "you impatient boy. I will wait for you. I will wait all the evening if you wish." Then I assured her I would be there. We paused for a moment, and I was about to ring off when I heard her voice, very low and trembling: "I am so glad—so glad."

In the lunch-hour I went to Leicester Square and met my old friend whom I had not seen since my holiday. There were now not so many birds flying over the streets as earlier in the morning, though many people were still followed.

We sat in a small tavern, drinking beer, eating sandwiches, talking. I told him about my holiday, but he did not seem interested. There was something restrained about him. I knew the reason.

"You're unusually quiet," I said.

"And you," he returned, "unusually and damnably good-tempered."

Then he told me what I knew.

"It follows me about, like everybody else. And it's so stupid," he complained, "so damn silly. These things come from somewhere, they go somewhere, and I won't rest till I find a perfectly sound physical explanation of them."

"They go somewhere," I said, "that's true."

"You seem to know something about them," he said quickly. "Aren't you pestered too?"

I hesitated. If I told him the truth, would he ever believe it?

"Look here," I said, "you can get rid of this thing if you look it in the face."

"In the face!" He was silent for a moment. "I don't know whether it's got a face," he added in a low voice.

We came out from the tavern.

With an effort he recovered something of his old jaunty manner. I tried to explain that if he looked the bird in the face he would see something dreadful there, the creature would vanish, he would never suffer it again.

"A lot of fake mysticism," he objected. "I suppose you're aware that people have been killed by these things?"

"Yes, and do you ever remember a dead bird or even a feather being found? Is that fake mysticism?"

No, he did not remember, but there must be a natural explanation for that too. He seemed determined to prove that the birds were part of the natural system of creation.

"Then why don't you catch and kill the one that's worrying you?" I suggested. He had no answer.

I said, "Fred, if you want to come out of this business alive—stop asking for a natural explanation; look this thing in the face and let it do what it likes with you."

Our attention was drawn to a crowd gathered round a figure standing on a box near the National Gallery. The man was short, eccentric in appearance. I recognized him at once. He had a great mop of sandy hair falling down to his shoulders; a shirt with an open neck, exposing a bony, pink chest; and a fierce, bright expression on his small, foxy face.

"Why," I said, "it's the fellow we saw in the café the other night. The chap with the hair."

"He's found his vocation at last," said Fred. "Let's stay and listen."

We drew nearer. The man was preaching; flinging his arms about, clapping his chest, and shouting in a strident voice at his unmoved audience. "What did God send to the Egyptians? Lice, caterpillars, frogs. What does God send to you? Birds—birds! And what do they mean, my friends? They mean that you're a lot of miserable fornicators caught in a net."

There was a placard beside him, bearing the scarlet words—"DEATH AND JUDGMENT COME TO ALL."

As we watched, he induced himself into a veritable fury of scorn and denunciation, abandoning himself to that semi-insane state known as *hywl*. But a sublime allegiance to *hywl* depends upon the ecstatic support of a Celtic audience. Londoners were not so easily infected. Some heckled him, but he took no notice. His voice rose to a scream until we thought he would collapse in a fit.

"Serpents! Whited sepulchres! Hypocrites! What abideth? Faith, hope, and charity? Not in this new Babylon. Naught but sounding brass and tinkling cymbal. The spectres of the Apocalypse stalk in the land, and who heeds them?"

Phrase upon phrase from the Pauline tautologies, coupled with the semi-delirious but poetic ravings of John, the mystical friend of Jesus, tumbled indiscriminately from his mouth. There was something demoniacal about the man.

Near by was a statue; on this statue sat a large, black, skinny bird, not unlike a cormorant, only leaner and drabber, with a very foul smell. The preacher cried: "The birds are a judgment, fools—the birds are a judgment!" The solitary watcher flapped heavily into the air, fell upon the preacher, obscured him. . . .

The crowd drew away, women screamed. The inevitable ambulance arrived. I turned to Fred, "Do you still believe in the fortuity of these natural birds of yours?" Then I shook his hand and said good-bye, thinking I might not see him again. I actually never did see him again, though I have an instinctive and reasoned belief that he came out safely and re-established himself somewhere, as I did. For all I know, he may still be alive in some corner of this island, and wondering similar thoughts about me.

When I returned to the office later that afternoon I was long overdue my time. The Underwriter had been working himself up into a fury over my absence. My friends told me I was in for trouble, and I took a delight in preparing the words I should say to him. But when it came to the point, all my fine speeches melted away. He summoned me into his room about five, when the brokers had gone and he was alone. He asked me what I meant by continually absenting myself from the office. He said he could not tolerate my insolence any longer; he would have me moved to another department, where a strict watch should be kept on me. But the force of his words was entirely mitigated by the incessant raising of his head to the ceiling, by the wild and pathetic roving of his little eyes. In that last desperate assertion of his authority as my employer there was some vestige of manhood which I was compelled to admire.

I did not refute his accusations. But when he said, "I will have you moved to another department," I interrupted quietly:

"I shan't come to the office after to-day."

Though I knew it was cruel I could not resist. "Neither will you for much longer."

"Get out." His voice was thick, tied up in his throat. "Get out."

A practical sense of my position came to me. We were within a week of pay-day; I should need all the money I could get.

"There will be a month's salary," I reminded him.

His hand trembled. Suddenly I was sorry for him.

He wrote on a slip of paper and gave it to me. "Give this to the secretary," he said.

I left the room with the chit for my wages in my hand. It was the last time I should see the place, and suddenly I felt affectionately towards it. There was so much of me in this prison, so many dreams dreamed over that long desk, so many poems written under cover of a register. I collected together pens, pencils, and various small belongings that were my property. I lingered upstairs washing my hands, looking out of the window over the roofs to London. I came down again, said good-bye to my friends, and was saddened by their apathetic reception of my news. Nobody cared. Why should they? I was foolish to prolong my stay another moment. With a sentimental gesture I took the pencil and signed my name in the book for the last time.

I came to the lift and thought for a moment to go down and say good-bye to the old book-clerk. But I dismissed the idea. It was idle to look an inch into the past; already, all this was dead.

As I came to the door I saw a taxi waiting. On the roof was a small fussy-looking bird, preening its feathers in an endeavour to induce them to cover up a large bare patch near its tail. I had never seen a bird quite like it. It was a dull yellow in colour, with a very skinny breast and small legs. Its head was fat as a plum and quite as bald. It seemed top-heavy.

I stood on the other side of the road looking at it, wondering what the creature reminded me of.

Then a man came down the steps of the office, hastily opened the door of the taxi, and stepped inside. The bird tittered and poked its head over the side of the roof, looking down towards the window. The driver accelerated his engine. I heard a scream . . .

So bird and Underwriter were borne away out of my life. And he is another whose fate is unknown to me.

*

The second of those three days. That also is clear to me, like a quiet landscape held within the bounds of a slim frame.

A *quiet* landscape—— Yes, for all the strange things I have told
you, what I have to tell you now is perhaps the strangest; something for which I have never found an adequate explanation. But
when you are dealing with supernatural happenings, what explanation will ever suffice? Before I describe the second of those last
days I want briefly to recapitulate the events of the preceding
weeks. By so doing the extraordinary quality of that quiet day
will be seen all the clearer.

For six or seven weeks, since the beginning of August, from
the moment when I had first seen a swarm of strange birds
coming in a dense cloud over the river Thames—London had
been tormented by winged creatures such as nobody had ever
seen before. The advent of these pests had been received with
that philosophic resignation so peculiar to the English people.
When, however, the creatures began to break up into smaller
bodies, to invade our private and public activities, to attack and
cause the deaths of hundreds of citizens, they were regarded with
increased trepidation. By the middle of September no habitation
of man was free of the birds. They had become so general a phe-
nomenon as to be accepted without question. In the last few days
almost every person in London had been shadowed from place
to place by a bird; there was no way, apparently, of getting rid of
these sinister attendants. Yet even this preposterous situation, so
embarrassing and so ominous, could not entirely destroy the sto-
ical temper of the grievously tried people. They still struggled to
retain their outward composure and dignity; they would not, on
any account, admit the fear they felt in their hearts.

Meanwhile the whole country was stricken by a drought
which had dried up the crops and withered the fruit. No rain
had fallen for many months. Sickness fell upon thousands, and
famine—that spectral brother—seemed imminent. The Government at Westminster, weary of attempting to maintain peaceful
relations in the continent of Europe, had almost abandoned its
negotiations with the League of Nations—a league which had by
now dwindled to a half-hearted syndicate of small and unimportant powers. Beneath so much oppression the majority of people
bore upon their faces the marks of suffering, of long, sleepless
nights, of ceaseless worry. The entertainments with which men

sought to divert themselves were collapsing through lack of support. Great meetings were held in a colossal hall in west London, where journalists, priests, politicians and scientists spoke passionately of the need for a mobilization of the forces of peace. Finally, as you know, a special service of religious intercession was to take place.

This is a picture, however inadequate, of the utter gloom which pervaded the City that September when the sun rose more fiercely every day in the hard, burning sky. Augment the picture of your own imagination, because the sharper this wretchedness appears to you, the sharper will appear the ensuing gaiety and light-heartedness on the morning of that second day when it was announced from every town in the island, that the birds had vanished back into the mysterious sphere from which they had emerged some six weeks ago. Yes, they had gone. . . .

The feeling of relief, of freedom, was apparent in every person you met. A laughter which had not been heard for a long time seemed to ripple over the streets. And the disappearance of the birds was not all that gladdened men's hearts. For as the day continued, a slight breeze awoke and began to stir faintly over the crinkled leaves and dust-heavy flowers. It was barely audible, but it seemed to us like the faint breath of a sick man in whom one had given up all hope.

What I chiefly remember is the beautiful quietness of that day. I had forgotten how often the air was full of the harsh noise of the birds until London seemed like a rookery, only a hundred times less companionable. Now these sounds had gone, and in their place we heard the soft music of a little wind, sighing gently over the land.

I had not to go to Leadenhall. Waking up with this thought I could not accustom myself to it at once. I had told Lillian the previous night, and she had not received the news very favourably. She had been in bed most of the day, unwell and irritable. Annie had plagued her with stories of the birds she did not wish to hear. Then my news had added to the burden on her spirit.

"What are you going to *do*?" she had asked wearily.

"I'm going to buy a car, and take you away, a long way, where we can look at our lives and get them straight."

"Yes, but what are you going to *do*? You can't go on looking at life for ever."

In the morning she came down to breakfast, and I first began to realize the changed nature of the day when she told me she had slept well, the first time for many days. She was smiling, full of jokes. I knew that something unusual had happened, and at first I wondered whether she had opened her windows and come out of the ordeal as I had. I questioned her discreetly.

"Weren't you—worried in the night?"

"No," she said. "No, not once. I expect it was all my eye, don't you, son? I believe I imagined it. They say you can imagine such things."

She seemed a changed woman.

"I heard of a girl once," she continued, "who imagined she had swallowed a spider in a glass of milk. She got so ill they actually had to operate on her. Fancy that, now!"

It struck me that her gaiety was assumed. I went out and was so amazed by the quietness and the change over everything that I could do little more than wander about the streets in a half-bewildered delight. It was hard to believe what had happened. I bought a newspaper later and read that the disappearance of the birds was not confined to our neighbourhood. I telephoned my friend Fred, and asked him what it was like in the City. He told me that it was all clear, and that he personally was annoyed with the birds for leaving us before he had had time to examine them properly and arrive at some sane conclusions about them.

While still in the telephone-box I had a strong inclination to call Olga and ask if I could walk up to Hampstead and see her. But a second thought prompted me not to. It would be better to stay with Lillian to-day, to try to talk to her, and perhaps arrange to bring Olga to see her to-morrow.

On my way home I passed a small fancy shop and was suddenly reminded of the candles I had wanted for the empty sticks on the bureau. My mother was in such a good humour, so light-hearted, they would please her to-day. So I went into the shop and bought two tall candles, white, with tapering points.

"There, Mother," I said, unwrapping them and showing them to her.

"Why, they're lovely. They make you think you ought to have a service, don't they?"

I laughed and set them in the sticks. With my arm round my mother's waist, we looked at them and agreed, that they entirely altered the appearance of the dark corner.

"Shall I light them?" I asked.

"Oh no, you extravagant boy," she said. "Besides, it would spoil the look of them."

I could not quite understand how lighting candles could spoil the look of them, but I did not argue the point.

Later, I talked to her and tried to make her see that my leaving Leadenhall was inevitable, and better to come soon than late. "What I plan," I said, "is that you should have a long holiday with me somewhere. Perhaps Wales. We can leave Annie to mind the house."

She said I was mad, compared me to her father, sighed, and laughed. It was strange and delightful to have tea with her later in the afternoon, with the windows wide open again. She laughed and joked, and we played the fool with each other.

"To-morrow," I said, "I shall go up to town, see if I can find any old cars——"

"You'll break our necks," she said. "I'm sure you can't drive. I don't know how any one does it."

"Rubbish!" I scoffed; "it's as easy as walking."

"Well, dear, I don't find that very easy," she said.

We took the newspaper and looked at some advertised cars, discussing what particular make we should have. Looking back, it seems to me that we were figures in an ironic drama, instructed to laugh and be merry by a supreme playwright. And all over London in a thousand homes that evening, I dare say similar scenes were being enacted.

Towards sunset I took her out. She had been half afraid of going, but I encouraged her. It was her first walk outside the house for several days. We went up to the ridge. Here is the crystallization of that quiet day. The same scene as I set for you earlier in the story: the tennis players, the wooden seats, the lethargic railway, the distant spires and chimneys—and over it all a long feather of wind, so slight as barely to stir a leaf in the plane trees. But wind—wind; a breath from another country.

We sat and talked a long while. "I want to bring Olga to see you to-morrow night," I said. "You will love her, and she you."

My mother was dubious. "I'm never any good with strangers," she said. "But bring her if you like, son."

The tennis players had left the courts; it was quiet, almost dark. We heard the wind sighing from many miles away, in the west. Where the sun had set there was a barred window of red light left in the sky. We watched its glow fall and fade till there was nothing left.

"Why, son," said my mother, "it'll soon be winter. That sunset reminded me of winter somehow."

She murmured half to herself the words of her old hymn:

> "Shadows of the evening,
> Steal across the sky."

As we turned to go and surveyed for a moment the long black shape of the Alexandra Palace, there were tears in my eyes.

When we came back to the house, "Let us light our candles, Mother," I said.

But, "Oh no," she replied, "it would be a shame to waste them."

I talked to her in her room.

"You'll open your windows to-night, won't you?"

"Not to-night," she replied quickly. "I needn't yet, need I? Besides, I should catch cold. The wind's rising. I believe we shall have a storm."

I sighed, left her, and walked up and down the street before I went to bed. I noticed then that almost every window in the street was shut, despite the still warmth of the night. Why had they laughed all day, I thought? Why? When they must shut windows at night——

It was a brilliant starry sky, with no moon. I heard the distant sound of the wind like one long-continued note gradually coming nearer.

*

The third day. I rose early, for I had not been able to sleep very well. Incessant during the night had been that distant note of the wind, rising by imperceptible degrees to a long, uneasy moan. It was a sound so strange to us that I could not accustom myself to it. From the west, from over the Atlantic, storm-clouds were being slowly driven towards our island. There should be cause for nothing but rejoicing in that I told myself; and I tried again to sleep. But I could not. Before dawn I rose and switched on the light. I tried to read, but my mind was too full of thoughts. In a mechanical sort of way, hardly knowing why I did it, I began to assemble the few books that were of any value to me.

Then it suddenly came into my mind—why am I doing this? Thus taking stock of my few possessions as though I stood on the eve of a great change in my life? My practical self assured me, I might very soon be going away somewhere with my mother and Olga. It was as well to decide what books I should take.

I remembered it was the day fixed for the intercession service in the Cathedral, and I decided I would go. Then I would have lunch with Fred, and ask him to help me in buying a cheap car; he was the sort of person who would know about such things. Later, in a day or so, I would drive my mother away somewhere, perhaps to Wales. If she made any objections, I would just put her in the car and drive off; she would very soon admit that she liked the change. But before all this I had to see Olga and have some definite plan to put before her. I would not bring her to see my mother that evening; I would talk to her first.

All these half-formulated plans were very well, but recurring in my mind was that practical phrase of Lillian's, "What are you going to *do*? Yes, but what are you going to *do*?"

I answered it half-heartedly, aware that I contradicted those decisions I had made two weeks ago upon the mountain. I said, "I will write; I will spend my life juggling with words; working out upon paper some clear and philosophic attitude towards existence which is not yet mine." I heard a milkman's cart rattle along and the man whistling some popular tune to himself. Soon the world would be awake. But for a moment I was alone while everybody slept; I was stealing a moment from time. I felt that I had the power to arrest the progress of the sun and keep those blinds drawn so long as I wished.

I looked up to the sky. Eastward was pure dawn, with a rose-coloured streak lying in the last green vault of night. But westward, a long strip of black cloud pressed low on the horizon. And from there came the wind. I felt it slowly chilling my body until I began to shiver. It was colder than I had known it for weeks. I was reminded of another morning when I had risen early and gone to the swimming-pool and seen the birds thick as ploughed earth on the surface of the water. Barely a month ago, yet it seemed like a different existence. We had been half amused then by a lot of birds. And now they had all gone; the world was returning to normality. I looked all around me, on to roof and into tree. There were no birds.

I heard the click of the letter-box in the front door; the morning newspaper had been delivered. Wanting to see whether there was any fresh news of the birds, I ran up to get it. By my mother's door, with the newspaper in my hand, I paused, then knocked.

"Come in," she called. Then, as I entered, "Why, how early you are!"

"Did you sleep well?"

"No, not very well. I kept hearing the wind and I thought we were going to have thunder."

"There's a bank of cloud coming up from the west," I told her. "I expect we shall have rain at last."

I went to my bedroom with the paper. Spread out in huge black letters were the words, "HAVE THE BIRDS VANISHED?" And a leading article commenced—"These are the words on everybody's lips."

It appeared that all the previous day there had been no sign of the birds. "The proposed gas attack was abandoned," declared the paper; and added, "It is hoped that such a dangerous measure will never now be found necessary."

I saw another column headed "Rain in the West." At a late hour last night a heavy south-west gale had launched itself on the coasts of Cornwall, and rain of exceptional violence had fallen. Little wooden beach-huts had been smashed to pieces by the wind, and somewhere a large-tanker was ashore. Habit compelled me to ask—were we interested? I laughed. They could be as interested as they liked in Leadenhall; it no longer concerned me.

At breakfast we spoke about the change in the weather. My mother was still in good spirits, but a little uneasy. She continually rose from the table and crossed to the window, looking out and remarking at intervals that "Regular pea-soup was on the way."

"If you go out," she said, "you had better take a coat. That is, if you're still bent on this silly idea of yours."

"Yes," I replied. "I think I shall go to St. Paul's."

"There doesn't seem much need to pray for rain, does there?" observed Lillian. "Since it'll probably come down in bucketfuls before long."

I left soon after breakfast. Annie was cleaning the door-knocker and told me to be back early if it came to rain, as my mother hated a storm.

"All right, Annie," I said. And I made some jocular remark. She did not reply, but scowled and rubbed the polish furiously into the brass. I think she bore some grudge against my cheerfulness; I could not encourage her to smile or joke. Poor Annie. . . .

The service in the Cathedral was at eleven-thirty. By ten when I left the house, the bank of cloud had risen higher in the sky and soon threatened to obscure the sun. There was a breathless silence hanging over everything; a subdued excitement in the patter of people's feet along the pavement. Men at the station, who two days ago had been heavy-faced and speechless, were standing in groups together, looking up to the sky, pointing to the cloud. "Rain, rain"—the word was on everybody's lips. "Strange," remarked somebody, "it should come on the very day of this service in St. Paul's."

In the carriage they talked of the change in the weather with heightened and quick voices.

"Well, with rain coming and the birds gone," said a little man who was in the habit of addressing the world at large, "we all return to normal."

"I suppose the birds *have* gone?" came the dubious voice of a thin man with a red, scraggy neck.

"You bet your life, sir," replied the little man, nodding his head rapidly and sucking his teeth in a confidential sort of manner. "Y'see," he explained, "I have a theory; quite simple. They were driven over here by bad weather. We shall find out one day where they came from. Undiscovered island in the Atlantic—mark my words, sir. Couldn't find their proper home, as you might say. Now here's this rain coming and—phoosh! Away they go. After the sun, y'see. Can't bear rain. Felt it coming. Birds always know. Why—you wouldn't believe——" And he went on at great length to tell us a story about a pet jackdaw he had had as a child; a story which he told so amusingly that we sat and listened to him, hardly noticing how the light slowly darkened outside and the air through the open window seemed to get thin. It was a curious scene. I remember suddenly the long, squalid names of the drab stations we passed—Haggerston, Canonbury—as we drew towards Broad Street.

The little man had finished his story.

"Yes, but these birds," objected the dubious one, "where do you suppose they are now? Tell me that."

The little man waved a hand as though he had birds up his sleeve.

"Somewhere in the Far East," he affirmed. "Mark m'words, gentlemen, mark m'words!"

"Pity," said his antagonist in a bitter voice, "you didn't catch one like that jackdaw of yours. The Natural History Museum would have been glad of a specimen." The man opposite me leaned over and touched my knee. "Excuse me, do you mind if we have this window up a little——"

"No," I said. "Of course." And I suddenly realized I was cold.

I took an omnibus up Broad Street, wondering at the extraordinary air of excitement which the expanding cloud cast over everybody. Very few people talked about the birds; everybody talked about the rain which seemed imminent. Hanging on a thousand arms, I saw that the umbrella had returned to London. The expression on people's faces was carefree and jovial; conversation was light and careless, as it had always been.

On that journey to the Cathedral I realized that I was one of the few not affected by this return to normality. Nothing seemed normal to me. The sky where now the great cloud surged slowly

up to meet and extinguish its adversary the sun, was a menace.
The cries of people gathered in groups on the pavements I
passed—"The cloud, the cloud—rain, rain——"—were like the
spasmodic yappings of a ventriloquist's doll. All along Cheapside there were such groups of people, talking in quick, joyous
voices, and pointing to the sky. "The cloud, the cloud—look at
the cloud—rain—rain is coming at last!"

By the time I reached the Cathedral close on eleven, to wait
for a seat in the great crowd of people who approached the building on every side, the sun was half obscured in the dusty-looking
hem of the cloud. A watery light fell over the City. The cloud,
farther west, had thickened to a dense unbroken blackness. It
seemed to grudge the expulsion of the rain it held, like a person
who has a rare treasure to show you in a box and will not lift the
lid.

I stood in a long queue outside the north door, slowly trailing my way in. The crowd thickened behind me. Hundreds had
come on the impulse of the moment, a religious impulse which
prompted them to give thanks to God for the cessation of the
drought. I heard many of them saying they had not intended to
come, but they felt that they must.

Eventually, after a long wait, I got into the north transept of
the Cathedral and found a seat.

Far away in the west I heard the wind, mounting like the
oncoming rush of water down a mountain-side. . . .

*

The Cathedral was shaped like a cross, and as you stood in the
centre of the cross where the two shorter arms—called tran-
septs—extended on either side from the main trunk—nave and
chancel—you looked up into the inverted cup of the great dome.
In my early days it had been dark and mysterious; as though you
saw into the hidden depths of a thick cloud wherein nebulous figures swayed and soared. Then to look up into that dome was to
receive something of the true mysticism of religion. But recently
they had cleaned the paintings in the dome, revealing enormous
paintings of God, or one of his prophets, sprawling over the

world. Previously, in the darkness of the dome it had been possible to feel that the Deity might indeed have his dwelling place somewhere up there. The latter-day revelation of him was a cold disappointment, probably because the paintings were bad.

Spanning the dome like a hoop was a gallery, very high up, in which the curious could make experiments with the whispered voice which, because of some acoustical quality, would travel from one side of the dome to the other.

Built up in tiers, under the dome, was the great choir which had been collected from smaller churches around London and the suburbs; men and boys, perhaps three or four hundred of them, all dressed in white smocks called surplices. Some of the boys had frills of starched linen round their necks, and some of the men had sacks of drab autumnal colours slung over their shoulders. These were hoods. To one side of the chancel, built high up, was the organ, with pipes projecting from various galleries and some very large ones, called thirty-twos, lying horizontally. When I entered the Cathedral, the organist had already begun to play some dim prelude of his own invention. It was mournful, solemn music, and did not seem to balance the whispered excitement of the people, who already saw this service as one of thanksgiving, rather than one of supplication.

I sat hemmed in at the back of the north transept. Only by craning my head could I see anything of the choir. I studied the form of service that had been given to me at the door. I remember that it commenced with the prayer that Jesus taught his disciples, *"Our Father, which art in Heaven."* After that, the people were invited by the officiating priest to repeat a general confession of their sins. This was a very common formula in churches. Following the confession, the Archbishop was to give an absolution, which meant that everybody was "forgiven." Then came some sentences between priest and people. Let me see—what were the words? *"O Lord, hear our prayer: and let our wail come unto thee."* Something like that, I imagine. Then there was a hymn honoured and revered by all people of this island: *"O God, our help in ages past."* After that, more prayers and a reading from the Holy Book. Then I remember, while all the people knelt, the choir was to sing the penitential psalm of the Hebrews, *"Have mercy upon*

me, O God, after thy great goodness," set to music by some early
Italian composer. This was to be followed by an address by the
Archbishop.

Nothing was heard in the Cathedral except the rustling of service papers, the distant drone of the organ and the whispering
of people. Nobody spoke aloud, for it was considered a mark of
extreme irreverence to use the natural voice in church. This was,
I suppose, why they always had so much music and singing, since
the strain of whispering could not be maintained for long.

As each person settled into his place, after having first crouched
over the chair in front in the travesty of private prayer which
tradition expected all to adopt, a deeper quietness fell. Slowly it
began to grow darker. A stain of weak sunlight that had fallen
through a high window, making a shallow pool on the heads of
the singers, dried to a thin yellow streak till nothing was left of it.
A murmur of approbation arose when, through the great west
door, the Lord Mayor of the City with his Corporation entered
in procession up the nave. At the head was a flamboyant individual carrying a massive gold mace; then the gowned gentlemen of
the Corporation, the portly aldermen of London, the masters of
ancient City guilds and companies; finally the Lord Mayor himself—whose gold chain of office seemed to drag him down to the
ground, and whose three-cornered hat bedecked with feathers
and held before his breast, seemed to imply that he was concealing something which he did not wish us to observe.

The procession passed into the chancel; the organ swelled out
and played something more appropriate to civic dignity. Some
lights in the chancel were turned on, for by now it was not easy to
read the words on our papers. It grew near the half-hour. Outside
we could hear the buses and cars thundering past, the hoot of
motor-horns, and sometimes the clatter of a train over Ludgate
Bridge at the bottom of the hill. But above this we could hear,
mounting to a higher and less monotonous note, the sound of
the wind.

I stirred in my seat as the conductor appeared and walked on
to the platform before the choirs; a tall bent figure with a large,
sallow face, pendulous jaws, and a crop of grey curly hair like
sheepskin. He stood there fingering his conducting stick and

spasmodically scratching his thighs as though he were irritated by a flea. I saw him bend down and whisper to a slim, orange-haired youth who seemed to be his personal attendant. I think he had mislaid something, and I watched, interested, as the youth hurried out, and, coming back presently, handed his master a little box. From this the conductor extracted a small medal on a silk ribbon—the sign of some order, I presume—which he hastily—as though he hoped nobody had seen—put round his neck.

Now all seemed ready. The clock was a minute to the half-hour. We waited only for the Cathedral choir and the priests to enter and take their special seats in the chancel.

The clock struck; the vergers closed all doors to prevent the entry of any more people; we heard the Cathedral choir, in some side aisle, singing their vestry prayers. Then they entered, and everybody stood up. It was hard to see. I craned my head sideways between two very tall hospital nurses who stood in front of me. A faded, elderly gentleman on my left nudged my elbow. "Now we shall have some nice singing," he said. I nodded abstractedly, not wanting to talk to him; he was a cadaverous and slightly offensive figure.

I watched the procession. First a cross, carried by a youth. Then twenty boys, all looking somewhat ragged and unkempt. Then about a dozen men who swaggered in with their heads high in the air and their hands clasped behind their backs. Then a verger with a silver wand, followed by a great many priests and one or two obscure bishops from the colonies. I recognized one priest as an acquaintance of mine: a tiny figure with a flat, triangular face, coal-black hair, and a slavering chin. He looked as though he had just been playing a trombone or some such unwieldy instrument. Then came another verger with another wand—followed, after a space, by the Dean of the Cathedral. And finally the Primate himself, the Prince of the Protestant Church of England: the Most Reverend sage known as the Archbishop of Canterbury. He was a spare, frail individual with knotted brows and a bent back. Before him went his chaplain with an intricate and extravagant pole of gold, studded with jewels and shaped like a shepherd's crook. This was his pastoral staff, and we were supposed to be his sheep.

The organ sunk lower; heads—though not so often knees—were bent in prayer; and a quiet, well-mannered voice from the chancel commenced the words "Our Father"—words which immediately rustled all over the great building as everybody muttered the prayer. The service had begun.

I found my thoughts wandering. Why had I come here? If I wanted to hear the singing or the address, I could have heard it on the wireless in my home. All over the country now people would be listening, so that the service was lifted from the mere confine of this building and carried to one vast outpouring of prayer over the entire island. But I could not believe in it. There was something so appallingly self-conscious and complacent about this crowd of people in their approach to their God; something so essentially weak and faithless masquerading as strong and faithful. The priests, who had so shabbily drifted in just now—how faded, how archaic they were. They seemed to me to have only historical interest, like the tombs and monuments in the Cathedral. The great crowd of surpliced singers, how vain they were of their voices and their little musical distinctions. The Lord Mayor and his silly men, how pompous they all seemed—like comic old engravings which had sprung to spasmodic life. The conductor kneeling on his dais, how proudly he relished his exalted position.

As I stood up with the others to sing to "God, our help in ages past, our hope for years to come," I said to myself, "These are arrogant thoughts; cast them out." And I tried to sing. But the very words, "O God, our help in ages past," seemed a confession of people's inability to believe any longer in their God. "Our help in ages past, our hope for years to come——" Suddenly, it all seemed intensely pathetic.

Now it grew darker, so dark that all the lights in the Cathedral had to be switched on. It seemed as though we had leapt suddenly into a late January afternoon. As the lights came on, so the excitement of the people spread like a spark amongst straw. The hymn had ended with a great reverberating blare of the organ, a sound which at other times would have greatly moved me. Now we were kneeling and listening to prayers being read by the Archbishop. His voice wavered up into the dome and could barely be heard. He was asking that the nations might be bound together in peace and concord. "What dangers we are in," he said, "by our unhappy divisions——" As he prayed, and the people said "Amen" we heard suddenly, above the noise of the passing traffic, a new sound: not wind, not trains, nor the drone of many engines. First we heard it as a sharp, plucking noise on the west window; a metallic tapping of the glass, like finger-nails flicked upon the pane.

I raised my head. The Archbishop had paused before a prayer which appealed for rain. The sounds from the window quickened. Still the Archbishop waited. People began to murmur, raising their heads, looking behind them to the west window.

Suddenly, in a high, thin voice the Archbishop began to pray, voicing the common desire of his people in the prayer that he improvised. "O God, our Heavenly Father, who hast vouchsafed to hear our prayers and to open the clouds above us as thou didst for thy servant Elijah——"

A thousand heads turned round to the window, where now the metallic tappings grew louder, more hurried. The wind rose in a sudden thud, hitting the Cathedral like sacks beaten against a wall. "Hail!" whispered somebody. And I heard a voice beside me saying, "The old man shouldn't have said it; no, he should have waited." It was the cadaverous individual who spoke. I looked at him and away quickly, for there was an unpleasant smile on his face. He frightened me in a way I could not understand. The face and voice seemed familiar.

One word grew and carried itself round the Cathedral. "Hail—hail!" It seemed impossible that the excited people could stay kneeling any longer. Now the choir was throwing the melancholy cadences of the Miserere from side to side. I saw the conductor as he waved his stick turn his head nervously to the west window, then back again. The Archbishop had gone into the pulpit and was kneeling in prayer. Everybody turned their eyes upon him approvingly. He was their Elijah; he had prayed and the rain had come. Even now the sweet, sharp hail pattered brokenly on the glass.

How many had heard the sound of a beak upon glass and

failed now to recognize it! Or is a hailstone composed of the same substance as the bill of a bird?

We heard a scream then. We heard the faltering tinkle of broken glass on a stone pavement. We heard a harsh croaking of malicious glee. We heard the flapping of a thousand wings.

Then there was a great crashing of splintered glass, and a thick swarm of birds, mighty as eagles and dull black, flew in one solid phalanx along the nave, a few inches above the bowed heads of terrified people. Without hesitation they made for the whispering gallery in the dome. Before we could realize what had happened, that glittering hoop in the cup of Heaven was densely lined by a thousand black shapes.

Through the broken window the wind swayed and roared in fury.

*

To speak of the dreadful chaos which ensued within the next few minutes is a task that I confess I shrink from. No words of mine can ever describe that cataclysm to one who did not know that great City and its Cathedral. For perhaps twenty seconds the most deadly silence prevailed. The birds had stopped their vile chattering and sat so still above us that I could imagine they were nothing but a black circle painted round the dome. We heard only the roaring of the wind through the smashed window.

The Archbishop behaved with dignity. He did not attempt to leave the pulpit, but stood there with his thin yellow hands on the reading-desk, his head cast down, apparently deep in thought.

Suddenly he broke this dreadful stillness. Kneeling down, he prayed in a loud voice, a thin, vibrant voice which cut through the silence. It was now as dark as twilight in winter, and the wind began to moan and howl its way to gale force. The man at my side turned to me and said, "Well, now, there'll be trouble." He had apparently been gifted with the same prescience as myself, for he did not seem in the least disturbed or surprised by what had happened. I looked at him, and as I met his thin, cunning smile I was again afraid, I did not know why.

Suddenly there was movement from the dome. The Archbishop raised his head with a look of anguish as a bird swooped down from above, whirling its drab wings, and fell upon that haunted face. We saw only the flapping of wings over the side of the pulpit and the forlorn waving of the old man's arms.

The thought rushed through my mind; if something could induce all these people to stay quietly in their places; to pray as that old man is doing, and face their Demons, a miraculous ease and happiness could fall upon the City.

But the descent of the bird into the pulpit; the immediate descent of another who declined in a great curving flight towards the conductor on his rostrum, drove the people to instant action. And the only action they could consider in their panic was to make for the doors and get outside.

Once that deadly thing called panic seizes a large gathering of people no power on earth, no reasoning of any sort, can quell the pandemonium that breaks loose.

The conductor, intent upon nothing but his own safety, broke madly through the ranks of singers, scattering the music desks to the ground and sweeping terrified boys aside in his senseless effort to escape. Two or three boys and some women near the chancel screamed out aloud.

Reason and control broke. A thousand chairs were spilt sideways; the air was filled with terrified screams and the hoarse shouts of a few who tried to restore order. Every person who had, a minute before, been kneeling quietly in that Cathedral, burst madly out of his place in a terror-stricken flight towards the first door he could find.

In the centre of the choir I saw a billowing mass of white figures. The bird had seized the conductor and forced him to the ground. In a moment not one member of the choir remained in his place. They too ran blindly out towards the nave, some leaping madly over desks and chairs, some trampled and left wailing on the ground. "The crypt, the crypt!" I heard somebody shout.

Around me, people fought their way out. I held firmly on to a pillar in order to maintain my balance, for I saw that if I fell to the ground, I was lost. Struggling fiercely to escape were the two stalwart, masculine-looking nurses; I saw them push aside an old woman in their path who was slobbering hysterically. When I tried to help her, she snarled at me like a wounded cat who wants to be alone.

Standing firm and secure in this wild knot of struggling figures was the cadaverous man who had been seated next to me. He seemed impervious to what went on; he was thin, tall, like a dark statue, and an evil smile curled in his white face, like smoke in a flameless fire. He saw me holding on to the pillar.

"I'm safe, you see," he said, "I'm safe. They can't touch me." I turned away from his smile, so corrupt and malignant. Again I asked myself where I had seen the face before, and again I could not remember. I did not understand why he should be one of the few to escape. But now I think I do. . . .

Suddenly the birds in the dome, who during the last few minutes had done nothing but contemplate this shocking scene in dismal and abstracted silence, swooped down in one unanimous drive and broke up over the heads of the scattering people.

It is hard to speak of what happened. . . .

Nobody cared now for anybody else. Hundreds were trampled to death, and those who ran screaming, with hands over their eyes, were soon brought to the ground by the pursuing birds and either torn to pieces or smashed to pulp under a stampede of heels. To attempt to rescue a single person from this turmoil was a task beyond me or any one. It would need all my power of control to save myself and somehow get to my mother and Olga. I knew that I should not be attacked by the birds; but I stood in as much danger as any one else of being trampled to death. There was only one thing to do: to retreat to some hidden corner of the building and there wait till the crowd had thinned; it was madness to try to approach the doors at present.

So I attempted this. As I came cautiously away from the pillar, a gigantic bird whirled past me and buried his talons in the face of one of the nurses. I tried to avoid looking; it was a shameful thing that anybody should witness what I had to witness. I saw again the man with the evil face, smiling triumphantly, unmolested by any bird; and a deathly terror filled my heart.

I forced my way towards the chancel. I saw the Lord Mayor with a bird strangely like his three-cornered hat, fighting and shrieking up in one of the stalls. As I came near the pulpit, the pale figure of the Archbishop rose for a moment and held out his arms as though trying to speak. On his face was an expression of pure ecstasy like that of a blind man who sees for the first time, and knows that the world is lovelier than he had ever been told. Then his body shivered and he sank to the ground.

I got into the chancel. Lying over the choir stalls with sheets of music and books scattered amongst them, were the senseless, bloody forms of young boys, priests, and choirmen. I saw one fat old priest running round and round in insane little circles up by the high altar, crying pitifully as a great bird darted above, playing with him as a cat with a mouse. On the altar the two massive candles had toppled sideways; from one of them the hot wax sent a noose of thin blue smoke into the air. I stood between the choir stalls, not knowing where to go or what to do. Some aldermen of the City came running towards me and I drew aside to avoid them.

Suddenly, as I stood there, not knowing what to do, I was startled to life by a mighty, cacophonous burst of sound from the organ, as though all the notes had been depressed at once with every stop drawn. The sound went on, a gasping and wheezing of a thousand pipes. I could not bear it. It seemed to me the most terrible noise of all. Even the shouting, the screaming, the wailing of the wind, and the cries of the birds were not so hopeless a sound as the last savage lament of this dying organ. I thought of the organist lying over his keys, sounding his own death music with his lifeless body.

By now the chancel was almost empty. I stood looking down the nave where people still fought their way out, with birds, black as night, swarming after them. I began to feel cold. I was alone. Was there nobody else who sought and could obtain freedom as I did?

Standing there, with the organ crying like a tortured and infuriated beast, with that forlorn figure, the Prince of the Church, lying dead in the pulpit, I pressed my hands to my eyes, to my ears, trying to ignore all this horror. "There is nothing left," I told myself—"nothing left of the life you knew; it is all wiped away, and you, you have to go on living." And for a moment I was not sure whether I wanted to live; I felt it might have been better for me to have been crushed to death than to find myself living in this dying world.

I was driven out of these thoughts by a sudden roar of voices from the west door, still thick with struggling people. I looked up. I saw the crowds break away, fall back, and for a moment I could not understand what had happened. Then I knew. In face of the crowd who were already trying to escape, a mass of terror-stricken people from the streets was attempting to force its way into the Cathedral. Those outside driven in—those inside driven out. I shuddered to think what I might find when eventually I did get out. There was now an appalling confusion at the west door, thousands opposing those who tried to escape the building, and with the thousands who ultimately broke in and forced the others back again, as many birds. They ran now, this new body of people, up the nave towards the chancel, surging over broken chairs in a demented frenzy. For a moment I could not move nor realize my danger, spellbound by this dreadful sight.

A waddling little priest, with his surplice torn and bloody, came panting towards me and clutched my jacket; over his head circled a shrieking bird. "What shall I do—oh, what shall I do?" Saliva trickled down his flat red chin. The crimson hood on his back was streaked with a long dribble of mud-coloured ordure.

While we stood there with the bird wheeling overhead as though waiting for a more opportune moment to attack, the crowd from the west thundered nearer and nearer the chancel.

I took the priest's arm and dragged him away with me. "Come away," I shouted in his ear, "before we get trampled to death——"

He could hardly move; I had to tear him along by his surplice. We ran towards the altar and left the chancel by another gate. Behind us we heard the others smashing their way over the stalls and lifeless bodies. We came to an aisle, down towards the west by another path. Within a few feet of us was a throng of raving men and women. I jumped up into the protective shelter of a massive monument to some belligerent soldier.

I crouched down under a marble catafalque, and leant over the side to drag up the priest. But I was too late. The bird who had followed us, pounced upon him; in another second bird and man were lost under a torrent of stamping feet. A rabid mob of people swarmed past me. In their terror they fought and tormented one another; many tore their nails down their own faces as though to blind themselves.

I buried my head down by the cold marble, closed my eyes, and shivered. I could no longer look on these things. But I could not prevent myself from hearing the mournful wailing and crying of the tortured people, nor, above those sounds, the frightful din of the organ and the rushing of the wind.

I stayed there with my eyes closed, slowly getting colder. When I opened my eyes and looked below me, I saw a heap of bodies, torn clothes, blood, twitching limbs. I raised my head to the broken panes of a window opposite. As I looked at the desolate sky, the wind suddenly raged against the jagged hole and tore away the remaining glass. The sky and the wind terrified me. I would rather the rain poured down from that iron sky. Yet this thought reminded me that if I stayed much longer in this dreadful place I should never get away before the rain fell. The thought of Lillian and Olga raced in my head. I was driven to action.

I jumped, clear and wide, recovered my balance, and fled towards the west door. There were still people wailing and crying in the Cathedral. By the door I encountered a swaying mass, and with no thought now but for my own escape, I hurled my way into the midst of them, determined to get out.

A sharp pain in my hand made me cry out aloud. I withdrew it quickly from the teeth of a woman dressed in expensive clothes. I met her eyes and shuddered; her face was contorted in madness. I broke away from her, but she pushed towards me and tried again to attack me. I felt my passions rising, the passion of self-preservation, so deadly. I wanted to kill the woman, to kill any who got in my way. But as my thoughts turned thus, an enormous bird covered the woman with its wings.

Breathless and sick, I stood gasping against a pillar on the steps of the Cathedral, the wind dashing against my face and deep down into my body.

*

It is strange how in moments of great stress, the most insignificant object by its very imperturbability can recall us to the reality of existence. Standing on the steps of the Cathedral, hardly aware as yet of the horrible confusion in the streets before me, feeling that I had come through some dreadful dream and that I was but slowly waking—I was jerked back to a realization of the truth by the sudden consciousness of the stupid, hard black hat which all this time I had been holding in my hand. God knows how I had kept it! But there it was, this domed hat with a dent in the middle, otherwise unharmed, utterly contemptuous of the fact that it might be the last bowler hat left in the world. I looked at it and shook my head in bewilderment. What did it mean? What business had it to be alive?—for truly it seemed to me to have a secret life of its own. Yet though I resented its imperviousness to disaster, there was something tangible and realizable about it which filled me with a strange comfort. Here was this hat in my hand; I was still alive, the hand that held it was mine.

The whirring sound of engines above sharply reminded me that if I stayed here for long I should certainly never emerge from the City alive. I looked up and saw a fleet of aeroplanes flying low. Mingled with them, blacker than the blackness of the cloud which had now drained sunlight from all the sky, I saw birds flying in and out amongst the machines. I heard shots. In the square below I saw mounted police, and soldiers hideously masked with oxygen-laden appliances, making frenzied attempts to drive the people into shops and offices. Whether there was any organized purpose in this shepherding of the people I did not know; but I suppose they hoped to drive every one into shelter and then give a signal to the aeroplanes to expel their fumes of poison gas. They never succeeded in this plan. For suddenly, one of the aeroplanes, overpowered by the birds, turned over and came spinning to the ground, falling with a hiss of sharp flame into the middle of Ludgate Hill. An omnibus loaded with people and black with birds crashed into the flaming wreckage of the aeroplane. Almost simultaneously a powerful car travelling at a great speed, with a monstrous bird stretched over the hood, lurched sideways to avoid the bus and swerved into a shop doorway thick with people.

I saw then only a ribbon of flame and figures running, red and wet.

As I stood there trying to summon enough courage to get away, people still hurled themselves frenziedly up the steps. "The Cathedral, the Cathedral!" they cried. There seemed to exist a belief amongst them that, once inside with the doors shut, they would be safe. I pressed myself back against the pillar as they swayed past me. They were the last of our civilization to claim the sanctuary of that old temple. Already the shoutings and screamings were dying away to a silence that would be more intolerable.

Curious sounds stand out in my memory. A horse neighing; a cataract of broken glass in shop windows; the grumbling of forsaken engines in car and omnibus; the bitter sound of children wailing; a cat crying; and, most singular and haunted of all, dance music from a high-powered wireless set broadcasting from some continental town.

While I stood there, half insensible to what went on around me, a new sound clanged abruptly in my ears. The Cathedral clock struck two. When I heard that, and saw that the steps were slippery with the foul mess of trampled bodies, that the streets were ready to crack under the stagnant weight of burning traffic, I threw my hat away with a cry, and saw the last of it tumbling down the steps till it rested unconcernedly against the belly of a dead horse.

I could escape. I would.

I heard a chuckle of laughter and turned, startled. There was a man skulking behind one of the pillars; I did not need to look to know who he was.

"Only you and me left now," he said.

"There will be others," I spoke in a low voice, not looking at his face.

"Others—yes, a few. And what do you think they will do?"

"I don't know."

I could not move. I was held by his voice, for suddenly I remembered it as the same voice that had sounded over a marble table one night in a café.

"I tell you what they will do," he said. "They will build it all up and start again in exactly the same way until——"

"No!" I said. "No!"

But my words seemed to choke in my throat.

"Yes, they will. And I shall help them. I shall——"

With a great effort I turned and faced him, sick at the sight of his narrow face, his changeless smile. It seemed to me that he was blind in his right eye, and when I saw that, I was heavy with fear.

"I've seen you before," I said steadily.

"Yes," he said. "Oh yes—we're old friends."

He advanced towards me as if to link his arm in mine.

"Come," he said, "let us have a little fun——"

My hand shot out as though independent of my brain. I knocked him sprawling against a pillar. But as I ran down the steps I heard him laugh, a high, complacent cackle.

I ran wildly towards a little alley where I knew there was a telephone-box. Quickly I turned aside as I saw the crushed head that lay athwart the door. I did not yet realize that such things as telephones were to be of no further use to man. When I ultimately found another box and got inside, no amount of turning the dial could connect me with my number.

Desperate with the thought of Olga and Lillian, I came out to Cheapside and ran wildly towards the Bank. It was difficult to make any progress, for the street was in utter chaos. Hardly a shop window remained intact; merchandise of every description was scattered about in the road; cars had mounted the pavement and charged into sheets of glass; I saw their drivers inert over the wheels. Whirling in the hurricane that now seethed over the City as though to suck everything into its invisible pocket, was a bombardment of news-sheets, coloured material from drapers' shops, hats, garments, a vagabond assortment of worthless trinkets. Strangest of all were umbrellas that had been blown inside out; a canvas chair that sailed aloft from the broken windows of a large general store. Mingling with these gale-driven inanimates, the birds darted and swooped upon the thinning crowds of maddened people. The wind blew from the south-west, but the birds, flying from the east, compelled their victims to run in face of the wind. If they staggered and fell, exhausted by the fury of the gale, it was not many seconds before a pursuing bird pounced down with a clacking of wings. I managed to reach the end of

Cheapside. There, panting for breath, I paused a moment, standing in the partial shelter of the open doorway of a jeweller's shop on the corner.

How curiously inanimate objects stand out in the memory. Rolling down towards the gutter, I remember a large silver cup of the type coveted by athletes. In the murky light its sheen was emphasized. I stared at it like an idiot. It reminded me of my bowler hat, possessing the same power of detachment and scorn for all this destruction. What athlete would claim it now? It might, I thought, lie there for centuries. For who could begin, who would ever dare to begin to build up the City again?

"They will build it all up and start again in exactly the same way."

The words came back to me. I could not believe them.

Fire from wrecked lorries and cars licked its way towards glass-shattered buildings. Some hoarding a few yards along the road was crackling in flames, a noise which sounded like derisive laughter. I suddenly thought of the park where wild animals from all over the world were herded together. What would happen to them?

I realized that I was not alone. A bright-faced, middle-aged man, clad in a nightgown and an overcoat, stood before me.

"Exthuthe me, thir," he spoke in an excitable, lisping voice, "but can you tell me the way to Chanthery Lane? I jutht want to inquire about my money. Quite a thum, you know."

I stared at him.

"Chanthery Lane," he repeated impatiently, "the Lane that ith in Chanthery." He leant over and whispered to me. "I too wath in chanthery, thir. But I got out thith morning, you thee. Now, if you would kindly thyow me the way."

His eyes were glittering; his mouth trembled with incipient laughter. I pushed past him and ran away quickly. Were madmen from lunatic asylums all that were left to roam the shattered streets?

"No," I cried aloud. "There are others, there must be others."

But I saw none.

I realized by now that to attempt to catch any trains to the northern suburbs was fanciful. I did not even possess the courage to descend any of the underground railways, for the steps were a hideous sight, cluttered with bodies and the grotesque fuel of the gale. Hordes of people had stampeded down to the railways hoping to escape. I shuddered as the wind whistled in and out of those bloody caves.

I crossed to the Royal Exchange and again pressed my hands over my eyes. For lying across Threadneedle Street like a mighty dismembered arm was an iron girder that had fallen from the scaffolding of the Bank of England; pinned under it, a tortured mess of splintered steel, smashed glass, wheels, horses, pieces of human beings. A dozen or so solitary birds hung like lean vultures over this heap of wreckage. At least, I thought, nobody will lie there long in agony; the birds will not be satisfied till they have claimed their last victims.

I stood again in the square where weeks before the pretty winged visitors had first alighted. And as I stood there I perceived for the first time the engraved words in the pediment of the Exchange:

"The Earth is the Lord's and the Fulness thereof."

I wanted to weep. But a merciful hardness closed round my heart and would not let me.

I felt a hard, metallic drop upon my bare forehead; another, and another. Rain was falling. I realized with all my running how intensely cold I was, shivering as though I had just come out of an icy pool. The rain fell, slowly and ponderously at first, stinging and pecking my head like globules of ice. Presently, I knew, it would burst down in full force and I might be trapped in the dying City.

Again I ran, and coming down a little street by the Bank, towards a place called Moorgate, I saw, standing outside a church door strewn with twisted bodies, a forlorn and battered-looking car with a head hanging face downwards over the wheel.

I ran towards it like a man who finds an old friend in a foreign country. Then I stopped dead.

An old friend?

Why was the car a pale blue in colour with a tattered black hood drooping half over the back? Why was the tumbled head covered with such gleaming gold hair? Where had I seen such a head before? Where had I driven this old car before?

It seems to me still, as it seemed to me then, when I lifted up
the bloody face of Ivor, that of all the terrible things that happened in that day, this was the most terrible; that a lad who possessed all the beauty of the earth and could crystallize it into a
single note drawn from a violin, should have come to the City to
"see life" and only have met his death.

That hardness which had begun to close like a protective
armour around my heart, broke. I could do no more than fall
down by the side of the car, weeping because Beauty had been
defiled.

*

I did not stay long. I still knew I could live; that here, delivered
into my hands through the tragedy of Ivor's death, was the
instrument which could bear me to freedom.

I lifted the body into the back of the car. I did not know what
I was going to do with it, but the thought of leaving it here for
worms to devour, refused acceptance in my mind. He should
be left somewhere in the open country beside the woods and
streams which were his natural heritage. So I lifted him into the
back, unable to look at the face—for I had never seen a dead body
before, and I could detect nothing of that repose which poets had
assured me lingers like moonlight over a dead face. This form
of lifeless matter was repulsive to me; the hand that could never
again hold a bow over a violin string, had lost all the beauty it
once possessed.

I started the engine and began to drive, nervously and slowly.
It was bitterly cold and the rain began to beat against the glass-
screen in front of me. I realized that I had forgotten to raise
the hood. Stopping, I got out, put up the hood and the cracked
yellow side-screens, and got in again. With the car now closed
around me I felt a new security; a feeling of warmth began
to flood over me. The smell of the petrol, which I generally
detested, seemed to me now the most consoling smell in the
world. When I found that I had not forgotten how to steer, that
the accelerator respected my touch, that I could change gear
without much grinding of the engine, the old feeling of elation

began to return to me. I was like a child who has found a favourite toy.

I drove on, very slowly, for the streets were so thick with obstacles that it needed all my skill to circumvent them. I began to forget that Ivor's dead body lay in the back, that the shops and houses I passed were empty shells of the life I had known. I knew only that the rain slashed upon the canvas hood and trickled through a small hole down my neck; that the wind threatened to lift the frail old car into the air; and that by careful control of the wheel in my hand and the pedals under my feet I could and must reach north London and the outer country.

The farther away from the City I drew the greater became the stillness. I took as many side streets as possible, for the main roads were often impassable. Sometimes I saw solitary birds in pursuit of half-demented figures. One incident stands out in my memory. A corpulent man came running towards the car, crying at me to stop and take him. He was an extraordinary sight. Apparently he had been in a barber's shop, for his face—down which a great cut painted a line of blood—was still speckled with the lather of shaving soap. Sticking into his collar were little bloody pieces of cotton-wool. He shrieked at me to stop, and my foot was on the brake. But round his head I saw a great bird flying. I drove on, hardening my heart, knowing I could do nothing for him.

I remember, too, in some sordid houses, seeing the shapes of women lying half out of windows, their arms swinging in the wind, their hair fluttering about their heads. But I was so intent upon the driving of the car, my eyes fixed always on the road immediately before me, that I noticed little.

It was late in the afternoon as I drew near Finsbury Park. The sky, thick yellow from east to west, seemed to gape open to release the torrent of rain that poured without ceasing, until the streets and gutters were bubbling like mountain streams. I came under a railway bridge, along a street that I knew well but which now seemed barely recognizable. Out in the road was a drenched mass of crushed fruit, raw lumps of meat, old books, broken bits of cheap furniture, carts, twisted bicycles, ragged materials, and twined in and out of this sodden heap, trampled corpses lying as though thrust deep down into the steaming pavements. I took a side turning where there were no shops, and here it was easier to drive, though even more desolate. In many of the houses windows were smashed and doors swung wildly on their hinges.

I was afraid now. The zest of driving had worn off. I only knew that I was shivering with cold, and that presently into one of these houses I should have to go. I dreaded what I might find there.

I came to the beginning of the long street. Under the railway arch at Stroud Green a train had tumbled over, spilling its carriages in a smoking pile in the road. I had to make a detour and come by another route to the ridge. On the top I stopped a moment, looking over to the vague outline of the Alexandra Palace, caught in the low sky. A dull redness flickered about the decapitated tower as though the place were smouldering. Some scaffolding upon the lopped tower had crashed to pieces in the gale. It was a melancholy sight. I wished with all my heart that it could be swept away, the whole vast building, so colossal a record of the cumbersome insignificance of the labour of men.

I drove on down the hill and, without stopping to think any more, drew the car up outside the house. To my dismay the door, like so many others, was wide open. I ran in, knowing that if I did not run, I should never go.

I called:

"Mother, Mother!——"

There was no answer; only the wind moaning round the house. I ran into the kitchen and stumbled over the body of Annie lying by the door. Quickly I left the room, having assured myself that Lillian was not there.

I called again, loudly, terrified of the sound of my voice, not daring to go upstairs. Still there was no answer.

I paused, listening to the wind and the rain, to the clock ticking in the hall. I turned towards the door, telling myself it was no good; she was dead—she was dead somewhere upstairs, and I should only torture myself looking for her body.

But as I thought this, almost glad to find an excuse to leave the house, I heard a moan, somewhere from below.

"Mother, Mother!——" I called again.

The noise came from the cellar, underneath the house; a place where there were no windows and it was all darkness. I heard it again, a dreadful moaning of a lost person in a lost place.

I ran to my room to get a candle and matches, and returned to the cellar door, under the stairs. As I opened the door, a thin gust of air blew out the candle. I lit it again with shaking hands. The gust of air fluttered past me down into the cellar.

I heard a scream.

In the flickering light I saw her crouched in a corner, her head pressed into her hands, rocking her body to and fro. My candle spat as a sharp breath of air whistled near it.

Then I saw the bird, small, grey, and ghostly, circling round and round blindly like a bat.

I ran to Lillian and put my arms round her, but she started away from me and cried:

"Who is it?"

"Mother, I've found you; I've found you at last. Open your eyes. Look at me."

She opened her eyes and looked at me; a wild haunted face in the candlelight; a face grey with distress.

"You—you——" she muttered.

And then suddenly in a fearful scream as the bird darted upon her upturned face, "Christ—Christ! You've let it in—drive it off—oh, drive it off——"

"Yes," I shouted. "Yes—I've let it in at last, and thank God I have. You must see now. You must see. Open your eyes, Mother! *Open your eyes.*"

She struggled like a maniac as I held her arms. She looked at me for a moment and seemed to understand. The bird alighted on her face, dug its claws sharp into her chin. Suddenly her struggling ceased, and she shivered to stillness with a long sigh. I closed my eyes and waited, holding her still in my arms. The fluttering of wings grew less; the sound of my mother's breathing grew lower until I wondered whether life still beat in her.

My heart sank like a stone in water. I was deathly cold and hungry. I opened my eyes. I saw my mother's face, calm and peaceful in sleep. I listened for the beating of her heart and heard it, like a faint ripple of water, so slight that I thought the smallest movement would curb it. There was a small cut on her chin; I noticed how white her hair was. I saw no sign of the bird.

I carried her out, and wrapped her in blankets. I filled a bottle with hot water and placed it at her feet. Then I laid her in the car, in the seat next to mine.

All the time I said to myself, "She will live; she will live." And Olga—Olga would be waiting for me. I knew now that fate could not deny me this. With an amused shock of recollection I remembered that I had arranged to see her this evening.

Before I left the house, the old home I was never to see again, I filled a large basket with bread, butter, meat, and other food that I found in the larder.

I came into the front room. Something prompted me to touch a note on the piano; but I closed the lid quickly before I should be tempted to play any more.

I took three or four bottles of wine from the cupboard, and pouring out a glass, drank some, while I chewed bread hungrily.

For the moment I could think of nothing while I ate and drank, slowly relishing the return of warmth to my body. But as I stood half-turned towards the window, my mind wandered to an evening recently when I had looked out of this window, dreaming of flowers; of flowers and——

I turned round sharply to face the cold, naked candles.

I struck a match and held it to the wicks. Slowly the small flames rose without flicker until the dark corner glowed like a sunlit puddle on a wasted heath. The spent match burnt my fingers and dropped to the ground. I held my hands on the bureau and my head fell forward.

Suddenly I left the room and closed the door.

I came back to the car with my basket of food. I saw the figure of my mother huddled in rugs beside the steering-wheel, her head hanging forward loosely, her mouth half-open. "It would be easier to drive," I thought, "if I put her in the back." But there was a mound under a dark grey rug. . . .

Then I knew that I could take Ivor no farther. Quickly I carried his body inside the house and laid him on the bed in my room. As I did so I exposed his face and turned away towards the open window. The rain had splashed a pool on to the dressing-table and trailed a thin stream into a half-open drawer, drenching handkerchiefs, collars, and ties. I closed the window sharply, and as I came to the door, passing the bed, I touched Ivor's body.

I shut the door and stood outside for a moment. I was cold again.

I came to the outer door and closed it for the last time. For a moment I stayed looking at Riveria, the house next door. A broken jar of imitation tulips had fallen out through the smashed window. These were the flowers, I thought, and I was the mourner——

As I stood there, with the rain still beating on my head and the wind howling, I saw in the western sky a faint honey colour, a thin strip of colour thrown out by the sun as it began to fall behind the clouds. I remembered that only a few days ago I had never wanted to see the sun again. Now it seemed that in this remote light in the western sky lay the promise of a new sun to flush over the awakening earth. And a great joy flowed into my being, so that I shivered no more and barely felt the rain that drenched my clothes. Already the horror of the day seemed to have become clouded as a dream.

I only stood in that wasted little garden for a few seconds. But time does not know of such things as seconds; I was related to an experience outside the measuring of clocks. Yet that the old humanity could still speak, could still sound its cautious note, was suddenly made clear to me in the striking of our old marble clock in the front room.

One—two—three—four—five. . . .

Tea-time. The hour for winter firelight and the charitable cup; the hour when tired men return to their families and read the evening paper, with their slippered feet stretched out before the fire; the hour when labour gives place to pleasant conversation and amusement. Tea-time——

The clock had struck that hour for me, and for the rest of that day until the next day, it would go on striking hours. Six—seven—eight. Supper-time. Nine—ten—eleven. Bedtime. Midnight. A new day. A new day——

Through the window I saw the two candles, their thin flames alive in their own secret world.

Then I was afraid. Afraid of the ghosts that already began to haunt the works of men; afraid of the clock that could strike because of the life man had left with it.

Afraid—because five strokes had no more significance, yet still sounded. Afraid—because two candles would burn till their last drop of wax had melted.

I ran into the car and drove off without looking back once, towards Hampstead. I heard beside me the faint breathing of my mother, regular and easy.

POSTFACE, BY ANNA

The house is very quiet, the boys are asleep. Thinking of the day that has just passed, I rose from my bed and read again the last sentences that my father dictated to me two days ago. I have been so close to my father in the last few weeks; it is hard to know that he has withered, his body now ashes upon the earth.

"I heard beside me the faint breathing of my mother, regular and easy." When he had spoken those words, his voice shook a little and he said, "Anna, I am tired. You shall hear the end of my story to-morrow." He went to his room and would not let anybody help him up the stairs. Then, perhaps in his sleep, he died; when we came to him in the morning, we found it impossible to believe that he was not asleep. Berin was the first to speak.

"Mother," he said to me, "he is dead." He looked at me with an expression that I cannot forget. It is strange how my youngest son has the power to touch me more than his brothers. My brothers and sisters came here with their families. We carried his body to the little hill that rises like a loaf of bread behind our house. Roger, Allan, and Berin had prepared a pile of faggots and ash logs, lined in the centre with a hollow of moss and dried leaves. Into this bed, we laid my father. Ivan, my eldest brother, set flame to the twigs. We watched silently as the flames grew and spread up until they licked their way over my father's body, and covered him from our sight. We came home, ate and drank together, telling tales of him and my mother Olga when we were children. Then dusk came, and Ivan with his brothers and their wives, my sisters with their husbands and children, left for their own homes.

I was left with Berin, and as we sat over the fire thinking of these things, "Mother," he said, "I have written a song for the Elder. Can I sing it to you?"

183

I said yes, and he sang these words:

> *"Since the tree waves its branches*
> *Answering the wind;*
> *Since the bird flies to the clouds,*
> *The river falls to the valley,*
> *The flower blooms under the sun,—*
> *Since nothing backward turns,*
> *I, too, flow on.*
> *Nothing is made to falter,*
> *Nothing to die.*
> *Life is a flowing onwards,*
> *Sleep is a ledge in the fall,*
> *Death is a lake in the mountains,*
> *A quiet abiding in time,*
> *A longer sleep."*

I wish my father could have heard the song.

By his bedside was a sheet of paper with these notes written on it: "The towns with forsaken shops and dead people. The old priest. Leaving the car and taking a faster one from a garage. Tell Anna about the cold roast chicken in the empty café at St. Alban's. . . ."

These are clearly notes intended for the final sections he wished to dictate. Now I can only use my imagination to picture the many terrible scenes he must have passed before he reached this country. If, however, I am unable to end this story as he would have ended it, it is possible for me to reconstruct something of the beginning of his new life here. My brother Ivan, who is fifteen years older than myself, was not born in this house. He was born in the house of the Welsh schoolmaster in the village down in the valley, some ten miles away. Ivan has told me that he remembers his grandmother, Lillian, when he was a little boy. He liked her very well, she used to ride him up and down on her knee and sing a rhyme about Banbury Cross which is all he can remember of it. She died when Ivan was about four years old.

A little later my father and mother, with the Welshman,

moved into the ancient farmstead which we now inhabit and which had been the property of the schoolmaster's father. Ivan does not remember the schoolmaster's wife at all. And he did not know of the son, Ivor, whose name was never mentioned.

It is thus to this schoolmaster that we owe our present abode. Here I was born, and all my brothers and sisters, except Ivan. Twenty-five years ago from this house I was wedded to Thomas the woodcutter, who loved me well as I loved him. We left this house and began to farm our own land from the cottage in the Valley of Mallynth. Nine years later I returned here with my three boys, sad at heart, glad to find the peace of my father and mother. Thomas had been killed by a falling tree; my little girl, my first-born, had died of a fever. In this house I found comfort in the growing beauty of my boys and the wisdom of my parents.

Here, then, for sixteen years I have lived a full and happy life with no time to consider what sort of a world it is beyond these few miles that are visible to us. When my father travelled to the City, twenty years ago, we were curious enough to know what he had seen. But he would say nothing, even to Olga very little. Now he has told me, I have written it all down, and you—my brothers, sisters, and children—must one day read it as certainly he intended you to.

*

I think over all that I have written down these last few weeks, the strange and terrible story of my father's early life, and I am sad to think that so many questions I wished to ask him can now never be answered. Even many of the words which he used have no meaning for me, though he tried often to explain them. I never cared to break the flow of his memories with questions, and at the end of a day's work he liked to put aside the past and talk of the happier present. What was the true meaning of the Birds? I have tormented myself with this question. I cannot try to add anything to what my father related. You—my brothers, sisters and children—must think what you will. We know that millions of people were killed, and that the world as my father knew it, passed away. We know that cities were destroyed and that men and women became the prey of savage birds such as nobody had ever seen before. My father reveals to us his own belief as to the true nature of these creatures; perhaps we must accept this and ask no more.

Yet there are still questions which cry out to be answered, and none more so than in his description of the man he met in the café and his later meeting with him on that last dreadful day. Why would not my father make himself clearer to me here? I know that there was much in his mind which he would never speak of. Who was this man? Is he somewhere still alive? Is he the living embodiment of that dark spirit our ancestors called Satan?

I am writing late at night, alone, with the ancient hills of Wales around me. And I wish I had never written "is he somewhere still alive . . ."

I look out of the window. The embers of the fire have nearly died away. Nothing but ashes is left of my beloved father's body. What do I believe—that he has gone somewhere to join my mother whose love for him and us bound all our lives together?

I do not know. But I am glad he lived so long, to enjoy all those blessings of life which we hold here, unclouded by the miseries which engulfed the old world, in the days before the Birds came.

END.

CPSIA information can be obtained
at www.ICGtesting.com
Printed in the USA
LVHW042159270122
709588LV00013B/616